MEDICAL THRILLER
A DR. BRYCE CHAPMAN NOVEL

REDEMPTION

BRIAN HARTMAN

The most difficult thing is the decision to act. The rest is merely tenacity."
-Amelia Earhart

For Cheryl, a wonderful mother to our children
and a chronic enabler of my dreams

Content Warning

Guns/Hunting (no one is harmed)
Attempted suicide / Mental Health

If you need help, please call the National Suicide Prevention Line at 800-273-8255 or the National Suicide Prevention Hotline at 988.

Chapter One

Death is a curious thing. To some it can be a relief as it ends a prolonged period of suffering. Others may see it as unnatural and much too early. Still others may see it as both, for the unnatural death of one person could lead to the end of suffering for another. Which is the greater wrong? Can a singular wrong make a right? The man laying silently under the king-sized bed believes it can. He did not seek out knowledge of the evil that is inside Kent, but once he learned of it, he could not ignore it.

Kent Carpenter leads a very private life. It's easy to maintain privacy at work when your desk is inside one of the hundreds of cubicles that fill three floors of an office building. As an IT consultant, the work is done with computer screens rather than direct human contact. Messages rather than phone calls. As long as the work is done correctly and on time, there's not much need for human interaction. The drive home is no different. Anonymous cars play follow the leader down city streets, each going the same way but with different destinations. If done correctly, there is no need for human interaction. That's perfectly fine with Kent, since many humans are disgusting creatures. Perverse, repugnant creatures. Kent should know, he is one.

Leading a private life is sometimes the creation of a shy person or one lacking self-confidence. It's easier to stay isolated inside oneself than to take the risk of opening up to the potential of being hurt. Other times, barriers are intentionally erected to hide behind. Covering personality traits that the rest of the world despises, rejects, abhors. Kent's privacy is born of the desire to avoid prison.

Today is ending like most days in Kent's depressing life. After a microwaved dinner and two shots of bourbon, he retired to his bedroom and sat down at his computer. He entered the twelve-character password to unlock the screen and then double clicked the icon named "Tor", an internet browser designed to provide anonymity to the user during online activity. By using specialized software and routers, it is able to strip identifying information from data, making it nearly impossible for others to track your activity online. This is perfect if one is worried about privacy, protecting their data, or hiding illegal activity. It is also a great method of accessing the dark web, a clandestine network of internet sites not readily available to standard browsers that is home to the online drug trade, pirated software, media and fringe pornography. The type of pornography that possessing could land one in prison.

This is the reason for Kent's privacy. Self-preservation by way of seclusion, where he is free to indulge in the rotting of his soul without an audience. Perversion and addiction lead to an interesting cognitive dissonance. In one sense, the psyche knows it's wrong, but that same psyche is addicted to it. The defense mechanism becomes isolation, deceit, and avoidance of those in society felt to be normal. Consumption of alcohol to numb that last faint whisper of a conscience. Except that tonight he does in fact have an audience.

Kent is a bad person, and he knows it. So did his audience lying under the bed. Kent had tried to stop drinking, tried to stop child pornography, but the addictions kept luring him back. Alcohol led to lack of inhibition and euphoria which led to rationalization, which led to the dark web. He realized this combination was probably going to either land him in jail or dead. Or perhaps both. But as with most addictions, the knowledge of the likely endpoint was not enough to ignore the siren song. Eventually rationalization wasn't necessary and simple resignation and acceptance was the new normal, combined with cheap bourbon.

The man under the bed had planned for this encounter months before. He had to enter the house and hide under the bed before Kent arrived home. Then bide his time until he could do what needed to be done. The planning and foresight were done with military precision. What he had not counted on was the difficulty of holding his emotions in check while Kent browsed his favorite websites. Disgust, nausea, and rage were welling up inside him and had to be controlled for the plan to work. Patience. Focus.

Eventually, the room darkened as Kent closed the browser window and began the bedtime ritual. Pajamas, teeth, and a strong sleeping pill. His doctor knew he didn't sleep well, but he didn't know the reasons for it. It was easier to prescribe an Ambien CR than it was to delve into the psychological reasons for the patient's insomnia. Kent was just as happy to end his night with immediate drug-induced slumber rather than face his recent actions while staring at the ceiling. Self-reflection and prayer at bedtime was something his parents had taught him during childhood as part of the bedtime routine. He gave that up when his addiction progressed and he couldn't face himself, let alone God. Ambien was a welcome addition to the night-time routine. Nearly instant sleep with no recollection of events. Just what the doctor ordered.

Kent's hidden visitor heard the pill bottle opening, heard the rattle of pills as one was poured into an open palm. He heard the swallow of bourbon and knew it would be only a matter of time until he could begin his work. Next was the sound of corrugated tubing rubbing across wood as the CPAP mask was pulled from the nightstand. Velcro rustled as the mask was applied to his face and then the gentle sound of airflow as the machine started up. Bedsprings creaked and groaned as Kent adjusted himself into a comfortable position.

After a few minutes the visitor heard Kent's breathing change to the steady rhythm of slumber. He checked his watch and waited thirty more minutes for good measure. Sleep was not good enough. He had to wait for the sleeping pill to smother Kent's consciousness. When he was satisfied enough time had passed, he rolled out from under the bed and got to work. Ten minutes later, he disarmed the security system, entered the code to rearm it with a fresh thirty second exit window, and walked out the back door.

Chapter Two

"Mornin' doc! You just missed all the excitement," said the chief of hospital security on his way out the ambulance bay door.

"Hey, Charlie, good morning. Glad to have missed it. I'm sure there will be plenty more where that came from though," replied Bryce Chapman, the physician arriving to staff the day shift in the emergency department. He had worked at Washington Memorial Hospital for the last ten years, signing on directly upon graduation from residency.

"Hah, you're right. The moon is full and society's ability to cope is empty. The coroner investigator is almost here, I'm going to wait outside for her."

Oh, that type of excitement. Nothing ends a shift quite like a coding patient. Rather than spending the last hour finishing with existing patients, handling admissions, discharges, and re-evaluations, exclusive attention is paid to a new and critically ill person. With luck, the patient recovers and is whisked quickly to the ICU for definitive management or the cardiac catheterization lab to open up a blocked coronary artery. Unfortunately, the patient often expires in the ED and notifying family and the coroner begins. The medical management of a coding patient is easy, it's the emotional and relational aspects that are hard.

There are two ways to enter the department from the ambulance bay, which is the closest entrance to the employee parking lot. The first is a straight shot down a long hallway that joins the hallway leading to triage and the waiting room. This route is often filled with moaning or vomiting ambulance patients on cots, patients being discharged, and family returning from a smoke break. The other way heads straight into the trauma resuscitation rooms and is the way Bryce heads ninety-nine times out of a hundred.

A quick wave of the hand past a black wall sensor opened doors to the trauma and resuscitation area. After just a few steps, Bryce was able to see the remnants of the resuscitation from beneath the privacy curtain. Empty boxes of epinephrine, a stylet from the intubation, and numerous empty saline flush syringes littered the area next to the bed. He also saw three shoes. One was a man's shoe. It had a well-worn sole with a repaired heel still in decent shape. Laces were left off this design in favor of Velcro, appropriate for its elderly owner. It was flattened, laying upside down. Defeated. Next to this shoe were two smaller shoes, perfectly parallel and fully expanded by the feet of their owner. A resuscitation room should be chirping with the sound of monitors, ventilators, and other diagnostic and therapeutic equipment performing various lifesaving and monitoring tasks. This room was silent, except for the soft sobs of a woman who now had a wedding ring but no husband.

Shaking his head, Bryce continued on through another set of doors to the physician's work area to begin his shift. "Hey, Bryce, about time you got here. I just had to code that guy all by myself," said Dr. Tom Sharpe, who was finishing his night shift.

"Yeah, sorry about only being ten minutes early to my shift today. Shame you had to run that code alone. If you had let the nurses, respiratory therapists, EMS crew, and techs help, maybe he would have lived," replied Bryce with a wink and a smile. Emergency medicine is a specialty well known for gallows humor. It's a coping mechanism to deflect the emotional stress that comes with seeing critically ill and acutely injured patients day in and day out.

"Yeah, well, I guess they helped as well. You know what I mean. Poor guy had widely metastatic lung cancer that was growing despite chemotherapy. Guess what his code status was?"

"Full code! He still had a few organ systems that weren't riddled with tumor, right?"

"You got it. His wife thought he was doing okay, and they were planning for a trip to Florida in three months," said Tom, shaking his head.

"Why don't you go ahead and get out of here. I'll go see this bronchitis patient," sighed Bryce. At least his day was starting off with an easy patient.

"Roger that, thanks. I just spoke with Ashley Saxon from the coroner's office. They're not going to investigate. The funeral home should be here in an hour to pick him up. He was an organ donor but with metastatic cancer he's not a candidate for donation."

"Ashley? I'm shocked she's not going to investigate," said Bryce sarcastically. "She might as well flip a coin anyway; I have not been impressed with her conclusions on previous cases."

"Are you suggesting the coroner shouldn't hire unqualified relatives?" gasped Tom.

"Exactly. Have a good day. Try to get some sleep," said Bryce as he logged in to the computer to begin his shift. *First patient, chest pain, room twenty-four.* He stood and headed down the hall toward the room. Jackie pulled the staffing assignment folder out and sank into a chair to review the assignments. Static and a chirp from the EMS radio broke the brief silence. "Washington Memorial, this is Medic 58 calling with a medical alert."

"Copy clear Medic 58, go ahead with your traffic," said a nurse into the EMS radio.

"We are a minute out with a woman in labor, this is her first child and she's about forty-one weeks. We can see the top of the head, but it seems stuck. We can't deliver it."

"Okay, we'll get the team ready, see you in trauma room one. Washington Memorial out."

Jackie Sirico turned toward Paula, the secretary. "Call up to NICU and labor and delivery to request staff for an impending delivery." As charge nurse, it was Jackie's responsibility to coordinate care and staffing in the emergency department.

The secretary picked up the overhead paging microphone and said, "Impending delivery thirty seconds out, going to room two. All available staff please assist."

"Where's Chapman?" Jackie said quietly, looking around for her attending physician on duty. She spotted him jogging down the hallway toward trauma. "Bryce, hang on!" she yelled as she caught up to him. They had worked together for years and saved countless lives as a team over that time period. The formalities had been dropped years ago at Bryce's insistence.

"Hey, Jackie, did you take that call? What's going on?" asked Bryce.

"Yes, she's forty-one weeks along, this is her first baby, and the medics said the child seems to be stuck. They can see the head but she can't push it out." They rounded the corner and approached the trauma room doors. Bryce waved his hand in front of the sensor and stood back as the doors swung open. "That's not good. Are OB and NICU on the way?" he asked.

"I had the secretary call for them but it's going to be a few minutes. Looks like we're on our own for a bit."

"Hey, we can do anything for a few minutes, right? Isn't that one of our mottos?" They joined the rest of the team in the room and prepared for the arrival of the patient. One nurse was heating up the infant radiant warmer and attaching monitor leads to prepare for the second patient. Others were preparing IV kits and sterile gowns and gloves to help the mother deliver.

Bryce grabbed a sterile gown and pulled on the gloves just as the EMS crew arrived. A loud scream announced their presence in the department. The mother was leaning back on the stretcher, both hands gripping the side rails, knuckles white as the sheet on the cot. "Ma'am, do not push!" commanded the paramedic as they wheeled her toward trauma room one.

Bryce was drawn to the obvious discomfort of the mother and then to the worried looks on the faces of the paramedics. They spent their lives in the trenches, pulling people back from the brink of death. They normally don't look worried. *Not a good sign.* Bryce lifted the sheet off the mother's abdomen and looked between her legs. A head full of hair was in the birth canal but too high for the ears or forehead to be seen.

"Let's get her moved over," he said, which initiated the lift and transfer procedure that the team members had literally done thousands of times before. This one was different though. This one had a head on both ends. "I'm Doctor Bryce Chapman, it looks like you're experiencing shoulder dystocia, which is a condition where the baby's shoulders are stuck and blocking further passage down the birth canal. How long has the baby been in this position?"

The mother looked at him deeply, eyes open and full of tears. "Don't let my baby die!" she begged. "Do whatever you need to, just get him out. We've been trying for years. I don't care about myself, just help my baby!"

"Okay, we will do our best. But how long has he been stuck in this position?"

"Doc, he wasn't that low when we got to her. I think he's been stuck a few minutes," said the paramedic. *A few minutes, damn. Hopefully the cord isn't being pinched and he's still getting good oxygen delivery.* "So we're out of time. Lay her flat, I want two people on each leg, flex her hips back as far as you can."

A nurse and the paramedic grabbed her left leg while the EMT and another nurse grabbed her right leg. They quickly pulled her knees up as far as possible. "Jackie, give suprapubic pressure when she tries to push next. You need to push that shoulder down below the pubic symphysis." He looked up at the mother and reassured her. "You can do this. I need you to push as hard as you can, right now!"

The mother took a deep breath and pushed with everything she had. Jackie climbed up on the bed and leaned down hard on the mother's abdomen just above her pelvis. Bryce placed his hands on the child's head and tried to firmly deliver the child. *Come on kid, get out of there! He didn't even budge!*

"Okay, pause. Next move everyone. I'm going to try to rotate him and then we're going to pull her legs and Jackie you're going to push again while she bears down." Bryce was able to get two fingers past the child's head and pulled the front shoulder toward the patient's left and then did the opposite with his other hand. *At least the cord isn't wrapped around the neck.* "Okay, push!" he ordered. Bryce again pulled down without success. *Damn it! We're running out of time.* "Where's OB?" he asked.

Bryce tried to insert his hand into the mother's vagina to remove an arm and facilitate delivery, but he could not gain access. "Someone get me the large curved scissors. We may need to do an episiotomy. It won't fix the shoulder problem, but it may give me enough room to get this arm out first. One more thing before we do that. Have her flip over and get on her hands and knees. That position can let gravity help and sometimes lets the baby come down. We're going to try this before we get more drastic and use the sharp pointy things." The team helped the mother flip over onto her hands and knees and Bryce put his fingers back in to try to spin the baby and get it out. "Okay, now push as hard as you can!"

Movement! Come on man, just a little bit more. Don't make me cut your mom or break your clavicle.

"One more big push, now!" he yelled. Bryce's downward pull combined with the mother's last effort managed to move the baby a full inch and then it stopped again. *God, help get this baby out. We're out of time.* The mother screamed again and suddenly Bryce's hands were full of a very large and very wet baby. "Oh, it feels different. Is he out?" yelled the mother, trying to look behind herself.

"Yes, good job!" said Bryce. Nurses surrounded him and brought suction and warm, dry blankets. The child began crying immediately after suctioning. Bryce clamped and cut the cord and then handed him to the nursing staff who placed him in the warmer and continued to clean and stimulate him. "Let's get her on her back and deliver the placenta."

After she was on her back, he unlocked the wheels on the bed and spun it so she could see her new son. "Marla, are you okay? How is the baby?" came a shout from behind the team.

"Oh honey, get in here. I'm okay, the baby is out and he's fine. They took great care of us."

A large man squeezed his way through the crowd and stood next to the bed. He leaned down and hugged his wife and then looked toward the warmer. A nurse was walking toward them holding their new son. "Here you go Mom and Dad; he looks beautiful. Congratulations." She gently handed the baby to the mother and stepped back, smiling at them both.

"OB here, what do you have?" asked a man in a surgical mask and gown. The team turned to look at the specialist who was no longer needed emergently. He looked at the parents and the baby with a confused look on his face. "I thought there was some sort of emergency that you needed help with."

"Yes, thanks for coming. We seem to have a whole department full of emergencies, but I've been in here delivering this beautiful boy and I need to go attend to my other patients. You can take over and deliver the placenta," said Bryce, stretching his hand out toward the OB doctor. Once the clamp had been handed over, he quickly examined the baby and then exited the room. Jackie followed close behind.

"The look on his face was priceless," said Jackie, busting out laughing. "He has no clue what it's like down here and what happened in the last few minutes."

"Right? I'm just glad that worked. I was about to break the poor kid's collarbone and cut her a bit. Was not looking forward to that," said Bryce, wincing as he finished the sentence. "Okay, back to work. I'm sure I'm a few patients behind by now."

Chapter Three

Bryce pulled up the tracking board for the department. Instantly he could see every patient in the department along with dozens of data points on each one. Color codes, flashing graphics, and columns of information told the story of how each patient was doing. Who was sick, who was likely stable, who could have probably been just fine asking someone at the bar why their pinky toe hurt rather than coming to the ER.

His third patient of the day fell into that last category. His name was Kent Carpenter. A triage category five. The lowest severity complaint. The triage nurse, who checks in patients and does the initial screening, assigns a category to the patient based on how ill the patient appears. A lower number means the patient is more critical and should be seen quicker than a patient with a higher number. It's one of the many systems in place to help prioritize care in a system that is chronically understaffed and overwhelmed. The triage nurse is usually very experienced with a good clinical sense of who is sick and who is not. It takes a lot to impress an ER triage nurse. They've been there, done that. An illness may seem severe to the patient, but it will be graded against the other patients in the department and the hunch of the triage nurse.

"Good morning sir, I'm Dr. Bryce Chapman. I'm the emergency medicine physician who will be taking care of you. How can I best help you today?" It was an honest question, one he said to each patient to begin the discussion; no matter how ridiculous their visit to the emergency department was. He learned early on in his career to ask open-ended questions, not to lead the patient to a particular answer. And to never trust the chief complaint entered in the medical record. Often patients do not reveal the true nature of their visit until they are one-on-one with the physician.

"Hi, Doc, I woke up today with a cough I just can't shake. I felt okay when I went to bed, but this morning I'm just feeling off."

"You've only been sick a few hours and really just have a cough?" asked Bryce with a hint of surprise. He often wondered why people felt the need to spend four hundred dollars on a co-pay for such minor complaints.

"Yes, that's about it. No fever. I felt a bit winded walking in from the parking lot, but I was fine once I got into the bed," answered the patient.

Bryce continued with a long list of questions, trying to tease out further symptoms or reasons to be concerned, striking out each possible critical diagnosis that the patient could have. A normal exam, normal vitals, and a benign history equaled a quick discharge with a large dose of reassurance. "I don't believe you have a serious illness at this point, sir. I recommend rest, Motrin or Tylenol for fever, and watching your symptoms at home. I'll get your discharge papers ready." Bryce glanced at his watch. 8:05 a.m. Only six hours and fifty-five minutes left until his week of vacation and a kid-free trip to the Bahamas.

"Dr. Chapman, can I speak with you a moment?" said the charge nurse, snapping him back to Indiana from his Caribbean thoughts.

"Sure Jackie, what's up?"

"I wanted to let you know we are understaffed again today. I had one nurse call in sick and the hospital reduced our full-time equivalents by two for the next sixty days. Please be patient with us as it's going to take longer to get IVs, labs, meds, and everything else done."

"They cut FTEs heading into influenza season?" asked Bryce, incredulous.

"Yep. It also coincides with the end of the last fiscal quarter. You know, the last chance the administration has to boost profits and claim their incentive bonuses in their contracts." She lowered her voice and looked at the floor. "We were short two nurses last night. When that code came in everyone came to help, which left two hallways without a nurse while we worked the code. We had an elderly patient fall and break his hip because no one was free to help him to the bathroom." Bryce saw a tear running down her cheek. "We do the best we can with what they give us, but sometimes it's just not enough," she said.

"Jackie, you and your team do an amazing job taking care of our patients. We'll find a way to get through this, and I'll try to find a way to convince administration to get the FTEs back. The team works best when we have all the players on the field."

Jackie rubbed the back of her forearm across her eyes, soaking the tears into the long-sleeved compression shirt she wore beneath her scrub top. "I hope so Dr. Chapman. I'm starting to doubt myself and my ability to run the department. At some point there's just not enough staff to do the job safely."

"And let me guess, it was you who had to apologize to the family after their loved one broke a hip, right? No one from administration came down to explain that this is simply a side effect of their cost-cutting decision and that we all need to sacrifice a bit for the bottom line?"

"Nope, all me. I can't keep doing this if nothing changes, but if I quit it would make the situation worse. I don't know what to do." Jackie leaned back against the wall and sighed.

"Hang in there. I'll talk to Dr. Tate and see if there's anything he can do." Bryce touched her forearm as he headed back to the physician work area. "Remember, you didn't cause any of this; you're a victim of it."

***

The rest of the shift proceeded as expected for Bryce. Chest pain, abdominal pain, a stroke, forgotten tampon, pediatric wrist fracture, and a random assortment of minor ailments rounded out the day. Finally, it was time to leave. Bryce checked his watch as he walked out. Only forty-five minutes after his shift ended. *Not bad.* He texted his wife to let her know he'd be home earlier than expected. His phone vibrated a response that he ignored while he drove home, but the second vibration indicated a call rather than a text. He grabbed the phone and saw Valerie's face on the screen.

"Hey babe, I'm on my way home. What's up?"

"Your parents are here and they're great with the kids, but I can't stand the constant suggestions of what we could be doing differently. Is this ever going to change?"

Bryce smiled but tried to speak without his facial expression coming through in his voice. "It probably will in a few years as they get dementia and forget what they've told you already. Then they'll simply repeat themselves every hour rather than just once a trip."

"Very funny, Bryce. Just get home, refill my wine glass, and take me to the Bahamas. In fact, do you want to get a hotel by the airport tonight?"

"Hey, they're not that bad. And they're really excited to spend a few days with the kids and connect with them. They raised me well enough to be worthy of you, right?"

"I guess. I'll see you in a few, but I'm refilling my glass now."

Bryce parked the car in the driveway and walked into the kitchen, finding his parents sitting at the table alone. Bryce hugged them both and sat down at the table. "Where's Val?"

"She said she had to finish packing," said his dad.

"I told her she should have done that while the kids were napping today, and then she could just sit here and relax with us instead of rushing to get ready to go. I always hated feeling rushed when we left on vacation," said Bryce's mother.

Bryce nodded his head in agreement. He knew that Val was completely packed and had packed everything for him also. He pictured her sitting in bed with a glass of wine and watching Netflix on her iPad. "Well, you know Val, she always wants to make sure everything is perfect. Just look at this place. If I stayed home with the kids instead of her, she'd have to work *and* clean up after me. Are you guys settled in? Do you need anything?"

"No, we're fine, son. It's about time for us to head to bed, anyway. We need to be rested up to keep up with the little ones tomorrow. Have a great trip," said his dad as he stood up from the table.

"We'll do our best. We'll have cell coverage on the island so call if you have any concerns. We'll try to check in with the kids a few times." He turned and headed upstairs to check on the kids and give them each a hug before walking back to the master bedroom. He did not see light coming from under their door, so he opened it slowly, only to see Val's face aglow from the iPad, a glass of wine in her left hand. She smiled at him quickly and went right back to her show. Bryce changed, climbed into bed, and fell asleep instantly.

Chapter Four

"Welcome to Exuma!" cheered the voice over the plane's loudspeaker after the plane slowed and began taxiing toward the small airport building. Passengers quickly followed with muted applause. Bryce and Valerie clinked their glasses together and smiled at each other. Drinks on the plane are certainly in order when you're on your first vacation without kids in years. They had just landed on a gorgeous, under-developed island in the Bahamas and were eager to get their vacation started. Fortunately, this airport had a single runway and gate so the usual taxi and docking protocols were much more rapid.

Valerie stepped out from the plane onto the mobile stairs and looked around. Palm trees, soaring white birds, a warm Caribbean sun obscured by occasional high clouds were exactly what she needed. After being at Bryce's side through medical school, residency, and having two children in rapid succession, she desperately needed a break. The truth was that his career success had come at the cost of an intimate relationship with her. What was once a marriage filled with lustful energy and fierce devotion had evolved into one with a "prevent defense" mindset, simply trying to hang on. Now the mutual goal was raising the kids, ensuring financial stability, and finding a way to get through each day. Neither

Valerie nor Bryce spoke of their hope for this vacation to change things, but they both hoped it did. It needed to. Counseling sure hadn't.

Bryce noticed his wife pause just after exiting the plane as she emerged into the sunshine. It's as if God trained His spotlight on her and she was letting the audience adjust their eyes. When they first started dating, he would try to sneak up on her and just watch her for a bit before she noticed him. Her beautiful blond hair and athletic figure looked nearly as good now as they did fifteen years ago. She would smile and act embarrassed when she'd spot him, but secretly she was flattered by the attention.

But that was then, and this was a vacation. "Val, come on. You're blocking traffic," chided Bryce with a quick slap on her butt to reinforce his words. His nudge brought her back to reality and she grabbed the rail to descend the steps, one hand fighting the wind for control of the hem of her dress. The years had been kind to Valerie, and earlier Bryce had noticed her turning heads in the airport between flights. Her pale-yellow sun dress and platform sandals didn't hurt either.

"This place is absolutely incredible," she said while they waited for their luggage. "That was the prettiest flight I've ever been on." The Bahamas are made up of seven hundred islands, of which only thirty are inhabited. Of those with an international airport, Great Exuma is the most remote. The flight from Miami is only three hundred miles which allows for a lower cruising altitude. This offers a better view of the crystal-clear Caribbean water, enhanced by the shallow depth and innumerable sandy shoals. The Exuma chain is a group of three hundred and sixty-five islands southeast of Nassau; one to explore every day of the year.

"Yeah, me too. Did you see all those deserted beaches? They gave me a few ideas. We need a bottle of rum, and then we'll pick up a boat and drop our inhibitions. What do you say?"

"I'll have to think about that. Making love on a pristine, deserted beach shouldn't be something left to crappy romance novels. Crappy relationships could use it to spice things up a bit too. "Okay Chap, maybe," she replied with a devious smile. Perhaps this vacation was indeed going to improve things.

They cleared the short line at customs and were soon standing in a gravel parking lot, baking in the sun.

"I think the car rental building is down this road a bit," said Bryce, struggling to drag his suitcase through the gravel.

"Tell you what," said Valerie. "Why don't I watch the luggage at this bar across the street while you go get the car?"

"Great idea. Get me something tall and cold." Bryce picked up the suitcases and carried them across to an outside table and then continued down the road to the car rental business.

Valerie flagged down a waitress and ordered two Painkillers along with a local draft beer. She was finishing her second drink when a bright red Jeep Wrangler drove up quickly and parked facing her table. The driver killed the engine and then stood up on the seat, his chest resting on the front roll bar.

"Hey, take a look at our ride. This is going to be a blast to drive." Bryce hopped down from the Jeep and loaded the luggage into the back seat before joining her at the table. He raised his glass in a salute and said, "Are you ready to leave our troubles behind and relax in paradise?"

***

"Hello, Washington Memorial Hospital Emergency Room," said the ER secretary.

"Hi, I was there two days ago and ... saw Dr. Chapman, is he ... there today?" sputtered the patient between coughing spasms.

"I'm sorry, he is not working today," replied the secretary. This is the standard response to anyone who asked. It's possible the caller has a grudge and wants to return to settle a score. Perhaps it's a former lover, a recruiter, a lawyer. No matter who the caller requests, the physician is not working today. Today it also happened to be true.

"Well, I was there two days ago and he sorta blew me off. I'm a lot sicker now, should I come back in and be seen?" The sentences were spoken in brief phrases, with pauses between them.

"Sir, we can't give medical advice over the phone. If you feel you need to be seen, we are happy to take another look at you," explained the secretary, again speaking the standard boilerplate response she was trained to provide.

"Okay, I'm going to come in, I can barely breathe," gasped the caller.

"That's fine, sir, please give me your name so I can tell our triage desk you're coming."

"Kent–" the first word was cut off by a coughing spasm. "Carpenter," was the squeaked reply before the click as the call was terminated.

Chapter Five

"Wake up, babe, we need to be at the boat in forty-five minutes!" said Bryce.

Valerie rolled over in the king-sized bed and stretched until she was worried her leg was going to cramp. "What time is it? And is that coffee I smell? And bacon?

"Yes, we're all prepared and ready for your enjoyment," smiled Bryce.

"We? Okay, I'm getting up," she said as she pulled herself up in bed and looked around. To her left was an open window with a view of the Caribbean sunrise. Turquoise water, birds floating in the breeze, and an empty beach that looked very inviting. Glancing around the room she saw Bryce putting food on a plate for her and laughed. "You're telling me you got up early, made coffee, bacon, opened the windows, but didn't have time to put on clothes?" she taunted.

"Hey, we're on vacation. And if I recall correctly, after the second bottle of wine we barely had time to take them off. I didn't want to risk any delays this morning, though it did make cooking bacon a bit of a contact sport. I may need help with some aloe in a bit," he winced.

"You're an idiot." The words sounded harsh but the smile and wandering eyes as she bit into her crunchy bacon made it clear these were words of endearment. This vacation was indeed exactly what they needed.

After eating and getting dressed, they hopped in the rented Jeep and headed for the boat dock. The beautiful water, beaches, and weather made Exuma a favorite status symbol for the wealthy. For two hundred and fifty dollars, you can be one of eight people on the tour through this beautiful area of the world. For fifteen hundred dollars, you can book the entire boat.

Bryce parked the Jeep in the marina parking lot, grabbed the cooler, and clicked the fob to lock the doors. "Did you just lock a car that doesn't have a top or sides?" asked Valerie.

"You can never be too safe," said Bryce with a smile.

They met the captain on the dock. He was average height but lean and dark-skinned from years of Bahamian sun. "I'm Kyle Lafayette, I'll be your captain and tour guide today. You've booked a private trip, so if you're ready, we'll shove off and get underway.

"Just the two of us? How romantic," said Val, leaning back into Bryce's chest.

Captain Kyle turned on the engines and once they were idling well, he released the dock lines. Twin 400-horsepower engines had the boat up on plane quickly as the captain navigated the narrow channels between the islands. Val and Bryce next to each other on the bow and stared ahead at the beauty as it passed by.

"That island is owned by Faith Hill and Tim McGraw," yelled Captain Kyle Lafayette over the noise of the wind and engines. "You can visit any of these islands, but you can only go as far as the high tide line. After that, it becomes private property. Up ahead are a series of islands owned by the Fry's

Electronics family. You can rent each of them independently if you'd like. Each one is themed for a different part of the world."

"David Copperfield's island is on the right. He has the largest Houdini museum in the world there. You can also swim with a titanium mermaid and play the piano if you'd like."

"I'm sorry, did you say swim with a titanium mermaid?" inquired Bryce.

"Yes, Copperfield has enough money to build interesting things like that offshore. It's sunk in about fifteen feet of water," replied Kyle.

"I think we'll skip that. Let's focus on pigs, iguanas, and James Bond movies," said Bryce. The boat stopped at a few islands along the way, allowing the Chapmans to swim with and feed wild pigs, feed grapes to iguanas, and walk beautiful, deserted beaches. This was a day that could last a month as far as they were concerned. "Let's go, guys, we need to get to Thunderball Grotto soon if we want to catch slack tide," implored the captain.

Chapter Six

"Washington Memorial, this is Medic 93, how do you copy?" blasted from the EMS radio.

"Medic 93, this is Washington Memorial, copy clear. Go ahead with your report," replied the triage nurse.

"We're en route to your facility with a thirtyish-year-old male, single-car motor vehicle accident. He drove into a bridge support. He was restrained, not much damage to the vehicle, but he looks rough. Pale, diaphoretic, respiratory distress. He's in and out of consciousness. Oxygen saturation was 73 percent but up to 92 percent on a non-rebreather. He has equal breath sounds but crackles everywhere. We'll be there in two minutes. He may need bilateral chest tubes."

"Copy that Medic 93. We'll see you in trauma bay two when you arrive, Washington Memorial out," said the nurse. "Paula, page out a level one trauma two minutes out. Thirty-year-old male, MVA."

Paula, the secretary in the ER for the night's shift, rapidly entered the information into the hospital's electronic paging app and sent the alert. Less than five seconds later, text messages were received by dozens of people on the trauma team. The hospital had closed its paging system six months ago and upgraded to phone-based applications and texting for communication. Anesthesia, X-ray and CT techs, respiratory therapists, lab techs, trauma surgeons, ER physicians and nurses, pharmacists, and others all received notification of the incoming trauma patient. A level one trauma patient is likely to be the sickest in the department and requires immediate attention to numerous problems at the same time. This takes a team approach, and Washington Memorial is the best in the city at it.

"Two minutes? That's all the lead time they gave us? Probably took them twenty to get the guy out of the car. I could have pissed and had a sandwich. Now I have to run a trauma with a full bladder and an empty stomach," whined Dr. Sharpe.

"I'll catheterize you while you are intubating if that'll help," laughed the charge nurse Jackie as she walked with Sharpe back towards their trauma bay.

They had barely arrived in the trauma bay when the doors swung open and medics rolled in with their patient. Clay Turner led the procession, per usual. Clay is an army veteran and loves to take the lead on serious cases. It wasn't a bad thing. He's an extremely competent paramedic. The guy everyone wants on their team when things go badly.

Dr. Sharpe stood ready, taking in the scene. The physical exam starts with using most of the senses. If things go well the sense of taste will not be utilized. A quick glance at the patient showed he was strapped to a back board with cervical collar on his neck, looking quite ill. His skin was pale, soaked with sweat, and he was breathing rapidly, but shallowly. Grunting noises were all he said and he was struggling against the restraints holding him to the board.

"Dr. Sharpe and team, I'm bringing you Kent," said Clay. "He was the restrained driver of a car verses bridge support this morning. Witnesses said he drifted over and hit it head on. They thought he looked slumped over before the impact. It took us a few minutes to get him out of the car, but the damage wasn't all that bad. His pressure is sixty, heart rate one hundred forty. Oxygen sat was 73 percent but is now 92 percent with the non-rebreather."

The team came together in a well-practiced maneuver to transfer the patient to the ER bed and roll him off the backboard while maintaining a neutral position on the neck. Dr. Sharpe began a quick primary survey focusing initially on the airway, which was open with no sign of obstruction. Next was breathing, which was abnormal. Shallow, rapid respirations and loud crackling sounds could be due to many things and few of them good. Multiple rib fractures, pneumothorax, a popped lung, pulmonary contusion, sternal fracture, or spinal cord injury were a few diagnoses running through Dr. Sharpe's mind. He ordered the patient placed on high-flow oxygen to help alleviate the work of breathing and buy some time to complete his exam before starting on the procedures that may need to be done. After breathing came an evaluation of the patient's circulation. Was he pumping enough blood to avoid shock? Were all extremities receiving adequate blood supply?

The patient's blood pressure was barely registering on the machine, only sixty-five over forty. A hypotensive trauma patient usually meant blood was escaping the veins and arteries and was pooling in places it wasn't meant to be. If not rapidly diagnosed and treated, the patient would die quickly. Tom Sharpe grabbed the ultrasound machine and began a quick, multi-faceted scan meant to evaluate for causes of the patient's low blood pressure. He scanned through the abdominal views looking for collections of fluid, usually indicating the presence of hemorrhage into the abdomen. Nothing. Next, he moved to the pericardium, the sack around the heart that can become filled with blood and not allow the heart to pump effectively. Nothing. Fearing a catastrophic diagnosis in the chest after negative abdominal imaging, he moved to each side of the chest expecting to find air outside of the lungs, causing increased pressure and respiratory failure. Nothing.

The patient had only been in the department five minutes and had already received more attention than most patients receive in hours. Two liters of fluid were nearly infused through pressure bags fed into large-bore IVs in each arm. Sharpe was starting to question whether this was actually a trauma patient.

"Hey, Tom, what do you have?" shouted Elisa Morales, the most aggressive trauma surgeon to stand under five-foot-tall in the history of the profession.

Chapter Seven

"There it is! Thunderball Grotto," said the captain as he backed off the throttle. The boat slowed and sank lower in the clear blue water off Staniel Cay as it came off plane and drifted to a stop. "Is that really where they filmed the James Bond movie?" asked Val.

"Yes, Moneypenny, it is," replied Bryce in his best Sean Connery voice.

He put on his mask and strapped a GoPro to his head. A red light indicated it was recording video. "Go ahead and grab your snorkel gear. I'll get us on a mooring ball and then you two can head in. The easiest way in is straight ahead under that sign. Depending on the tide you should have a foot or two of clearance and not need to swim underwater to get in. There are a few different exits, and some of them require you to swim through an underwater keyhole exit to get out. We got here a little late and the current is picking up after the tide change. Be careful about the current or you'll end up on Eleuthera." As the captain finished speaking, they were nearly knocked off their feet as the boat lurched forward, accompanied by a deep thud. The stunned captain turned around to see another boat had just struck their transom.

"Sorry, mate! Our brakes didn't work!" laughed the clearly intoxicated captain of a smaller, center console boat to the approval of his fellow intoxicated passengers.

Bryce walked with the captain to the back to examine the damage. Fortunately there didn't seem to be any yet. But they both knew to never underestimate the damage a drunken skipper can inflict to a vessel or occupant.

Bryce Chapman's gaze shifted back to the other boat's occupants when he felt an arm wrap around his waist. "Ignore them, they're not your responsibility. They're adults," reassured his wife. "Stop being an ER doc and just enjoy yourself. The captain said the current is going out and we need to be careful."

He smiled, kissed her on the forehead and agreed. "You're right, let's get in!"

Bryce checked the action cam position, donned his flippers, and leaned backward over the port gunwale, entering the water with a splash and completing the backward somersault underwater. In sharp contrast to the exuberance of her husband, Valerie climbed down the swim ladder and came alongside him in the water.

They proceeded towards the entrance to the grotto looking down as they swam. Countless fish darted among the coral, hoping for food to be kicked up as the flippers moved sand back and forth. To the right was a small underwater opening that required ten feet of underwater passage to get through. Jagged outcroppings and bends made the path more difficult. They looked at each other and Bryce smiled around his snorkel. Valerie shook her head, and then both headed towards the main entrance. He took a large breath and dove under, swimming the twenty-foot channel entirely underwater.

Valerie sighed through her snorkel at her husband's antics and let the current drift her into the cave. Bryce had nearly recovered his breathing when Val made it through the entrance. Looking up they saw a hole in the roof of the cave with sunlight and vegetation streaming through. Breathtaking. The walls were uneven and full of outcroppings and large pits. Underwater were many schools of small fish, holding their own against the current. The edges of the grotto offered a perch to hold to and catch your breath or just enjoy the view.

"Hell yes! This place is incredible!" came a shout from the entrance. Bryce recognized the voice from the collision. *I see enough drunks at work. Why do they have to follow me on vacation?* Two other men followed shortly after and soon five adults were treading water inside the grotto. If you were not holding on, the current could pull you through and out into the bay. In order to stay in one place you had to keep moving, allowing fatigue to subtly creep in.

"Babe, swim into that patch of sun so I can get a picture of you," said Bryce, pointing to a ray of sunshine streaming in through the opening in the rocky ceiling.

As Valerie kicked her flippers to move, she accidentally struck the leg of one of the guys from the other boat. It was a glancing blow that likely felt no different than a fish brushing against a leg.

"Hey, did that chick just grab my leg? Tony, did you see that? Our little mermaid here must be thinking of spawning."

Tony, the captain of the other boat, spun around. "Is that right? Do you want to join us later? We have an entire island rented for the week. Your friend can come also. I'm sure he wouldn't mind making drinks for us." The three men were swimming toward and starting to circle Valerie, separating her from Bryce.

"Actually he's my husband, and he doesn't make drinks for jackasses." She put her snorkel back in her mouth and dove underwater. The area of the grotto they were in had a depth of about twelve feet at the moment, plenty of depth for a former Division I collegiate swimmer to dive and swim past the men. She surfaced on the other side of Bryce and was heading for the exit channel. By now the current had increased and was rippling the surface as it accelerated in the narrow channel. She paused at the entrance to wait for Bryce.

"Hey, where are you going, babe? We're just starting to talk to you," said Tony as he swam towards Valerie. His movement was stopped by a firm palm against his chest.

"That's enough. You've had your fun and now you're going to let us leave," warned Bryce while staring into Tony's eyes. His arm still extended and pressed against the drunk man's chest.

"Oh, you shouldn't have done that. No one puts a hand on me. I'll fight you here and now," yelled Tony, his words echoing off the rock walls.

"No, you won't. You're drunk. Just go get on your boat and sober up before you head back to your island to continue your sausage fest," taunted Bryce. He instantly regretted the words the moment they left his lips. His training as an emergency medicine physician had taught him to react quickly and reflexively to serious situations. Contemplation and rumination are great on the medical floor during rounds, but the ER often requires immediate action based on instinct. When a man is threatening your wife, it's not a time for contemplation. It's a time for action.

"Sausage fest?" laughed Tony as he swatted Bryce's arm away. "Let me show you what happens when you insult a regional boxing champion, you bastard." The words were spewed out as Tony's arm cocked back, ready to deliver a blow straight into Bryce's face. What Tony didn't realize, is unlike in a boxing arena, he was taking a swing while moving backward thanks to the strong tidal current. His right hook passed two inches shy of its target, his momentum spinning his body to the left. Not to be outdone with stories of glory days, former high school state soccer champion Bryce extended his leg and kicked Tony as hard as he could in the side. This created distance between them and backward momentum that Bryce used to head toward the exit.

"Val, get on the boat and tell the captain we need to leave. I'll watch your back," he yelled over his shoulder while spinning back around towards the other group. What he saw shocked him. The kick he delivered had sent the already spun-around Tony straight into the side of the grotto, smashing his face into the rock. Propelled by the force of his kick and the power of the current, Tony's face was cut in several places and bleeding into the water. He was missing a central incisor, the socket dripping blood and making his voice sound like Mike Tyson. Bryce kicked backward again and put the snorkel back in his mouth as he heard the group yell and begin to charge after him.

"Follow him, I'll take this other exit and get ahead of him," screamed Tony as he headed for the underwater exit.

Bryce's confidence nosedived when he heard that, making him pull against the current as hard as he could. He cleared the entrance to the cave just as Valerie climbed on board the boat. The captain had the engine running and was removing the mooring line from the bow cleat, eager to follow Valerie's shouted advice once Bryce was on the boat.

Bryce was halfway to safety when the first of two men cleared the cave entrance. Twenty feet separated him from his 800hp getaway vehicle. Valerie yelled encouragement to him and prepared to help him up the ladder. Scurrying up a ladder in swim fins is no easy task. The captain held a fishing gaff in a ready stance at the bow of the boat. The best weapon in a fight is the one that you have. Gaffing a man would be a new experience, but he assumed it'd be much easier than a flopping tuna. He hoped to not find out. Bryce cleared the ladder, and the captain placed his hand on the throttle.

Chapter Eight

"Elisa, glad you could make it," said Dr. Sharpe. Most trauma resuscitations start with the ER physician while the trauma team assembles. The ER is in charge of managing the airway and the patient until the trauma team arrives. "This guy drove his car into a bridge and was nearly dead when EMS arrived. Blood pressure is sixty over nothing; he's in shock with a negative ultrasound for blood, pneumothorax, and no significant injury found. If you ask me, I think he was sick and then crashed his car. We're blasting fluids into him, and I've ordered imaging, labs, and antibiotics. I really don't think we need you; this should be an ICU admission for sepsis."

"Interesting interpretation. They pull a guy from a wrecked car and you're telling me he's not a trauma patient? I'd rather have a CT scan than an ultrasound by an ER cowboy. Let's get him down the hall to the scanner," she replied.

"I'd prefer to not send him down there right now. His systolic pressure is sixty," argued Sharpe.

"Which is exactly why we need to diagnose his injuries so I can take him to the OR and save his life," snapped Dr. Morales. "Does he need to be intubated?"

"I'm afraid if I intubate him, the positive pressure in his chest would lead to cardiovascular collapse. His pressure is sixty!"

"Okay, ER, thank you for your airway management evaluation; the trauma team will take it from here. Someone call CT and tell them we're on our way. Donut of truth, here we come," called Elisa Morales to anyone close enough to hear. She unlocked the bed, placed the monitor on the foot of the bed, and began pushing the patient toward radiology.

"Don't you want to start pressors to stabilize his blood pressure first?" shouted Sharpe as the team headed down the hall. He shook his head, flipped the gloves into the garbage can and walked back to his workstation. Three patients had come in while he was handling the trauma and it was time to play catch up. *I'll just read about him later when I finish my chart.*

Tom Sharpe scanned the chart of a seventy-five-year-old man with severe mid-abdominal pain. That's never a good sign. That patient won the "who is sickest" game of the patients needing to be seen and earned the prize of a jaded ER doctor entering from behind door number one.

"CODE BLUE, emergency department, CT scanner," blared through the overhead speakers in the department. *You're kidding me, that freaking surgeon.* Tom excused himself from the room and jogged down the hall towards CT.

Chapter Nine

Bryce turned around to survey the scene they had just es-
caped from. What had happened? *How had our perfectly*
romantic excursion turned into a trip from hell? He saw
the two men who had followed him out the main channel
but did not see Tony. That was odd, considering he took
the shorter route out. He quickly scanned around his boat;
fearful the ringleader was about to board their vessel. His
scan revealed nothing.

"Hold on, wait a second!" he yelled at the captain.
"Where's their friend? He never came out."

"Who cares? Let's get out of here," begged Valerie. She did
not enjoy confrontation.

Bryce saw the concerned looks on the men's faces as
their friend failed to appear. One dove under the water and
quickly surfaced with a look of panic. "Help! Tony's stuck in
the underwater exit. He's not moving!"

Son of a bitch.

Bryce pulled his mask back into position and dove back
into the water. He was eighty feet away and it felt like he was
swimming in molasses. The clear Bahamian water allowed
him to see Tony floating lifeless in the underwater opening.
Able to see, but not help. It was torture to a man who has

dedicated his life to helping others. Even those he had just smashed their face in.

With twenty feet to go he felt someone next to him and looked to see Valerie passing him. Her muscle memory combined with adrenaline was no match for Bryce's amateur swim technique. She reached Tony first, but was unable to pull him to the surface. He was clearly caught on something.

Bryce dove under and found Tony held tight against the rock, his back sliced raw from struggling against the sharp coral. *What's he stuck on?* His arms and legs were free. His mask had fallen off and was resting on the bottom. The only other possibility was the swimsuit. Quickly Bryce reached behind Tony and grabbed his suit, feeling it caught against a jagged outcropping. He pulled the suit in every direction, but it would not budge. The synthetic fibers were too strong to be torn by hand with minimal leverage. His lungs burning, Bryce resurfaced and gasped for a breath of air. He screamed for the captain to bring the boat closer as he dove under again. This time he planted his feet on either side of Tony, squatted down, and grabbed his swimsuit. He twisted the suit in his fists and stood up, essentially performing an Olympic deadlift. The fabric tore, and Tony floated free. Bryce kicked off the rock and dragged Tony to the surface. Valerie elbowed him out of the way and reached an arm around Tony's chest, dragging him to the boat twice as fast as Bryce could have done.

Their captain helped pull Tony onto the boat and laid him on the deck. Bryce yelled for someone to call for help. It was the right thing to do, but the wrong place to do it. There was no help. They were in the Caribbean, eighty miles from the nearest hospital in Nassau, with no roads and no ambulances. The Bahamian Coast Guard would be by in a few days.

"Mayday, Mayday, Mayday, this is power boat Purple Haze at Thunderball Grotto, Staniel Cay. Requesting immediate medical assistance for a drowning. Repeat, power boat Purple Haze at Thunderball Grotto, Staniel Cay, requesting immediate assistance for a drowning." The captain's voice was urgent yet calm as he sent out the distress call on the radio.

As Bryce cleared the gunwale, he leapt onto Tony and began chest compressions. There is no use in feeling for a pulse when the patient has been submerged several minutes and lifeless for at least a minute. Chest compressions on a patient with a pulse are annoying and can cause some injury, but the risk of waiting a bit to do a definitive pulse check outweighed any potential harm.

As he was compressing the chest, bloody froth bubbled out of Tony's mouth. Bryce knew what was coming and he steeled himself for it. *What's the worst that can happen?* With that on his mind, he leaned down, sealed his mouth over Tony's, pinched his nose shut, and blew air into lungs that were full of saltwater. Valerie took over chest compressions with the cadence and depth adjusted by Bryce for maximum effect.

Tony's friends had boarded the boat and were trying to help, but were unsure how. Bryce sensed their dilemma and asked them to pray for their friend. All sense of inebriation vanished as the seriousness of the situation sank in.

After several rounds of compressions and breaths a pulse check was done, yielding nothing. Valerie resumed compressions as the captain scanned the water hoping to find someone who could be of assistance. He saw a wave runner heading toward them at full speed, doing at least sixty miles an hour through the uneven chop. It slowed as it neared their boat, and the driver tossed a bag to the captain. "It's our AED, it's all we have," yelled the man on the wave runner. He had come from a luxury yacht anchored in deeper water who heard the radio call. *Thank God for wealthy elderly people in the yachting community. Without them, there would be no AED on the boat right now.*

Bryce smiled and couldn't believe their good fortune. How did an AED arrive in the middle of paradise? He unpacked the device and dried Tony's chest, applying the pads to the right upper and lower left lateral chest. He gave two more breaths and then asked Valerie to pause compressions while the AED assessed the rhythm.

NO SHOCK ADVISED.

The computerized voice spoke the words to the dismay of all on board. It could mean that Tony actually had a good electrical rhythm and didn't need a shock. Or it could mean he had absolutely no electrical activity and no shock would be beneficial. A dead heart cannot be shocked. Only a heart beating out of rhythm or in fibrillation can be shocked with an expectation of benefit.

Valerie continued chest compression as Bryce continued breathing for Tony. The foam from his mouth had lessened, though Bryce still wanted to vomit. The minutes ticked by as CPR continued. They were without IVs, nurses, medications, airway equipment. Stranded in paradise. Once again, a three-hour tour led to disaster.

"Power boat Purple Haze, this is sea plane Turbo Beaver. I am two minutes out from your location, I'll be landing from the west and am available to transport your patient if needed."

Bryce laughed. He worked at the largest trauma hospital in a major US city and sometimes it took two hours to get an ambulance to transport a patient to another facility. In ten minutes flat he had a plane on standby in the Bahamas. This string of luck meant it was time for another pulse check and AED evaluation.

SHOCK ADVISED. CHARGING. STAND CLEAR.

Bryce's heart leapt. Asystole, or a lack of electrical activity, was a death sentence. Restarting a heart that wasn't beating is extremely rare. Correcting a fatal rhythm disturbance at least has a chance at survival.

He looked around to ensure no one was touching the patient and pressed the button to deliver the shock. Tony's body jerked as two hundred joules of energy coursed through his chest. Valerie was watching the machine and Tony to see what happened when Bryce directed her to resume CPR.

"We restart compressions right away and then do a pulse check in a bit. If his heart restarted it's still going to be beating inefficiently for a little bit," he explained. Valerie nodded; he was still teaching even on vacation in the middle of a code. That's why he's earned a prestigious teaching award three times in ten years.

The ever-increasing engine noise confirmed the sea plane had landed and was headed their way. The pilot cut the engine and drifted to a stop against their boat. Tony's friends met the plane and tied a line to it to keep it close.

"Come on, you have to save Tony. Please!" they implored.

"Let's stop and do a pulse check," Bryce said to Val, who stopped compressions and placed her hand on Tony's wrist, feeling for a pulse while Bryce did the same at the neck.

Chapter Ten

Sharpe entered the CT suite and saw a nurse straddling the patient while doing chest compressions. The radiology tech held a button to slide the gantry out to remove the patient from the scanner. "What the hell happened?" he yelled as he approached the scanner.

"We were just getting ready to inject contrast for the chest CT when his heart rate dropped and then he went asystolic," explained the nurse.

"Just get him back to the trauma room and we'll do this there," he snapped. Dr. Sharpe grabbed the airway kit and began bagging the patient as the team wheeled back towards the trauma bay. Dr. Morales rushed past them calling ahead for a thoracotomy tray.

Sharpe shook his head. *A thoracotomy? For a septic patient? Has she lost her mind?*

The bed slammed to a stop as the nurse stepped on the brake, locking the bed back into position. Sharpe called out for the airway equipment as he prepared to intubate.

Clay Turner stepped up to take over compressions. Paramedics are experts at CPR, and Clay was in excellent shape. Capable of extended compressions without taking a pause. Exactly what benefits patients the most.

"Let's give a milligram of epinephrine and make sure the fluids are still on pressure bags. I want liters three and four going," he directed.

"No, the patient needs blood. He's a traumatic arrest. Fluid will just dilute his anemia more. Give him two units of packed red cells on the rapid infuser!" shouted Elisa Morales. "And where's my thoracotomy tray?"

"You're giving blood to a septic patient and cracking his chest? Is this a new protocol I'm not aware of?" Sharpe couldn't believe what he was seeing. He passed the breathing tube into the lungs and confirmed its placement by listening to each side of the chest as the respiratory therapist squeezed the bag to inflate the lungs. Air went in smoothly but returned with thick mucus secretions that began to fill up the tube.

"Clay, speed it up and push deeper," instructed Sharpe as he noted the chest compressions to be slow and not relaxing enough between them. "You need to allow the chest to fully recoil between compressions."

"Hey ER, thanks for the airway. This is a trauma patient. American College of Surgeons states a traumatic arrest who loses pulses in the department should undergo an immediate thoracotomy. This could be lifesaving. We're opening in fifteen seconds," she declared while ripping open the sterile surgical tray. She had donned a sterile gown in record time and was prepping the chest with iodine.

Sharpe stood in disbelief. Clay held compressions as Dr. Morales made an incision from sternum to armpit on each side, as deep as the scalpel would go. This exposed the deeper muscle layer and ribs that made up the chest wall. She then grabbed a large pair of surgical scissors and cut the muscle between the ribs on both sides. The final move was cutting through the sternum with a serrated wire saw. Her surgical technique was flawless, impressing everyone in the room. It wasn't every day they got to see a human cut in half.

Next she expertly cut open the sack surrounding the heart. Sharpe saw her eyes squint as each step in the process failed to yield the expected finding. No blood. No large pocket of compressed air in the chest. Only massive amounts of adherent mucus on the lungs. Like someone let Slimer from *Ghostbusters* loose in the man's chest for a few days.

"Huh, no blood. Can we resume compressions?" asked Sharpe from the head of the bed.

"Yes, of course. Someone do open cardiac massage while I do a laparotomy," ordered Dr. Morales.

He had to give it to her. She just would not quit. The line to do chest compressions was usually long. It's a tiring physical activity that requires frequent rotation to maintain effective compressions. Open cardiac massage lines are twice as long because the story telling and coolness factor for having performed it is off the charts.

"Who here actually knows how to do open cardiac massage?" asked Sharpe. He was answered with silence. "That's what I thought," he laughed as he moved to the patient's side and reached his sterile gloved hands into the chest and began squeezing the heart from the bottom, careful to not pinch his fingers and to keep the heart parallel the floor. Sometimes you pull rank to boast or use your position for personal gain. This time he did it to try to save the life of his patient.

"Wow, there's no blood here either," stammered Dr. Elisa Morales.

Sharpe looked down and saw the open abdomen of his patient. Or was it his dissected anatomy cadaver? They were starting to look so similar it was hard to tell. At this point the patient had received four liters of fluid and two units of blood. He still did not have a pulse and had no electrical activity on the monitor. Dr. Morales looked at Sharpe and said, "I don't think this is a trauma patient. If he makes it, call ICU to admit and manage his care."

"If he makes it, you're going to repair these divots you left in your playing field. I tried to tell you this guy was septic. Look at his lungs. There was literally pus oozing out of them when we bagged him. Someone send a culture of that to the lab. Everyone wash their hands well. We don't want whatever he has." Fifteen minutes into the code, Dr. Sharpe pronounced the patient dead. There was no more use in trying to resuscitate him. He had a zero percent chance of recovery. "Okay team, good job. This was good practice for when we might be able to actually save a trauma patient. Leave all the lines and tubes in place until I talk to the coroner," he said.

Clay stared at his patient, his hand on the wrist confirming the lack of pulse. "At least you will hurt no more." Several team members slapped him on the back in a show of support as they filed out of the room.

Once a code has ended and the patient dies, and awkward silence usually follows. There is a room full of disappointed people who tried unsuccessfully to make a meaningful difference in a life. They tried to fight the grim reaper and were unsuccessful. Conversation slowly picks back up, quicker if family is not present. The floor and surrounding area are cleaned of debris from the code and the patient is draped in a respectful fashion.

Tom Sharpe found Elisa Morales as she was stepping onto the elevator. She was the type of person who could never admit a mistake. She always had to be right.

"Hey, next time would you mind listening to me? I had that patient figured out."

"He was going to die no matter what we did. I could tell that the moment I walked into the room," she countered.

"Maybe so. But at least he could have died without a surgeon hacking him in half." He said the words as the door to the elevator closed. He was disappointed to not get to see the look on her face or get a response. He figured he'd hear about it from administration eventually. Who cares? They can add it to the list of other complaints against him for inappropriate comments. Fortunately, the list of positive letters from patient families vastly outnumbered the complaints of colleagues. When that no longer mattered to administration, it would be the day he planned to retire, Sharpe told himself.

Chapter Eleven

"I think I feel a pulse!" announced Valerie. Bryce felt the carotid artery bounding beneath his fingers and high-fived his wife. He leaned in for a kiss to share in the moment of celebration only to be pushed away with a look of disgust. Apparently, she wasn't into kissing guys whose faces were covered with other people's blood and vomit. Quirks like these are good to remember in a relationship. He made a mental note to remind himself of this one.

Bryce noted Tony still wasn't breathing, but had a good pulse. He asked someone to look through the AED bag to see if there was a mask to help deliver breaths.

"Here, is this what you want?" asked one of Tony's friends; the one who started the inappropriate talk with Valerie just a few minutes ago.

"Perfect. Thank you," responded Bryce, much to the relief of Tony's friend. Clearly glad to have done something to help.

"Hey, Cap, see if that pilot is ready to get us out of here. We need to get him to a hospital. He's not going to get any more stable than he is right now." The captain jogged back to talk to the pilot. The plane's cockpit door opened, the pilot stepped out, and then reached behind him to adjust seat positions.

"Wait, that pilot looks like–" Valerie's sentence trailed off as her brain rejected the message her eyes had just delivered. *It couldn't be. He should be on a stage with a microphone, not flying a plane in the Bahamas.*

"Let's go, y'all, let's load him into the back and head to Nassau. My Turbo Beaver can get him there in thirty minutes if we get movin'." The unlikely group of adversaries turned rescuers picked Tony up and carried him toward the plane while Bryce continued delivering breaths and checking his pulse. They laid him down on two seats, and Bryce knelt on the floor next to him.

"Val, did you hear the name of the plane?" smirked Bryce.

"Shut up, don't ruin this moment, you dork," she said, flashing him a smile.

The pilot handed back a portable oxygen tank and mask along with a headset to communicate during the flight. "Val, I'll call you when I can. You were great back there. Captain Kyle, can you make sure my wife gets back to our villa?" asked Bryce as he leaned out the door.

"Absolutely. Godspeed, my friend."

Bryce reached forward to grab the door and swing it shut. He was unfamiliar with the interior and struck his head on the fuselage while ducking back in. He shut the door and secured the latch. The pilot called on the radio for the group to untie the plane and push them away. When they had drifted a safe distance, he started the single Pratt & Whitney turbocharged engine and accelerated into the wind for takeoff.

Valerie and Kyle helped the others gather their items and delivered them back to their boat. "Do you guys know how to operate this boat and how to get home?" asked the captain, who was genuinely concerned for their well-being, despite what they did to his customers and nearly killing one of their friends.

"Yes, we'll be fine. This whole thing sobered us up pretty quickly. Thank you both for helping Tony. Sorry for what happened back there. I guess we drank too much and started acting pretty stupid. We owe you for saving Tony's life."

"He's not out of the woods yet," reminded Val. "But let's talk about this in a few weeks when we've had a chance to process what happened." She gave them Bryce's name and cellphone number. She wasn't about to give out hers.

The captain backed their boat away and looked over to Valerie. "So... can I count on you for a five-star review on Trip Advisor?"

She burst out laughing as the weight of the moment lifted. "Absolutely. But here I am on a boat with you while my husband is being whisked away into paradise by the number one country music artist in the nation. That's my fantasy, not his," she said with a sigh.

"Selling as many albums and concert tickets as he does certainly have its benefits. He bought himself that island about two years ago," explained the captain as he pointed out a small island to the north. "Let's get you back to the dock and we can split the last two beers."

Chapter Twelve

Dr. Bryce Chapman held his ID out to the security badge reader and walked into the ER. He'd been away for seven days and felt more refreshed and rejuvenated as he could remember in years. His shift today started at 10:00 a.m., a nice way to get the day going. The department would not be very busy yet and he was able to see his kids before heading to work. Often the life of a rotating shift worker meant one could see their family before or after a shift, but not both. The 10:00 a.m. shift would have him home by 7:30 p.m., in time for a bedtime story and hugs before enjoying a few hours alone with Val. And he had an amazing story to tell his colleagues. ER doc goes to paradise, gets a tan, saves a life. Telling stories of interesting cases often fills the down time between surges in patient registrations.

"Hey Bryce, welcome back. You look good," said Tom Sharpe.

"Thank you, my friend, I feel good. If you're ever in the mood for incredible beaches and sex, I highly recommend Exuma."

"I'll keep that in mind, but do you think Val would want to go back so soon?"

"Hah, not what I meant, you jerk," replied Bryce with a laugh. "Besides, we're doing great now. I don't think she's thinking about leaving me for any of my partners at the moment."

"That's too bad. As good as you are, I'd like to remind you that I still hold the record on cath lab delivery. That should count for something."

"Trying to impress a woman by telling her you do things faster than anyone else doesn't sound like a good pickup line. Anyway, you should have seen me in action at Thunderball Grotto."

"Look, it was just a joke. I'm not interested in watching."

"No, we were snorkeling, and someone drowned. We got him back and then Colton Hix flew us to Nassau."

"Oh, come on, I know we love telling stories of heroics, but that's a bit much. You saved a drowning patient with no supplies and then a country music star showed up and flew you guys to a hospital?"

"Absolutely. And get this, I even beat the guy up before he drowned because he and his drunken friends were going after Val."

"Well aren't you a knight in shining armor! But I don't recall the knight resuscitating the attacker after he defended the queen. That is a new twist, one worthy of the great Dr. Bryce Chapman," he said with a flourish of the hand.

"It was incredible how the community responded. Someone brought an AED and mask over from a mega yacht via wave runner. Then Colton shows up in his sea plane from his private island. Pure luck we got him back. I even did mouth to mouth on him initially, despite his smashed and bloody face. By the time we landed in Nassau he was beginning to move on his own. I think he's going to be fine. Absolutely amazing."

"You did mouth to mouth on a guy with a bloody face? Did you get Hep C and HIV testing on him?"

Bryce stopped cold. His heart sank. No, he did not think about that. "Why do you always have to ruin my good stories?" Bryce said with a shake of his head. *How could I be so stupid? I rinsed my face in salt water before getting on the plane. Why didn't I ask the hospital in Nassau to obtain labs for blood exposure tracking? I need to track down Tony and ask him to consent to testing. I've already had sex with Val, did I expose her to HIV and Hep C?* He was dreading this conversation tonight. Suddenly he wished he was working until after she would be asleep.

"Sorry, my friend. I'll order the hepatitis panel and HIV on you for baseline testing. If you can't get the guy tested at least you can track your own results to make sure you don't convert."

Tom Sharpe found Jackie and explained what they needed. She pulled Bryce into an empty exam room and prepared his arm for the blood draw. "No good deed goes unpunished. Sorry, Dr. Chapman."

"Thanks. It was still the right thing to do. The odds are very slim that he'd have anything and even if he did, that I'd catch it from him. But it still makes me nervous."

"Absolutely. Let your wife know I'm thinking about you guys. And great job saving that guy. Don't tell the other docs, especially Sharpe, but you're my favorite," she said with a smile. She popped the tourniquet off his arm and removed the needle. After placing a bandage on his arm, she inverted the tubes a few times to mix the blood and preservative.

"Thanks, Jackie. The feeling is mutual." Jackie was a veteran and did an incredible job training the new staff on how to be a good ER nurse. An ER has a high turnover of nursing staff and techs. Many newly graduated nurses start in the ER as a way to get experience in IV starts, managing a broad variety of patients, and critical care training. It is very difficult to start as a floor nurse and then move to the ER. The mindset is so different that it's a difficult adjustment if someone has much experience in other areas. Controlled chaos is an accurate term. The constant turnover leads to fresh faces and new names to learn.

Bryce walked back to the physician's work area and sat in front of his computer. It was time to get to work. "Hey, can I talk to you for a minute?" asked Tom, taking a seat next to Bryce.

"Sure buddy, what's up?"

"Do you remember a younger guy you saw with the sniffles the day before you left for vacation?"

Bryce felt a twinge of panic. Conversations like this never lead anywhere positive. "Vaguely. Do you mean the guy who had been sick about five minutes and came to the ER?"

"Yes, your chart said he woke up with a cough and runny nose. Anyway, he came back in two days later and died. Overwhelming sepsis, but he crashed his car on the way to the hospital and presented as a trauma. Elisa Morales cracked his chest and abdomen in the ER when he coded. I think it was a medical arrest and then his car bumped into something, but since it was called in as a trauma she was involved and took over. It was so strange, his lungs were covered in pus, but your chart said he looked fine and had normal vitals two days prior."

"The guy looked absolutely perfect. I wasn't worried about him at all. Did he get an autopsy?"

"No, the coroner said he had cystic fibrosis and a pneumonia death was to be expected, but they are presenting the case at the Trauma Morbidity and Mortality meeting tomorrow morning and we have been asked to be present."

"Oh wonderful. I can't wait." Bryce turned back to his computer as Tom Sharpe grabbed his backpack and headed home for another day of sleep. Life as an emergency physician was hard enough on a normal day. Now, Bryce had to do the job while second guessing himself and dreading what was to come. Flashbacks of an event in medical school that nearly made him quit came flooding back. When a patient dies unexpectedly, under unclear circumstances, the last thing a doctor wants is the blame placed on them. Fortunately, today was a standard shift with bread-and-butter cases. A few sick patients, one cardiac arrest, and plenty of walking wounded. He managed to have the waiting room empty when his partner arrived to relieve him at the end of his shift. Bryce left quickly, planning to finish his charting at home. It was a lofty goal, one he rarely met.

Chapter Thirteen

"Bryce, get in here! Colton Hix is on the news," yelled Val from the kitchen.

"So? Why is he on there?" came the reply from the garage.

"He's talking about the rescue he helped with in the islands last week."

"So, do you just hang out in the Bahamas waiting to rescue people with your plane?" asked the attractive reporter as she smiled at Colton.

"I wish. I was down there with my family to relax after the tour we just finished. We were at the dock about to go fishing when I heard the distress call on the radio. We're only a few miles from there, so I figured I would go over and see if I could help."

"What did you see when you got there?"

"There was this couple doing CPR on a guy in a boat. A wave runner had just thrown a bag onto the boat, I guess it was an AED, that thing that shocks your heart. The guy was doing mouth to mouth while his wife did chest compressions. It was like a scene out of a movie."

"Are you going to make a movie out of the experience?" asked the reporter. "And if so, can I be in it?"

Colton laughed. "No, ma'am, I don't make movies. But I am writing a song about it. It's one of the ways I've found to deal with events that happen in my life. It was such a moving thing to be a part of. Raw, beautiful. People helping people, without regard for their own safety. I would love to meet that couple again someday and buy them a beer. All I did was fly a plane. They saved his life."

"Well, without you stepping up to help he might not have made it either. Colton Hix, thank you so much for being with us today. And when that song is finished, we'd love to have you back for a live performance if you'd like."

"That would be wonderful. Thank ya'll very much. Dr. Chapman, if you're out there, well done, sir."

The news broadcast switched to a story about an upcoming vote in Congress and Valerie quickly turned it off. She set the remote on the counter and spun around quickly. "Did you hear that? Colton Hix wants to buy us a beer."

"I never thought I'd be mentioned on the national news. At least it was for something positive and included beer," replied Bryce.

"I'm going to reach out to him on social media and see if I can make this happen."

Bryce watched her grab her phone and open Twitter. "Are you really going to try to setup a date with a country music star right in front of me?"

"Whatever. You'll be there too. Maybe you can make drinks for us," she added with a wink.

"Hey, too soon. You can't quote Tony's friends, you know where talk like that leads," he laughed. "No more fights for a while, okay?"

"Fine. What are the rules on play fighting and then making up after?" she asked as she stepped towards him and grabbed his arm. Her fingers slid up his forearm and under his sleeve when they hit the bandage over his blood draw site. She lifted the sleeve and looked at him. "Did you get blood drawn today? What happened?"

Bryce let out a long sigh. "I talked to Tom Sharpe and told him about our events in the Bahamas. He asked if I had Tony tested for Hepatitis C and HIV since I did mouth to mouth on him while he was covered in blood. I hadn't even considered it. So I had a nurse draw my blood, and I'll need to try to track Tony down to see if he'll get tested. Until then, I am not sure we should be intimate, I'd feel terrible if I gave you one of those diseases."

Valerie grabbed his other hand and leaned in close. He wrapped his arms around her in a gentle hug. "Well, we've had sex since then, does it really matter at this point?" she asked.

"I think it does. It would be very unlikely for me to contract one of the viruses, and then have it replicate fast enough to have enough of a viral load to be able to pass it along in such a short time. I have no idea how long it takes to be able to pass something like that on after contracting it, but I don't want to take any chances."

She sighed and considered what he said. "Well, isn't that pleasant. What a way to ruin a great story for us. So what does this mean? No kissing? No sex? What about a condom?"

"I'm not going to kiss you through a condom," said Bryce, trying to soften the mood.

"Be serious for once, will you? This is important to me. And I assume it would be for you also?"

"Look, it's a low-risk situation. Odds are he has no diseases and even if he did, it's a low risk that I would convert to positive. But it's not a zero risk. I don't want to put you at any risk at all. I think condoms would probably be fine, but how much risk are you willing to take? I couldn't forgive myself if I gave you something. Kissing should be fine as long as my gums aren't bleeding, or I don't have open sores in my mouth."

"You really know how to set the mood, Chap," she trailed off while looking away.

Needle stick exposures are just one hazard in working in medicine. All healthcare workers who deal with sharp objects and patients are at risk of contracting HIV, Hepatitis C, and other diseases from their patients. It's always in the back of the mind during procedures, but practicing universal precautions and assuming everyone has a terrible blood-borne disease has reduced the incidence of transmission to healthcare workers.

"Whatever you think is best. But try to get him tested soon, okay?" She kissed his cheek and headed upstairs. Bryce watched her walk away, a view that motivated him to get started on that answer immediately.

Chapter Fourteen

"Dr. Chapman, what are you doing here so early? Your shift doesn't start for two hours," said Paula.

"I'm here for a meeting. I get to defend myself in front of the hospital medical staff. I can't wait."

"That doesn't sound pleasant," said Paula, shaking her head. "Well good luck, sir, I'm rooting for you."

"Are you ready to get this over with?" asked Tom Sharpe as he and Bryce walked down a hallway in the hospital. Tom carried a small cardboard box in his hand, decorated with fancy artwork and advertising a local bakery.

"Absolutely. I'm sick of the trauma team dictating our care in our department. You were one hundred percent correct. That patient was in florid sepsis and shouldn't have been a trauma patient at all," said Bryce. He had reviewed the chart extensively and spoke with everyone involved in the care. He even spoke to the paramedics who had transported the patient from the scene.

"Can you imagine if I ran into their operating room and started performing procedures on their patient that I knew nothing about?" replied Tom.

"I would actually love to see that," Bryce grinned.

"And don't let them say you missed anything on that first visit. I reviewed the chart. I would have done the same thing.

He shouldn't have even come to the ER the first visit," Tom said. "I have a plan for today. It might ruffle some feathers but I'm going to make a point in a dramatic fashion. Do you trust me?"

"Trust you? Val and I drove home two hours from a soccer tournament to have you repair my son's facial laceration. Of course I trust you."

"Thanks," he smiled. "I remember that. When I ask, just hand me this scalpel."

Bryce took the instrument and considered what his best friend might be planning. "One question though, what's in the box?"

"Who are you? Detective David Mills? Wait and see."

***

The two ER doctors entered the hospital auditorium and took seats down by the front. The room was full of surgeons, residents, medical students, and a few administrators. "Hey, Ash, good to see you," Bryce said over his shoulder at the ER director sitting behind him.

"Good morning, gentlemen. Glad you could make it. I've talked to Elisa Morales; she's planning to defend her actions strongly. Tom, she's planning to file a complaint against you to the medical staff council for insulting statements you made to her by the elevator."

"Insulting statements? Are you kidding me? She literally cut my septic patient open from stem to stern. I simply asked her to listen to my input before doing that next time," Tom said.

"Well, I'm sure it's going to come up today, so I wanted you to be prepared."

Silence replaced the muted conversations as the chief of surgery strode to the podium to begin the weekly Morbidity and Mortality conference. This was a time to discuss cases where errors or bad outcomes occurred in an attempt to identify ways to improve. The goal was to improve patient care and educate all involved. It was not a process meant to direct personal attacks or launch accusations, but intentions are often unrelated to outcomes.

The first few cases were straight forward without much discussion. A gunshot wound to the head who died on the way to the hospital. A suicide patient who died after a month in the ICU. "The next case is Kent Carpenter, single-car motor vehicle accident. Presented in shock, and arrested in while undergoing CT scan to evaluate for injury. Dr. Morales, can you comment on what you found?"

Bryce and Tom shared a sideways glance. How was she going to handle this? Dr. Morales walked to the podium and adjusted the microphone down to her level.

"Thank you. I responded to the trauma one activation made by Dr. Sharpe in the emergency department. When I arrived, the patient was clearly in shock with a systolic pressure of sixty. Initial workup by the ER staff was not able to determine a significant injury, so I proceeded with the patient to CT scan. I was concerned he was going to die before I had a chance to save him. While in the CT scanner, he lost his pulse. We then brought him back to the ER where we attempted traumatic resuscitation. I did a bedside thoracotomy looking for reversible causes and when this did not yield any, I opened his abdomen hoping to find a fixable cause. Standard trauma protocols; executed appropriately. The only abnormality I found was purulent material adherent to the lungs. This ultimately grew Pseudomonas aeruginosa. The autopsy report confirmed he had cystic fibrosis which explains his severe pneumonia from this pathogen. Further review of the record showed he was seen in the ER two days prior at the onset of this illness but unfortunately no testing was performed and no antibiotics were prescribed. By the time he tried to come back, he was too far gone to even drive to the hospital, let alone survive to discharge."

She ended her presentation looking at the floor and shaking her head. A surgical resident asked a question about her technique for the clamshell thoracotomy. He was asking to be taught how to perform the procedure, rather than asking when it should be done. Several questions were directed at the ER team, focusing on the first visit and lack of a workup. Bryce stood and walked to the podium to answer the questions. Dr. Morales stepped to her left to make room.

"Hello. Dr. Bryce Chapman, ED attending. I saw the patient on his first visit. He had very little past medical history and to my knowledge no active medical problems. The patient told me he had felt fine the night before but woke up with a cough and malaise. He had symptoms for two hours when I saw him."

"Why did you not do an X-ray, or at least prescribe antibiotics for him?" asked the surgery chief.

"For a patient with two hours of symptoms? Because it's not indicated. His exam and vitals were normal. There was nothing to do. Have a good day. Come back when you have an emergency."

"Well, obviously he did, and then he died. Do you think he would be alive today if you had prescribed him antibiotics at that first visit?"

"No, I don't."

The chief smirked. "How can you say that? He died of sepsis from severe pneumonia. Isn't it a bit absurd to claim antibiotics would not have helped?"

"Sir, have you read the chart? He had multi-drug resistant Pseudomonas. If he had received antibiotics, it would have been for community-acquired pneumonia, not MDR Pseudomonas. Anything I put him on would have been completely ineffective. Though the side effects of inappropriate antibiotics may have hastened his death."

The chief paused for a moment. The cowboy ER doctor did have a point. "Okay, thank you, Dr. Chapman. Now I'd ask Dr. Sharpe to present his opinion of the second visit."

Tom leaned back towards Ashford Tate, "Let me know what they say after I walk out. And sorry for making you clean this up," he added. He stood and walked to the podium carrying the small paper box. He walked past the podium, opened the box, and held it out toward Dr. Morales. "Elisa, can you hold my jelly donut while I address this distinguished audience?"

"If I have to, but this is not a jelly donut. It's cream filled," she said with a tone of annoyance, taking the box from Tom.

"No, it's jelly filled. I specifically asked the bakery for a jelly-filled donut, and they put a sticker on the box that says, 'Jelly Donut.'"

"That's all well and good, but this is a cream-filled donut. I can see plenty of cream and I don't see any jelly," she replied, pointing at the cream spilling out of the fill hole.

"No, you're wrong. It's my donut, your opinion isn't necessary. I'll even prove you wrong. Dr. Chapman, scalpel please." Bryce had been watching the scene unfolding with a curious grin. He knew what was coming. The audience was quiet as they took in the drama occurring at the podium. This was much better than rounding on patients. Bryce reached into the pocket on his white coat and handed his friend a number-fifteen-blade scalpel.

Tom Sharpe grabbed the donut from the box Elisa was holding and laid it on the podium. He yanked the protective cover off the blade with an aggressive arc of his left hand. He then raised his right hand above his head and stabbed down into the pastry, making a wide, messy incision across the donut while muttering, "I know there's jelly in here somewhere."

"What are you doing?" yelled Elisa. "You're a lunatic!" she said, wiping cream filling off her white coat.

"I know what I'm doing! I was told this was a jelly donut and I'm going to prove it to you," Tom said, while digging around quickly with his finger. "Huh, no jelly here. All I see is this thick yellow stuff. I must have made my incision in the wrong place. That's an easy fix." His arm again raised high above his head and came swooping down, making another large slice in the donut. "Huh, no jelly here either. I'm beginning to wonder if this actually is a cream-filled donut."

Bryce was doing his best to not fall to the ground laughing. There was no one in the hospital who could make a more in-your-face point than Tom Sharpe. And today he was even outdoing himself. Elisa looked down at the sugary carnage on the podium. "What the hell is wrong with you?"

"Sorry, I guess you were right. It is in fact a cream-filled donut. Do me a favor, call the coroner and see if he wants any of it. I'm going to head back to the ER."

After that comment, Dr. Tom Sharpe picked up the empty box, licked some cream off the scalpel, replaced it in the sheath and headed for the door. Bryce leaned into the microphone and added, "meeting adjourned," before following his colleague out the door.

"Dude, that was absolutely hilarious!" said Bryce, jumping into the air and pumping his first.

"Thanks, I hope they finally realize how they treat us in the ER. I am done bending over and just taking it. Poor Ash, I wonder what's happening in there now."

Chapter Fifteen

The Morbidity and Mortality meeting ended quickly after Tom's performance. Stunned silence gave way to muted whispering that ended when the chief of surgery stepped up to the podium and formally dismissed the audience. Ash headed back to his office to prepare for the next meeting with the hospital attorneys and the plaintiff's malpractice attorney.

He finished typing an email and stood up. It was only five minutes before the meeting, yet he was finding several meaningless tasks to stall the inevitable. He hated these meetings. He spent his days as director of the emergency department developing treatment protocols, reviewing concerns from other departments, advocating for more resources, more nurses, more support from the hospital administration. As difficult as those tasks are, he much preferred them to what he was about to do.

He had become a father figure to the doctors in his group. His experience and gentle demeanor had endeared him to all those who worked with him. He cared about his partners as a father would his children. And now he had to go speak to the family of someone accusing his colleague of malpractice. A negligent act that led to the death of their loved one. Bad outcomes are unfortunately part of practicing medicine; the question here is whether the bad outcome could have been foreseen and whether an action was omitted that could have prevented it. He would have to be compassionate with the family who lost a loved one while defending his physician and company from a malpractice lawsuit. It's a difficult task to tell a grieving family who is accusing someone of malpractice that they are wrong, and have it not come across as uncaring.

Ash walked into the hospital conference room and shut the door behind him. No sense leaving it open since he was clearly the last to arrive. He saw the family of Kent Carpenter seated on one side of the table next to their attorney, Lorena McCarthy. Smiling a greeting, he walked to the other side and sat next to the two hospital attorneys. "Dr. Tate, thank you for joining us. We were just finishing introductions," said Lorena without a hint of an accent. Her voice only gave away her Irish heritage after a few whiskeys. She could hide the accent when she wanted, but not her appearance. Fiery red hair and a few freckles highlighted a head that stood a bit taller than most women. She used the accent from time to time to highlight irony or drive home a point. If you heard a Celtic accent, it was time to grab your legal pad, because something important was about to happen. "My name is Lorena McCarthy, and I'm representing the family of the deceased, Kent Carpenter. His former spouse, Rebecca, as well as sons, Robert and Chris.

"Pleased to meet you," Ash said smiling at Rebecca and the kids. *What are the kids doing here? Who brings two young children to a meeting with lawyers about the death of their father?* He looked at Lorena, then the kids, and then back at Lorena. She smiled warmly back at him, clearly proud of the props she had at her disposal to influence a compassionate jury.

"I'm sure you have reviewed the charts for both of Mr. Carpenter's visits to your department. The first time he was seen by Dr. Bryce Chapman and dismissed rather quickly. The second visit was with Drs. Tom Sharpe and Elisa Morales. Our contention is Dr. Chapman failed to meet standard of care in evaluating Kent's complaint of cough and shortness of breath. No imaging was performed, no blood work was ordered, no antibiotics were prescribed. He was in the department a total of twenty-five minutes. While that may be good for throughput metrics and win praise from the hospital administration, it clearly was too short to properly evaluate a patient who would die two days later. We are also naming Drs. Sharpe and Morales as we believe they also breached standard of care. He did not require a thoracotomy or laparotomy, and these procedures made it less likely to survive the severe sepsis he presented with."

Ash looked to his side and caught the eyes of the hospital attorneys. They also seemed surprised the lawsuit would include the second visit. By the time the second visit occurred there was likely nothing that could have been done to save the patient. Why add it to the suit?

"That's right, we are naming three physicians and the hospital as defendants. My client is suing on behalf of her children and for her missed child support payments. We believe we can prove all three breached standard of care, and these actions directly resulted in the death of Kent Carpenter. I have drawn up the lawsuit but have not filed it yet. I am hopeful we can agree to a settlement prior to court proceedings."

"What terms are you proposing?" asked a hospital attorney.

"Nothing more than my client could have provided his family had he still been alive. Lost wages for forty years of employment, Social Security benefits up to the average life expectancy, interest on financial investments he would have made, and compensation for the loss of companionship and guidance a father can give his children." She slid a piece of paper across to each attorney and Ashford Tate. "Four million dollars."

She might as well have said forty million. Anything above a few hundred thousand was likely going to be refused by the hospital and physicians. If a malpractice suit ends with a judgment against the physician or a settlement in lieu of a judgment, it is reported to a national database and is counted against the physician forever. It is more difficult to get a job, to get malpractice insurance, to get credentials at a new hospital. Malpractice suits have many more elements at play than simple compensation to a patient or family for a bad outcome.

"We will need to discuss this offer with the hospital and the physicians involved. We can have an answer to you by the end of next month," replied the hospital attorney.

"Seven weeks? No. Sorry, lads, we don't have that kind of time. I need an answer by the end of this month," replied Lorena, the inflection of her voice rising as the last word cleared her lips. Her head tilted forward and a little left. "I plan to file the first of next month."

"Okay, we will do our best to give you a response by then," he replied.

"Ma'am, I did review the charts for your ex-husband. For what it's worth, I would have done exactly as Dr. Chapman did at the first visit. There was no testing indicated based on his exam, vitals, and symptoms. Unfortunately, by the time he came back he was likely too ill to survive no matter was treatment was started. I am sorry for the loss you and your children have experienced. We'll be in touch with Ms. McCarthy as well," Ash said.

The meeting ended quickly and the parties went their separate ways, except the lead attorney for the hospital. "Dr. Tate, can I have a word?"

"I figured you'd want to talk about this. What is your side thinking?"

"We need to settle this, but not for four million dollars. That's untenable. It will be hard to defend the first visit in front of a jury. When she puts the kids in the front row and hypnotizes the jury with her voice and hair, we're going to be in trouble. I'll see if they're willing to reduce the settlement offer and then I think we should consider it. You know the juries feel bad for families and want to compensate them for the loss, even if it wasn't any fault of the doctor or hospital. They all assume insurance pays, and no one is really harmed."

"Look, I trust Bryce and would have done the same thing in his shoes. Let me talk to him and Tom and see what they think. I don't want to throw them to the wolves. Settlements follow us around forever. For a lawyer it's just a loss, for a doctor it's a scarlet letter. Dr. Chapman thinks something is strange about this one. No one gets that sick and dies without a little help."

"What are you saying?"

"Bryce thinks his patient was murdered. He's looking into a few possibilities, but it will be difficult to prove."

"Okay, let us know quickly. We only have three weeks until she files, and we will need several days to negotiate this settlement." Ash nodded and headed for the door; shoulders slumped toward the floor.

Chapter Sixteen

Bryce drove toward the hospital with a heavy heart. Ashford Tate had called a few minutes earlier to inform him there was a copy of the autopsy report in his office. Bryce had been waiting to read the coroner's conclusions, but now that it was ready for him, he was nervous to read the findings. "Thanks for the call, Ash. Have you read it yet?"

"I skimmed through it. Basically saying he had cystic fibrosis and a severe pneumonia due to Pseudomonas aeruginosa. No injuries from the trauma, though the trauma surgeon did cause a few."

"Yeah, no kidding. She filleted the man wide open. Honestly though, she thought it was the right thing to do and went for it. She'd probably make an excellent ER doctor. Why did they think he had cystic fibrosis? That doesn't make any sense. He had never been to any of the local hospitals for shortness of breath or respiratory complaints. And by the age of thirty-four we should have seen him dozens of times for respiratory illnesses."

"I agree with you, Bryce, but you have to consider the source. Our coroner is the best friend a criminal ever had. He's incompetent and signs off on whatever ideas his investigators come up with. It doesn't help he's related to the one who investigated this case," said Ash. "I need to run.

Technically we should leave the report here at the hospital but take as long as you need to review it."

Bryce waved goodbye without taking his eyes off the report. He skimmed through the pages to the conclusion:

Kent Carpenter, 34yo white male, previously known to be healthy. Father had cystic fibrosis, presented to the hospital with symptoms consistent with pneumonia but no testing was performed. Subsequently worsened over the next two days and then called the hospital for advice. He was encouraged to return and was involved in a single-car accident on the way to the hospital. He was found to be critically ill and underwent thoracotomy and laparotomy in the emergency department that failed to find a traumatic injury.

It was noted that his thoracic cavity had evidence of excessive purulence, eventually growing out multi-drug resistant Pseudomonas aeruginosa. Given his death due the pathognomonic organism in cystic fibrosis patients and the disease presence in his father, we conclude the patient died of pneumonia due to cystic fibrosis. Smoking was not a contributing factor in his death.

Bryce sat the report on the table and leaned back in his chair. It didn't make sense. Cystic fibrosis is a terrible disease that leads to numerous respiratory complications and illnesses usually starting at a young age. Why had Kent made it to thirty-four without frequent visits to the hospital for pneumonia? He scanned the report to find the genetic testing results but could not find it, even on the second more thorough time through. "Where's the genetic testing?" Bryce wondered aloud. "How are they concluding he has CF without testing?" He looked for the investigator's name and found it near the top. Ashley Saxon, with a phone number listed to the side. He snatched the phone from Ash's desk and punched her number in.

"Saxon," said a voice after the first ring.

"Hi, this is Dr. Bryce Chapman. Do you have a few minutes to talk about the autopsy report on Kent Carpenter?"

He heard a sigh over the line. "Yeah, I have a few minutes. What do you need?"

"I took care of him on the first visit to the hospital. He looked great. I had no concerns for him being sick, especially with a chronic disease like cystic fibrosis. How did you conclude he had that?"

"Well, if you read the report, you saw his father had it, and it's an inherited genetic condition. And he died of Pseudomonas pneumonia, a classic finding in cystic fibrosis patients."

"Sure, but how did he make it to thirty-four without numerous visits for respiratory complaints? Did you guys test him to see if he carried two copies of the gene?"

"No, we didn't feel that was necessary. Our budget is already stretched thin, so in situations where foul play is not a concern, we try to close out the cases in a quick and cost-conscious way. We simply can't perform thousands of dollars of testing on every person that comes through as a coroner's case. We don't have the resources."

"I understand your budget restraints, but what if he didn't have CF and there actually was foul play involved? Don't you need to test your theory that there wasn't anything suspicious before certifying a death? I mean, you're diagnosing someone with a genetic condition without even testing for it. Isn't that making it easier on the bad guys to get away with it?"

"Doc, I don't like what you're suggesting. We do the best we can and are proud of the job we do. If you have a problem with it, take it up the coroner. Honestly, I get tired of these medical cases where the doctor misses something and expects us to find something to get them off the hook."

Bryce felt his face flush. He responded with increased volume and a tone of annoyance. "I didn't miss anything. Kent did not have cystic fibrosis. You are screwing me over here by saying he did. What does it take to run that test? I'll pay for it."

"That would be a huge conflict of interest and the coroner would never authorize that. We can't perform testing after the fact because the doctor doesn't like our findings."

Bryce was fuming by this point. He realized he wasn't going to get anywhere positive on this call. "Well, I think we're going to have to agree to disagree. Is there any way I can get a tissue sample to run the test on my own?"

"Sure, bring me a subpoena signed by a judge and we'll hand it over."

A subpoena would add weeks or months of delay, something he could not afford. "Fine. We'll talk again. Have a wonderful day." Bryce dropped the phone on the cradle without waiting for a response. He needed to run a genetic test on Kent, but he lacked a tissue sample.

Chapter Seventeen

"Why do you want me to get a CT scan? The kid is seventeen with a fever, right lower quadrant pain, and all surgical signs of appendicitis," asked Tom Sharpe into the phone, his hand held on his forehead.

"Because the days of surgeons whisking patients to the OR only to find a normal appendix have passed us by," said Elisa Morales.

"How do you feel about the radiation risk in a seventeen-year-old patient who has a lifetime to accumulate more ionizing radiation? What of the risk of that for a worthless CT? Just come stick a knife in him and get his appendix out before it ruptures."

"Excuse me, are you the same ER doc who hacked a donut apart in front of the entire surgery department to make fun of me for what you claim was inappropriate surgery? Now you're demanding that I operate without a clear indication? Is this the same Tom Sharpe I'm talking to now? ER doctor extraordinaire?"

Tom sighed. "Fine, I'll get the CT scan. I may be gone when it's back; Bryce Chapman is taking over for me today so he may call you with the results." He hung up the phone and buried his face in his hands. Pulling them slowly back through his hair he whispered, "Why can't we just treat the patient without performing useless tests?"

"Because everyone is too busy to do what we used to do," said Bryce, just arriving to work. "We spend all of our time documenting what we saw, what we did, and what we were thinking. We don't have time to actually see patients anymore. Easier to demand a CT scan because maybe it'll save a trip to the operating room."

"It took me four hours to get a urine sample back on a lady last night. Four hours! I got the rest of her labs, a CT scan, and an MRI while we were waiting to collect a urine sample. How is this possible?"

"You know exactly how. The hospital gutted our nursing staff, and we're short every shift, even before people start calling in because it's too nice out to come to work."

"I know, I know. There just has to be a better way. We can't keep cutting staff and increasing patient load without creating new problems or missing something serious."

"Dude, just go home. Have a morning beer and pass out. We won't fix the system today," said Bryce to his friend.

"Okay, but promise me we'll fix it tomorrow?"

Bryce nodded as he sat down and logged into the work-station. "Tell me what you have to turn over and get out of here."

"Just that one you heard me on the phone about. Seventeen-year-old male with right lower quadrant pain. He has appendicitis but Elisa wants a CT scan first before going to the operating room. I'll be in the office doing charts for a bit. We got slammed overnight and I'm way behind. If I go home, I'll never get them done." Tom pounded Bryce on the back as he headed toward their office and a little peace and quiet to finish his paperwork.

***

"Is Tom Sharpe still here?" Elisa Morales' voice carried through the emergency department like a distress call over water. It seemed to carry forever and anyone who heard it snapped to attention.

"He may still be in our office; it's down that hall, last door on your left," pointed Bryce. He watched her stride confidently down the hall, a sinister smile on her face. He knew they had not gotten along since they coded his bounce back patient, and her sneer made him nervous for what was in store for Tom. Bryce popped out of his chair and jogged down the hallway as Elisa opened the office door.

"Appendicitis, huh? You wanted me to slice that poor kid open based solely on your clinical suspicion? Good thing I'm not some cowboy doc and demanded you get a CT scan," she said.

"Okay, so what did the CT show?" asked Tom.

"Mesenteric adenitis. Classic mimic of appendicitis. The kid had diarrhea for a few days before this pain started. Any surgical intern would put that in their differential diagnosis list for a patient like this. Do they teach differential diagnosis in emergency medicine or do you usually just order the CT scan and wait for the radiologist to tell you what's wrong?"

Tom shoved the keyboard back, striking the monitor stand with it. He pushed the chair back with his legs and spun to face her. "How dare you come into my office talking to me like this! I made a clinical decision and asked you to see the patient, that's it. I'm glad the kid doesn't need surgery, especially on a day you're on call."

"Woah, woah, guys. Calm down. This doesn't help anybody." Bryce held his hands palms up, shoulders drawn back, and pumped his hands a bit as he spoke. Tom and Elisa turned to face him. "Can we bring down the temperature a few degrees? Is it possible this has nothing to do with the current patient and everything to do with Kent Carpenter?"

All three stood silently, staring at each other. The tension in the room melted as each took a big breath and nodded. "You're right, Bryce. I'm still pissed about that," said Tom.

"You're pissed? I'm being sued because Bryce missed a horrible pneumonia in a cystic fibrosis patient without even doing an X-ray," said Elisa.

"That guy did not have CF, not a chance in hell. How did he go this long without ED visits for various pulmonary issues? We had literally zero chest X-rays on the guy. He was here three months ago for a broken femur that was fixed by orthopedics. He was young enough that he didn't need a chest X-ray, but anesthesia didn't note any issues with the ventilator or physical exam abnormalities."

"But the coroner report said—"

"Elisa, the coroner is a veterinarian. He relies heavily on his investigators, and the one who handled this case is woefully incompetent. Their department is underfunded and with the crime and opioid overdose spike, they are too busy to investigate medical deaths very thoroughly. They grab any reasonable diagnosis and move on. Case closed," explained Bryce.

"A vet? You're joking. I thought they meant he served in Afghanistan or something," she replied. Tom couldn't hold his laugh inside and made a gurgling sound and then coughed a few times to cover it. "Shut up, man, why would I assume the coroner usually worked on parrots and snakes?"

Bryce smiled at the feeling of camaraderie that had returned. "Look, we're all on the same team here. Maybe we should figure out a way to think through this case instead of attacking each other?" Tom and Elisa both nodded in agreement. "Okay, so how do we prove he didn't have CF? He was cremated and we didn't obtain any labs other than that culture of his lungs that grew Pseudomonas," said Bryce.

"We need his DNA," Tom said.

"I don't have any. Do you Elisa? Tom?"

"No, but I bet I know who might," said Elisa with a grin. She held the smile without explaining further.

"Are you going to make us beg for it? Just tell us what you're thinking," said Tom with a sigh.

"Per usual, the answer lies in his surgical history. Do you guys remember what surgery he had and why?"

"Yes, he had testicular cancer and had a testicle removed three years ago. But there's no way the pathology department would still have a tissue sample from three years ago, would they?" asked Bryce.

"Probably not. But that's not what I was thinking. Have you two really never been involved in an orchiectomy procedure?" Tom Sharpe and Bryce Chapman both shook their heads slowly side to side. "Oh wow, it's one of my favorite procedures. What woman doesn't enjoy cutting a ball out of a dude? I've done a few in residency but I never got the chance to do two at once, it was always just one and usually for testicular cancer. Tom, keep asking me to operate on appendicitis without a CT scan and I may offer to perform my first bilateral orchiectomy ever. Pro bono of course." She punched him in the arm for emphasis.

Bryce felt bad for laughing, but it was hilarious to watch his friend get roasted by the tiny surgeon. "You still haven't told us how this helps us obtain DNA," Tom said, trying to redirect the conversation away from his groin.

"Whenever a patient needs to have a testicle removed, we recommend he put a semen sample in storage in case he ever lost his other testicle and wished to have children someday. It's likely Kent Carpenter stored a semen sample at a sperm bank. You just need to find where."

"And then what? Just walk in and place an order for a Kent Carpenter semen sample?" asked Tom.

"Elisa, maybe you could go in and pretend to be looking for a donor then scan through the sample photos until you find Kent's picture?"

"Bryce, that's disgusting. No. And besides, he didn't leave the sample to be a donor. He would have left it as an insurance policy. He wouldn't be in any sort of brochure. This is definitely a man's job. When you need an egg harvested, I'm your girl."

"I wish we had time to use the courts to subpoena the sample, but the hospital wants to settle this case immediately. I'll see what I can find out. Thank you both for being reasonable. Can we agree to work together, moving forward? You're both excellent doctors and our patients need you on the same team."

Elisa and Tom shook hands and agreed. Bryce wondered which was going to be harder, keeping these two friendly or stealing a semen sample. Both seemed rather ludicrous.

Chapter Eighteen

Valerie finished putting the kids to bed and found Bryce sitting in bed on his phone. "The kids said goodnight. They wondered if you were going to tuck them in also."

Bryce didn't look up from his phone but replied, "Yes, they are adorable."

"What? Did you even hear what I said?"

"Uhm," stuttered Bryce. "You said something about them going to bed."

"I told you the kids wanted to know if you were going to tuck them in. You're not even present. It's like there's a ghost of my husband laying in my bed." She walked to his side of the bed and looked at his phone. "What's so important anyway?" She saw the half-full glass of bourbon sitting on the nightstand and gave him a disapproving look.

"I'm trying to find semen storage facilities in town," he said. Valerie replied with a blank stare; she didn't trust her words at this moment. "Seriously. It's about that patient that died. We need to prove he didn't have cystic fibrosis. Elisa Morales thinks he may have stored a semen sample somewhere before he had a testicle removed for cancer a few years ago. It's our only hope to get a DNA sample to test for the gene."

"Okay, I guess that makes sense. That's better than you looking for one to make a deposit." She paused a few beats before continuing. "Actually, I'm not sure. I think I'd rather you be looking to make a deposit at a sperm bank than a withdrawal."

"I have a list of a few places to check out. I'll call them tomorrow and see if they have it."

"You think they're going to just tell you if there's a sample for a certain person? There are probably privacy rules in place. You'll have to think of a different way to find out if they have it."

"Good point. I'll come up with something." Bryce leaned over and grabbed his drink, downing the rest in a large gulp. "Night, babe." He clicked off his light and laid down on his pillow. Valerie raged quietly on the inside. Clearly, Bryce was not going to tuck the kids in bed. She shut the bedroom door loud enough to ensure Bryce wasn't asleep and tried to think of an excuse to tell the kids.

Chapter Nineteen

Bryce Chapman's shift had been slow and steady with very straight-forward patients, until a nurse jogged up to him holding an EKG. It was for a new patient who just checked in complaining of chest pain.

"Poor guy seems to be having a heart attack. What room is he in?" he asked. The nurse pointed to the last room in the hallway. "I think the one that now has four people standing outside it and a crash cart being wheeled in."

"Paula, can you page out a STEMI alert for the patient in room twenty-six?" he asked while hurrying down the hall. Bryce walked into the room to see a male in his mid-forties laying in the bed. His pale skin was soaked in sweat. They made eye contact as he walked in the room and Bryce could see the fear in his eyes. Smiling at the patient, he made his introduction and took a quick history.

The patient was forty-six years old and smoked. A bad habit in general, but disastrous for insulin-dependent diabetics. The complication rates for diabetes increase exponentially with tobacco use. His father had died of a heart attack at fifty and now the patient was doing his best to follow in his dad's footsteps. "Sir, the EKG confirms that you're having a heart attack today. The good news is this is fixable. Our cath lab team provides excellent care and they will be here in a few minutes to take you to the lab." Bryce looked at the patient's wife and spoke reassuringly. "We do this very quickly at Washington Memorial. Our chaplain will take you to the cath lab waiting room and the cardiologist will speak with you after the procedure is over."

Bryce then ordered aspirin, heparin, oxygen, and a loading dose of Plavix. The nurses placed the defibrillation pads on the patient's chest and attached the leads to the monitor. The nurse's phone chirped and she answered it quickly. "Cath lab is ready for us," she called out to the room.

Bryce checked his watch; the patient had been in the department for six minutes. The current record shortest time for a heart attack patient to stay in the ER was seven minutes, eighteen seconds, held by none other than Dr. Tom Sharpe. Bryce always felt like Tom cheated on that one. It deserved an asterisk. That case was at three in the morning during a snowstorm and it took the ambulance thirty minutes to make it to the hospital. The cath lab team had been ordered to sleep at the hospital to avoid weather related delays and were prepped and ready long before the patient arrived. And it still took him over seven minutes. The record was about to be toppled.

A loud mechanical pop was heard as the nurse unlocked the bed and began to wheel the patient out of the room. Six minutes, twenty-four seconds. Bryce smiled. "Good luck, sir. I'll be following along in the chart to see how you do. Congratulations on quitting smoking!"

Bryce stepped to the sink to wash his hands when he heard yelling from the hallway. "He's in V-Fib!"

"Get him back in the room!" yelled another nurse.

Bryce grabbed gloves and the respiratory bag hanging on the wall. When a patient has no heartbeat, he will not be breathing either. The patient was wheeled back and was now unresponsive. His wife was still in the corner, hand held over her mouth. A nurse started CPR as Bryce gave further orders. "Let's shock him immediately, 200 Joules on the biphasic, quick as you can. Give him 300mg amiodarone and have a milligram of epinephrine ready in case this shock doesn't work."

A loud tone with increasing pitch began after the nurse entered the settings in the defibrillator and pushed the *CHARGE* button. A series of beeps indicated it was charged and ready to deliver a shock. "Okay, everyone clear!" shouted Bryce. Compressions were held and all staff stepped back from the patient to avoid conducting the charge into their bodies. He pushed the *SHOCK* button firmly.

The patient's body jerked as the energy coursed through his chest. Compressions resumed immediately. The monitor is difficult to interpret during compressions due to the signal interference of chest movement. After the amiodarone injection was complete, Bryce called for a pulse check. The nurse held compressions and placed two fingers on his neck. Two other nurses did the same on various body parts.

"I've got a pulse."

"Me too!"

The monitor showed a normal rhythm, and the team felt a strong pulse. He was breathing again and starting to look around the room. Bryce pulled the respiratory mask off his face and reapplied the nasal cannula oxygen tubing. "What happened?" the patient asked, confused.

"You died for a bit there, but we got you back. Okay, let's get to cath lab." The team again began its journey down the hall to the cath lab. Bryce glanced at his watch. Eight minutes, ten seconds. *Damn it.* He wondered if the first time would count or if the second was going to be the official time. Either way, it will probably take several beers to figure it out with Tom next time they were both off together.

"Ma'am, I know that was scary, but I hope that was the last of the surprises today for you. He will have no ill effects from that brief code. I know the cardiologist who is taking care of your husband and she is excellent."

The patient's wife returned a nervous smile, offered her thanks, and followed the chaplain down the hall. Bryce realized he needed to urinate, badly. It had been hours since he had time to visit the bathroom and the Diet Coke fountain machine near the physician work area did not help matters. He grabbed his phone and headed for the employee break room.

> *A letter came for you today by certified mail. It's from the Department of Public Prosecutions in Nassau. Call me.*

He read the text from Val and felt a knot form in his stomach. What was this about?

> *I'll call when I'm leaving here in an hour. They probably want my statement as a witness to charge Tony. Maybe we can fly down for a deposition.*

The words looked good on his phone, even if they weren't what he was actually thinking. When his shift ended, he left immediately and drove home to see what the letter from the Bahamas contained.

Chapter Twenty

The kids went down easily, smiling and happy at having both parents home for bedtime, unfortunately a somewhat rare event. "They always sleep so much better when you're here to tuck them in at night. It's like they know their dad will always keep them safe and never let them die before they wake, despite their nightly prayers." She leaned in to kiss Bryce, but he pulled away.

"Sorry, I forgot," said Val. She kissed him on the cheek instead. "I'll meet you in the bedroom in a minute." She headed downstairs to the kitchen, poured two glasses of wine, and tucked the letter from the Bahamas under her arm. Bryce reached for a glass of wine and the letter fell onto his lap when Val extended her arm to hand him the glass. He picked up the letter ripped it open as Val sat down next to him. Their eyes scanned the letter simultaneously.

```
DEPARTMENT OF PUBLIC PROSECUTIONS
3rd Floor Post Office Building
PO  Box  N  3007  Nassau,  N.P.,  The
Bahamas

Dr. Bryce Chapman:
```

This certified letter is to inform you of pending charges filed against you for crimes committed in the Commonwealth of the Bahamas. Mr. Tony Proffit submitted an affidavit alleging felony assault by you at Staniel Cay.

You have thirty (30) days to respond to this letter and inform us of your plea. We have an extradition treaty with the United States, and you will be brought to our country to stand trial if you do not surrender voluntarily. If you choose to have a local attorney represent you, please kindly inform us immediately.

Sincerely,
The Honorable Judge Antonio Rolle

"You have got to be kidding me," sighed Bryce when he finished reading. "How can they charge me with assault when Tony was coming after you? He even threw the first punch."

"I don't know, Bryce," said Val. "But I'm really starting to wish we had never taken that trip." The words stung Bryce. This trip was supposed to be first step on their relationship's road to recovery. It had started out great and ended with them saving a life together. Now he was facing felony charges in the Bahamas, worried about Hepatitis C and HIV, and the recovery just hit a major setback.

"Val, I can sort this out. We just need to explain what really happened. He's obviously lying to the police. I wish I still had the video from the GoPro, but I lost it when we loaded Tony onto the plane. I hit my head on the fuselage but didn't realize the camera had been knocked off."

Val sighed and took a long drink of wine. "That is going to make it tough to prove, isn't it?"

"Yes, it will. We saved that guy's life, and now he's trying to ruin mine. Sometimes life just sucks."

"Where are you going?" asked Val when Bryce got out of bed.

"I don't think wine is going to cut it after this. I'm going to get some bourbon."

"Wine and bourbon? How about you just face your problems instead of trying to drink them away?" asked Valerie.

"What fun is that?" replied Bryce from the hallway.

Chapter Twenty-One

Tony awakened and looked around the room. *Where am I? Clearly a hospital, but which one? What happened?*

"Good morning, Son," said Niles.

"Dad, what are you doing here? What am I doing here?"

"You had an accident, Tony. You were snorkeling and somehow got into a fight. During the fight, you were caught underwater on a rock and drowned. A doctor happened to be there, and he and his wife saved you. You had over ten minutes of CPR before they got you back. Then you were flown to the hospital here in Nassau."

"Are you serious? I don't remember any of that. Who was he?"

"He's an ER doctor from Indianapolis. He's also the one who smashed your face in. I'm looking into what happened and will file a police report. I plan to talk to him next week."

"Woah, that's insane. I can't believe this. Thanks, Dad, you always look out for me."

"You're welcome, son. We'll find a way to make this right." Niles patted his son on the hand in an act of reassurance and then leaned back. This conversation was the third time he had explained it to his son today. The doctors said he had an anoxic brain injury due to being deprived of oxygen for so long. They said he would struggle with forming new memories and had lost many of his old ones. Simple tasks may be complex, and he would require significant assistance for quite some time. They gave him no guarantee of a full recovery. Niles could tell from the doctor's facial expression that a full recovery seemed unlikely. It was time to get him back to the States and to the best neurologists and rehabilitation physicians he could find. His lawyers could handle the legal aspects of the case for him. It helped that his company was incorporated in the Bahamas so the lawyers could deduct the personal matter as a business expense. He smiled. A silver lining to every situation.

***

Niles Proffit boarded his corporate jet, a Gulfstream G550, at the Nassau airport and immediately walked back to the small office on board. He felt the rumble of the engines as the pilots prepared for the return flight to the States.

He glanced at an email from his secretary and dialed the number for Bryce Chapman.

"Hello?" said Bryce.

"Dr. Chapman, this is Niles Proffit, CEO of Optimus Equity."

"Hi there. Do I know you?" said Bryce.

"My company owns Washington Memorial Hospital, and I am the father of Tony Proffit, someone you recently had an altercation with in the Bahamas, if I'm not mistaken."

There was a few second pause before the conversation continued. "Sir, that is correct. How did you get my number?"

"I own the hospital you work at. It wasn't difficult. Anyway, I talked to Tony and his friends, and now I'd like to hear from you. Why did you assault my son and nearly let him die at Thunderball Grotto?"

"What? That's not what happened! Your son was drunk and was being inappropriate with my wife. I held him back so she could get back to our boat, and then he tried to hit me. I didn't start this at all. In fact, I saved his life after he drowned trying to chase me."

Niles shook his head and closed his eyes. "That's quite a story, Dr. Chapman. My son tells a different one, and each of his friends agreed. So, who am I supposed to believe?"

"I'm telling you the truth. Talk to our charter captain. Why would I attack your son while I'm on vacation? We even went back and rescued him and then performed CPR until we got him back. Tony's lying to you."

"Well, isn't this a tough predicament we find ourselves in? Sounds like we're going to need the Bahamian courts to sort this one out for us. Fortunately, I do a lot of business here. They are used to seeing my plane on their runway and my money flowing into their local economy. As for your job, I'm not sure I'm comfortable having you work on patients at my hospital given these accusations. I will continue looking into the matter, but as a word of caution, I would start looking for alternative employment." Niles hung up the phone before Bryce could respond.

He stared at his empty hands and pondered the next move. *Do I push him away or keep him close where I can crush him?* He smiled and closed both hands tightly into fists before throwing a quick right-handed jab into the air.

Chapter Twenty-Two

Bryce woke up early for his shift and slipped out of the house quietly. He preferred the unexpected events at the emergency department to the expected ones at home. Valerie had become cooler towards him again; fortunately, he had bourbon and beer to warm him up.

"New patient, stroke alert, room two, heading to CT first," said a nurse into the overhead paging system.

"Really? That's the third one today," said Bryce as he threw his pen against the wall behind his computer monitor.

Paula turned around at the noise and outburst from the normally calm doctor she cared about. "You okay, Dr. Chapman?"

"No, I'm getting tired of the constant stroke alerts being called out. It completely disrupts our workflow. I'm judged on how quickly I see the patient, order tests, administer medications. Everything. And most of these are vague nonsense or psychiatric disorders manifesting as neurologic symptoms. It's a waste of our time."

"Well, I don't know about the medical side of things, but as someone who has been a patient before, I know I'd appreciate you taking care of me. You are usually so nice to everyone. Are you feeling okay?"

Bryce instantly felt embarrassed about his reaction. "You're right. I'm sorry. I've been under a lot of stress lately, both here and at home. I feel like I have no control over anything, and these protocols just make it worse. I'm not a marionette, I'm a real boy, damn it." He stood and walked down the hall towards CT.

Paula watched him walk down the hallway. "That poor man. I hope he gets over this soon," she whispered.

Bryce left the hospital exactly at the end of his shift, a rarity in his career. Normally he'd be skipping out of the department, but today he dreaded leaving. At least at the hospital, he usually dealt with other people's problems. Once he left, the problems he faced were all his. He walked into his house, grabbed a beer, and then sat down at the kitchen counter. "Bryce? Is that you?"

"In the kitchen."

Valerie came down the stairs and walked into the room. "Hey, you didn't text to let me know you were on your way home. I would have gotten dinner started."

"Sorry, guess I just forgot."

"Really? You never forget. What's going on?"

Bruce huffed loudly. "What's going on? Everyone is attacking me, Val. From every direction. I'm being sued at work. My job is being threatened. There's a warrant out for my arrest in the Bahamas." He shook his head and brought the can to his lips for a large drink.

"I know all of that. What I wanted to know is why you're stomping around like a toddler who didn't get his way." He stared at her and nearly responded but didn't. "Yeah, it's probably best you don't say anything for a bit. You think you're being attacked from every direction? What about from me? What about from the kids? Are we attacking you?"

He opened his mouth and began, "Val—"

"Nope, not yet. We are not attacking you. We're trying to support you. But lately you've turned into someone else. You've essentially stopped texting or calling me. The kids have asked me why Daddy doesn't want to play with them anymore. Did you know that?"

"Did they really?"

"Yes. Did anyone come running to see you when you got home?"

"No, but I came in pretty quiet."

"Bryce, their playroom is above the garage. The garage door opener shakes the whole floor." She paused a second for emphasis. "They heard you come home."

"Okay, okay. I'll go see them." He took the final drink of his beer and tossed the can into the recycle basket, conveniently located next to the drink fridge. He grabbed a second beer and headed toward the stairs.

Val watched him walk away and then entered the pantry to figure out a meal the kids would eat.

She didn't get very far into meal planning before quick footsteps on the stairs signaled a child was rapidly inbound. The sobs reached the pantry before she was able to turn around and see what happened.

Hannah ran into the kitchen calling, "Mom? Mom? Where are you?"

"Mommy's right here. What's wrong?" asked Valerie as she exited the pantry.

Hannah ran into Val's legs and hugged them. "Daddy came in and told us how messy everything was." She sniffed and rubbed her arm across her nose. "He said we needed to pick up all the toys and put them away."

"I'm sorry, honey. Did you tell him what you were making?"

"I tried. He didn't let me say anything. I just put it on the shelf and came to you."

"Okay, let me go talk to him. Is Noah still up there?" Hannah nodded. "You know what? When I was a kid sometimes my parents let me have dessert before dinner. Do you want some ice cream?" Hannah nodded again, this time with a slight smile. Valerie brushed her daughter's hair back behind her ear. "You're in luck, I found chocolate peanut butter ice cream at the store today. Do you think one scoop is enough?"

Hannah smiled bigger and shook her head side to side. "Two scoops," she said, jumping in the air.

Valerie laughed and fulfilled the order quickly. She held the chocolate syrup bottle up high and let it slowly drip into the bowl. Hannah's finger swooped through the air and caught a few drops of chocolate before being sucked clean a second later. She felt a twinge of guilt at teaching her kids to use food to soothe their emotions, but today she was in crisis mode.

Satisfied that the first fire had been put out, Val headed toward the stairs to check on Noah and Bryce. She did not like the condition of her family over the last few weeks. The kids had begun to withdraw into themselves and were less cheerful. Bryce was drinking more and not leaving the house other than to work a shift in the ER. She had been neglecting her own friends and hobbies as she struggled to keep their home life intact.

She found Noah sitting alone in the toy room. He was holding a small foam football and looking at a dark spot on the carpet.

"Hey buddy, what are you doing?"

"Nothing," replied Noah sadly.

"Was your dad in here?"

"Yes, he came in and told Hannah to clean everything up. I threw my football to him, but he didn't catch it. It hit his arm and then his drink spilled on the carpet. Dad said a bad word and then left."

"Wow, okay. I'm sorry, Noah. Your dad has been under a lot of stress lately."

"I don't know what that means."

"It means there're a lot of things happening in his life that are hard to deal with right now. Some of them are serious and we don't know how to fix them yet. He's also not sleeping very well." She left out the part about increased alcohol consumption.

"But why does he have to be mean to us? How does that help? Are we some of the hard things?" She felt tears begin to form and quickly walked behind Noah, sat down on the carpet, and pulled him into her arms. "No, you are not. You and your sister are perfect. Sometimes moms and dads don't always act the right way, and we take out our frustrations on those we care about most. Your father loves us very much, it's just hard for him to be happy right now. If you aren't happy, it's hard to be nice."

"I guess. I just wanted to play catch with him. And Hannah was making him something out of Legos. We wanted to make him happy," said Noah.

"That's very sweet of you, and I appreciate you trying. But we can't make other people happy. Happiness comes from inside you." She emphasized the point by squeezing him harder. "Other people can make it easier for us to be happy, but our happiness is up to us. Where is the thing your sister was making?" Noah pointed to a built-in shelf across the room. Sitting on the shelf was a rectangular Lego structure, still under construction. "Do you know one thing that makes Mommy happy?"

"What?"

"The beach."

"Yeah, me too," said Noah.

"Do you want to go to the beach?"

"What beach? We live in Indiana."

"I was thinking Destin. We could go see Granny and Grandpa. What do you think?"

Noah sat up and spun around to face her. "Yes, I want to go see them. Can we go fishing and get a boat?"

"Absolutely. We'll have a great time. Why don't you get ready for dinner while I talk to your father?" Val stood up and retrieved Hannah's project from the shelf and left the room. She found Bryce lying in bed with the lights off. His face lit from the light of his phone. She could barely see anything since her eyes weren't adjusted to the darkness. She flipped on both light switches, bathing the room in bright LED light.

"Hey, what are you doing?" said Bryce, pulling a blanket over his face.

"I'm sorry, you want to know what *I* am doing? I think you're the one who needs to answer that. You were short with me downstairs and then I tell you the kids are noticing something is off with you. So you go upstairs, tell them to clean up their mess, spill beer on the floor, swear at them, and then go hide in bed. That is not the guy I married. Something has to change, Bryce."

"Yeah, you need to turn off the lights," he replied without emotion.

She stared at the lump on the bed for a few seconds before letting out a loud sigh. "Okay, have it your way. I know you're under a lot of pressure right now, but the way you're handling it will not work in this house." She flipped the lights off turned to exit. "You know, the lights aren't the only thing you're turning off in this room, Bryce. The kids and I are taking off. Talk to you later." She closed the door hard and went downstairs to the kids. "Kids, go get in my car. We're going out for pizza. We have a trip to plan."

Noah let out an "All right!" while Hannah acted excited, but she didn't know why.

Chapter Twenty-Three

One week had passed since Dr. Ashford Tate last met with the hospital and Lorena McCarthy. That was long enough for the hospital to become antsy and ask for an update on the alternative theory put forward by Bryce.

"Dr. Tate, do you have any evidence that this patient was the victim of intentional harm? We need to determine our settlement offer before this case is filed in court," said the hospital attorney.

"I met with Bryce and we reviewed the autopsy report. It's a little strange that the coroner signed off on Kent having cystic fibrosis without genetic testing. Bryce spoke with the investigator and was told they have limited resources and could not perform advanced testing on decedents who did not show evidence of foul play."

"How would confirming he did not have cystic fibrosis prove he was murdered?"

"It wouldn't prove it, but it would certainly call into question why he was infected with such a rare bacteria."

"A curiosity will not be enough to delay this lawsuit. Do you have anything else?"

"Unfortunately, no, not at this time. Other than my unwavering support of Dr. Chapman and complete confidence in him as a physician," said Ash.

"I appreciate your confidence, Ash, but even the pope has a bad day. We'll begin drafting a settlement offer and are intending to deliver it before the end of the month. That's two weeks away." Ash nodded but didn't respond verbally. He simply let out a sigh and tried unsuccessfully to find another way to approach this situation.

***

Bryce opened his eyes and looked around the room. It was dark, Valerie was asleep next to him. He hadn't heard her come to bed after she took the kids to dinner. He had fallen asleep early and felt quite refreshed for the first time in weeks. Looking at his phone, he realized he woke up a few minutes before his alarm was set to go off. He quickly turned off the alarm and looked at his sleeping wife. His shift work meant early mornings on day shift and very late nights on the swing shifts. His arrival and departure from the bedroom at odd hours made it hard for her to sleep soundly.

Bryce showered quickly and put on his scrubs. He peeked in the kids' rooms and watched them sleep for a few moments before heading down to the kitchen. He never ate breakfast, but wouldn't leave the house without a travel mug of coffee in his hand.

He drove to work in silence, left only to his thoughts. He felt bad about how he had been treating his family and vowed to make an effort to change. He couldn't let the stress of work and legal challenges cost him his relationship with

Val and made a mental note to call her during his shift once she and the kids would be up for the day.

Bryce walked into the hospital, smiling, ready to start fresh. He greeted a few nurses and techs as he walked through the hallway toward the physician's work area. He found Dr. Ashford Tate waiting for him. "Good morning, Bryce. I wanted to stop by and talk to you for a second if you have time."

Bryce slowly set his backpack down on the counter and turned to face his friend and mentor. "Hi Ash, sure. What do you need?"

"I spoke with the administration regarding your pending lawsuit, the Kent Carpenter case."

"Yeah, I know which one. It's not like I have a bunch of lawsuits pending and you need to narrow it down for me," he replied.

"Sorry, that's not what I meant. Anyway, the hospital wants to settle this matter quickly and keep it out of the press. Lorena McCarthy loves to be in front of a camera."

"Well, at least she has the looks for it," said Bryce.

"She is rather mesmerizing, isn't she? I'm a sucker for the red hair and the accent," said Ash.

"Well, snap out of it. She's the devil, remember?"

"I know, but sometimes it's fun to dance with the devil. Anyway, the hospital told me they want this settled before the end of the month. They do not want it to go to trial."

"I'm telling you; something is not right with this case. The patient did not have cystic fibrosis. And no healthy person gets that sick that quickly without a little help."

"Are you certain of that?"

"I don't know, maybe. Honestly, it's the only thing that fits."

"So who did it? And how?"

"I have no idea," admitted Bryce.

"Well then, you had better get one in the next few weeks or you'll likely have a settlement against you in the National Provider Database. And you want to avoid that if at all possible."

"Okay, I'll work on it. Thanks for stopping by."

"Absolutely. I thought this was best done in person rather than email or a phone call. Oh, our locum tenens hire, Peter Thrasher, will be here tomorrow for his first shift. I showed him around a bit, and he knows the electronic medical record system already which helps. He uses a scribe so be prepared for an extra person hanging around."

A scribe is an assistant who works with the physician at the bedside, documenting the chart in real time. This allows the physician to focus more on the patient and clinical care rather than secretarial work created mainly to deny billing and defend lawsuits. Most scribes are college-age and interested in pursuing a career in healthcare. The bedside experience gives them an excellent view of a potential future careers and valuable experience to help them succeed.

"Dr. Thrasher? Are you serious? What a name. I can't believe we couldn't find anyone local to pick up these shifts. Is he decent?" asked Bryce.

"Seems to be. Has worked solo in critical access hospitals for the last few years. He probably won't know what to do with all the resources we have available here. My gut tells me you shouldn't let him meet Valerie. He seems to have an eye for the ladies. Anyway, we'll figure this lawsuit out. I agree with you; I don't think your patient had cystic fibrosis."

Bryce appreciated the consideration that Dr. Ashford Tate gave him. Managing a company is no easy task, especially when it must be done while managing relationships with hospital administration and other physician groups. It certainly would have been easier to send an impersonal email, but that's not who Ashford Tate was. And that's why he was beloved.

Chapter Twenty-Four

The department was busy today, and it was afternoon before Bryce realized he had yet to call Valerie. Stepping into an empty patient room, he pulled his cell phone out to call her, but stopped when he saw an unread text message from his credit card company. It had arrived two hours ago.

> *Hello, did you just try to spend $53.38 at Stop-N-Go in Nashville, TN? Reply YES if this charge is correct, or reply NO if you do not recognize this charge and we will initiate the fraud protocol.*

Bryce clenched his teeth and made a fist with his free hand. *Now I have to deal with credit card fraud on top of everything else?* He took a breath, tried to relax, and then put a call through to Valerie.

"Hello, Bryce," said Val after the call connected.

He heard some noise on the line like she was driving while they talked. "Hey, I got a text from our credit card company. Someone stole our card and used it at a gas station in Nashville, Tennessee. I wanted to let you know I was going to get it shut off and you'll have to use our bank card until we get a replacement. I'll have them overnight it to us." Valerie didn't respond. "Hello?" said Bryce.

"Sorry, I was thinking," she said. "Bryce, the card is fine. We just got gas there and we're back on the road. We're actually in Georgia now. The kids and I ate lunch at the rocket ship rest area. They loved it."

He let his fist relax and brought the palm up to his head. "What? You're in Georgia? Why? What's going on?"

"I think this is a conversation best delayed a bit until my fellow travelers are asleep. Can I call you back when it's a better time?"

"No, just tell me now. Where are you going?"

"We're taking a beach vacation to my parent's house."

"Seriously? We didn't talk about this. How long are you going to be there?"

"I don't know yet. Look, I'll call you back; now isn't a good time for this."

"You're damn right it's not. I'm at work trying to be positive and not lose my job, and then I find out my wife took my kids and is leaving the state?" His breathing sped up, and he paced around the room. His adrenaline was spiking, but he had no way to act to change the situation. No outlet for the energy.

"It's not like that. I decided it was time for some time away and a vacation for the kids, that's all. I was going to call you after your shift was over so I didn't distract you from your patients, but the credit card notification ruined that idea," said Val. "Sorry."

"Yeah, whatever."

"I love you, Bryce; I'll call you tonight when we get there."

He hung up the phone without responding. He pulled his arm back to throw his phone against the wall and made eye contact with a paramedic walking towards the room, pushing a cart with a patient screaming in pain. Bryce converted his arm movement to a stretch and waved at the paramedic to come on in. When the door opened, he could hear the screams of pain. Bryce considered starting a screaming match, pitting physical pain against emotional agony. To show the patient what a true, deep emotional scream actually sounded like. No, they were not in ten out of ten pain. Their family was probably still intact.

"Doc, this patient called us after falling at work. She tripped and fell against a file cabinet. Didn't really hurt anything other than her knee. There's a clear deformity. We think it might be dislocated."

Bryce looked down at the patient's left leg and knew immediately what was wrong. The kneecap had been pushed laterally and was outside of the normal groove in the femur that it was supposed to be in. Her knee was partially flexed and essentially locked in place. She was going to need it reduced in order to relieve the pain. No amount of pain medication will make a dislocated joint feel comfortable.

Bryce touched the patient's arm and said, "Ma'am, your kneecap has been dislocated. That's why it hurts so much. It's a two-second fix and I'm going to do it right now." He walked around to the patient's left side and placed his left hand on her ankle. His right hand cupped the dislocated patella. "When things are out of place, it causes severe discomfort. Unfortunately, so does putting it back in." In a sudden quick movement, he pulled on her ankle to forcibly straighten her leg while at the same time pushing the patella as hard and fast as he could. Like missing a vigorous attempt at hand clapping.

The patient began to scream but stopped as the pain had nearly gone away after a momentary spike. "Oh my gosh, I feel so much better now."

"So I do, ma'am, so do I. We'll get an X-ray, I'll put you in a splint and then we'll get you home to follow-up with orthopedics as an outpatient." He walked out of the room, passing a nurse as she entered to triage the patient.

"What's so funny?" asked the nurse while looking at the paramedic laughing in the corner.

"You just missed some classic Chapman. He looked like he was about to blow up his phone when we walked in and then twenty seconds later, he slaps her kneecap back in place and struts out like he sacked the quarterback."

"I'm sorry, who was that guy?" asked the patient.

The remainder of his shift was uneventful. The rare day shift meant he got to leave before rush hour. On a normal day he'd rush home to see Val and the kids but tonight he stopped at the local liquor store before continuing home.

Chapter Twenty-Five

Bryce sat alone on his couch, staring at the fireplace. Only a few months ago he was sitting here watching his kids rip into Christmas presents while sharing hot chocolate with Valerie. The room had been warm and cozy thanks to their presence and a crackling blaze in the fireplace. Now he sat alone, with a bottle of bourbon on the end table to his left. What had happened? He knew his marriage had not been perfect, but they had been working on it. The trip to the Bahamas was the high point in their years together. They even saved a life together! Yet here he was. Alone. Drunk. A medical malpractice suit pending, a criminal charge pending, his job threatened, and his family gone.

Normally three days off in a row meant fun times with the kids. Trips to the park, museums, movies. Now it was a reminder of how truly alone he felt. He reached for the bottle and poured another three fingers over the remaining ice. Actually, there was only a little bit left in bottle he thought, might as well finish it off. He had been sleeping on the couch since Valerie left with the kids. He didn't want to sleep in their marriage bed by himself. It didn't feel right. Next to the bourbon was his phone, a book, and a bottle of sleeping pills. With the kids gone there was no reason to keep them high in the medicine cabinet anymore.

Bryce held the glass in his right hand. Contemplating. He realized he'd need to go buy more bourbon tomorrow. This bottle had only lasted two days. The last one lasted four. Were the bottles getting smaller or was his despair getting deeper? He knew he couldn't continue like this. Valerie was young and attractive. Strong. She could easily remarry. The kids were young enough that they would grow to love their new father and forget about him. Valerie was too smart to marry someone who would be a bad husband and father. The life insurance policy would set them up nicely for the rest of their lives. If he died, the malpractice suit wouldn't matter. The arrest warrant vanished. The CEO would have to find another person to blame his son's character flaws on.

An overdose. Not the worst way to go, he figured. If he was found the next day, it wouldn't leave a mess like a firearm would. His family wouldn't have to clean anything up. The police and the coroner would take care of that before Val and the kids got home. The coroner. Bryce let out a laugh picturing the investigator standing over his body and declaring he died of polio or some other ridiculous ailment.

Bryce took a large swallow of bourbon and opened the bottle of sleeping pills. He then grabbed his phone and began to write an email to Valerie.

Valerie, I'm sorry I led you down this path in life. You deserve one of joy and fulfillment, not chaos and disappointment. I love you and the kids and hope you can forgive me. Mine is one life I don't care to try to save. The insurance and investment paperwork are in my desk drawer. Tell everyone I'm sorry.

He finished typing and stared at the phone. If he sent it now, she may see it right away and call for help, so he scheduled it to send tomorrow and clicked to confirm. Bryce grabbed the bourbon and finished the glass. No wounded soldiers on the battlefield of drinking tonight. He leaned over to put his glass and phone down and nearly fell off the couch. He grabbed the table to steady himself and pulled it over, spilling the contents onto the hardwood floor. The prescription bottle hit the floor and pills went flying in every direction. His glass shattered into several large sharp pieces. *Damn it. I can't do anything right anymore.* He stood to collect the pills. He didn't think it would take more than twenty to do the job, not even half the contents of the bottle. Why do doctors prescribe lethal amounts of medication in a single prescription? Perhaps he'd ask God in a few minutes.

Moments later, Bryce looked at the handful of pills he collected and the broken glass on the floor. He looked at the empty bottle of bourbon and realized he had nothing to swallow the pills with. *Damn it.*

He headed toward the kitchen, but the pain in his bladder diverted him to the bathroom. He always hated when patients came in having lost control of their bowel or bladder during their medical emergency. It's okay to have a serious condition, but at least have some self-respect and don't piss yourself. He didn't want that on his autopsy report. He stopped in the bathroom to relieve himself and continued to the kitchen sink.

***

"Kids, do you want to give your dad a call?" asked Valerie. They had just returned from an evening swim in the crystal-clear waters of Destin. "He's off today and would probably love to hear from you." They shouted their excited reply.

She let them use her phone's voice assistant to "call Daddy". The phone began to ring. After seven rings, it went to voicemail. The kids heard Bryce's voice and started talking to him. Valerie explained it was just the voicemail. They left a message to call back when he could.

Chapter Twenty-Six

A firm hand pounded repeatedly on the front door. Five raps in quick succession and then a pause. Seven raps in quick succession. Loud raps. Louder than was customary. Louder than was polite. Louder than someone with a hangover should have to deal with. Bryce opened his eyes and looked around. He saw the legs of chairs and kitchen cabinets. *Why am I on the floor? What happened? Why does my head hurt? Who was that pounding on the door?* He groaned as he sat up, and the throbbing in his head intensified. His right hand came up to rub his head and left a trail of some sort of paste on his hair and face. He looked at his palm and saw a glob of dissolved tablets smeared across his hand. The sleeping pills. Why did he have a handful of sleeping pills?

Bryce carefully stood up and walked into the bathroom to rinse the pills off his hand and face. He wasn't sure how much could be absorbed through his skin and didn't want to find out. He turned to empty his bladder and noted his pants were already undone, and someone had not flushed the toilet the last time. Since he's been the only one home for a while it's hard to blame Valerie or the kids. And the seat was up. He walked through the house trying to piece together what had happened. And who was that knocking on the door?

The family room contained more evidence of last night's events. A toppled side table, an empty bottle of bourbon, a broken glass, and sleeping pills strewn across the floor. Slowly, Bryce was piecing it together. He had talked to enough suicidal patients over the years to realize the scene he was looking at. The realization struck him like a sucker punch from Mike Tyson. Instantly a wave of nausea swept over him, causing him to run to the kitchen and grab a garbage can moments before retching uncontrollably. His breathing was fast, yet he could not seem to catch his breath. A constricting pressure gripped his chest. *What's happening? Am I having a pulmonary embolism?* He could feel his heart racing faster and his vision began to cone in like driving into a tunnel in the mountains. So this is what death feels like. He had hoped it would happen fifty years from now in his sleep with his wife at his side after a night of wild sex. Bryce tried to stand and get to his phone but his legs were too weak to hold his frame. He crashed forward onto the floor again with a gasped word, "Val–"

***

"Kids, let's try your dad again. Maybe he was in the shower last time." Valerie offered that excuse for the kids' comfort, but she knew Bryce would have checked his phone immediately after a shower. To be honest, he probably would have sent her a pic of his ass if things were better in their relationship. She missed those times. Smiling, she realized she actually missed the pictures as well.

***

The phone rang seven times and went to voice mail. Again, the kids talked to Bryce as if he were on the phone, only to stop mid-sentence when their mother reminded them about voicemail. *Where are you* Bryce? She was getting concerned.

***

A country song played loudly near Bryce's ear. He woke up on the kitchen floor for the second time in an hour. This new habit had to stop. He remembered feeling like he couldn't breathe, the chest pain, the vision change, and then nothing. He hadn't died. It was just a panic attack. Embarrassment overcame him as well as relief that no one was there to have witnessed it. The sound had been his phone's ringtone for Valerie; "She Don't Know She's Beautiful" by Sammy Kershaw. He remembered the night he chose that ringtone. They had attended his fifteen-year high school reunion and Valerie had stolen the show.

Bryce grabbed his phone to check the voicemail and call her back. What used to be a latest generation iPhone was now the latest generation phone with a shattered screen that would not respond to touch. Damn it. He must have fallen on it. They didn't have a landline, so he walked to the office and logged in to his computer to send her an email.

> *Val, I broke my phone and need to get a new one. I'll call you later today when it's fixed. I miss you and the kids.*

Love,
Bryce

He clicked send, leaned back in his chair, and immediately began doubting himself. Should he have sent more? He clicked on the "Sent Mail" folder and reread the email. No, it was fine. Short and sweet. As he was standing up, something caught his eye. There was an email in his sent items that was sent at 3:00 a.m. Was he up late sending emails while drunk? It was to Valerie.

He leaned forward and opened it, curious what profound truths he had shared with her. As he read what was clearly a suicide note, he felt the nausea return. The tightness in his chest returned. The inability to breathe returned.

NO! I am NOT going to have a panic attack.

He closed his eyes, focused on his breathing, and regained control over himself. Today was the first day he'd had a panic attack since medical school. That day had been the worst of his life and nearly cost him his future career. Today had been worse by an order of magnitude, though no one had died this time. Yet. He logged into Valerie's email account and deleted the message. He hoped she had not read it yet. Can a person casually ask their spouse if they happened to read any good suicide notes lately?

He stood and headed for the shower. A hot shower and fresh clothing could improve almost any situation. While drying himself, he looked in the mirror and made a promise to the broken person staring back at him.

Rock bottom. He had hoped to never experience what his addict patients did, yet here he was. Impulsive, self-destructive actions brought on by substance abuse that nearly cost him his life. His family may already be gone. It's called rock bottom because it's hard to dig a hole deeper than you're already in. What else could pile on to make things worse? His work life in shambles. His family in shambles. No matter what he did, it couldn't get any worse than it was right now.

Bryce made a promise to dig himself out of this hole. To recover his family along the way and eventually salvage his professional career. He also knew enough about substance abuse, mental health, and recovery that it was very hard to overcome these alone. He needed help.

"Yel-low," slurred the voice of Graham Kelly as he answered the phone.

"Graham, hey, it's Bryce. Long time no talk." Indeed. It had been over a year.

"Let me guess, same excuses? Life got busy, family, kids, and so on."

"Yeah, I get it. Busy down here too. So how ya' been?"

"Nothing to complain about, how are you guys doing?" asked Graham.

"Not good, that's why I'm calling you. Valerie took the kids and is staying with her parents in Florida. My job is being threatened by the CEO of the private equity group that owns our hospital. There's an arrest warrant for me in the Bahamas, and I'm being sued by a patient's family."

"Ouch. And you waited for all of that to happen before calling me?"

"I know, Graham, I should have called you earlier," Bryce said, rubbing his forehead.

"Well, what are you doing to sort all this out?"

"Mainly drinking heavily, running my wife and kids off with my behavior and attitude, and other self-destructive things."

Graham sighed. "That's not the guy I remember from medical school. The Bryce Chapman I remember rose to the challenge and kicked its ass. Remember that time fourth year?"

"Of course I do. But that was completely different. And looking at things now, maybe it would have been better if I had just quit medical school right then and there."

"That's ridiculous. Think of all the lives you have saved and people you have helped." Of course he knew Graham was right. But knowing and feeling are completely different. "Look, why don't you come up here tonight. It sounds like we need some time to talk through all of this. I'm here for you, my friend."

Bryce considered the invite for a moment. He did not have a shift for two more days and being in the house alone did not sound appealing. "Okay, yeah, I can do that. I'll be up there in about four hours."

"Perfect, I'll be waiting for you," said Graham.

Chapter Twenty-Seven

Traffic was light, helping Bryce make excellent time driving north to Graham's house. Actually it was probably closer to an estate. He turned onto the long driveway off a two-lane country road, unable to see the house yet due to a dense row of mature pines. The grass in the field was matted down in rows between the narrow tire tracks of an ATV. Bryce felt a twinge of jealousy for the life of freedom Graham found living in the country, where an acre of land could be bought for the price he paid for a one-car garage worth of ground in a subdivision. Why was land worth more in the subdivision? Ten times the price for one tenth the freedom and independence.

Bryce followed the driveway around a curve and through a break in the trees, revealing his friend's home straight ahead. He pulled into the circle driveway by the front door and waved to Graham, who was sitting on the front steps. "Hey buddy, good to see you," said Bryce as he exited his vehicle and walked toward Graham. His outstretched had was swatted aside as Graham wrapped him in a hug.

"I'm glad you were able to come up; it's been too long, Bryce. You look good. Have you been exercising?"

"Nah, just not eating much these last few weeks. Too stressed to think about food."

"Well that's what you're up here for. I've got some of my favorite relaxation techniques ready to go."

"Okay, but no massages. That would get weird. How long were you sitting on your steps waiting for me?"

"Only about thirty seconds. My phone beeped to let me know someone turned in the driveway and the video showed it was you, so I came out."

"Driveway alarms? Cameras? I didn't see any of that," said Bryce.

Graham smiled. "Exactly the point. Let's walk around to the garage."

Bryce followed his friend around the house toward the garage. He was already feeling better. The long car ride had been therapeutic. Hours of quiet time alone in a car to ponder the last few weeks. To make promises to himself and God of changes he had to make. Now he was walking in the clean country air with a good friend from when times were better. He hoped he had already hit rock bottom and was now reassembling the shattered pieces of his life into a ladder to climb out of the hole.

"What do you think? Look like fun?" asked Graham, slapping Bryce on the back. Bryce had been lost in his thoughts and hadn't noticed what was parked next to the driveway. His gaze rose from the ground and settled on what appeared to be two brand new ATVs. "Just got these babies last week. Suzuki King Quad 750s. They'll tow you across the field at fifty miles per hour and not even break a sweat," said Graham in a rapid, slightly higher-pitched voice. "It was either these or a Corvette, I like to think I made the right choice. The kids love 'em."

"They're beautiful. It's been a long time since I've ridden one though. What do you have strapped to the back?" said Bryce.

"We got coolers with food and drinks, a rifle for each of us, a chair, a blanket, and a few surprises."

"Surprises? Perfect, who doesn't like surprises? Let's go. Is your family home?"

"No, my wife headed to her parents' house with the kids for a few days," replied Graham.

"Yeah, same thing happened to me. I hope yours is just for a vacation though." The men climbed onto their ATVs and pulled the helmets onto their heads. Graham pulled out his phone and yelled at Bryce to pose for a picture. "Boy that takes me back! How many pictures did we take of us doing stupid stuff back in med school?" asked Bryce.

"Ha! Thousands. At least. And I still have them all by the way. Perfect blackmail material if you ever cross me. Okay, let's go. Fire it up." Graham showed Bryce how to start the ATV using the starter switch and throttle. Both machines roared to life and began the quick process of idling before they were ready to ride. "How do you know when it's ready?" yelled Bryce.

"When you're covered in dirt from my tires spinning out, you'll know you're good to go."

Bryce scanned the handles and controls, testing the brakes to ensure he knew how to stop. He had seen enough ATV accidents in the ER to realize the danger that often comes along with excitement. A loud noise to his left grabbed his attention. He turned to see what it was, and a cloud of dust blew into his face from Graham's ATV as he tore off into the field.

Bryce pulled the throttle lever quickly and the ATV leapt forward and the front rose a few inches into the air. He was nearly thrown off backwards but recovered and let go of the throttle. The second time, he eased into the throttle and soon was cruising at thirty miles an hour. He followed Graham in seemingly random paths through the fields, between trees, and even jumped onto the driveway to see how fast he could go. The cool wind whipped through his helmet and through his clothes, heightening the sense of exhilaration the power of the machine was already delivering. He felt alive and in control. So much better than last night. This was exactly what he needed. He let loose a primal scream as he pulled the throttle flush against the hand grip.

After ten minutes of joy riding in the fields, Graham pulled up next to Bryce and shut off the engine.

"So? Do you like them?"

"Dude, these are fantastic. I have been smiling non-stop since we got on them. You sure have a great setup out here. I wish we lived further out of the city, but Val likes the comforts of suburban life and quick access to stores and babysitters."

"Speaking of Val, how are things? Did you talk to her today?"

"No, I meant to on the way up, but I forgot."

"You forgot? On a several hour car ride with nothing to do but think? Come on, man. I didn't invite you all the way up here to have you make excuses. Why did you choose to not call her?"

"Okay, you're right. I didn't call her because I didn't know what to say. Promises aren't going to do it. It's going to take action, and I haven't done anything yet. Well, nothing productive. I've done plenty of self-defeating behaviors."

"Now we're getting somewhere. Let's head into the woods to the fire pit and we can talk some more," said Graham before starting the ATV. He waited for Bryce to get his running and then led the way down a trail deep into the woods. Bryce estimated they had traveled about half a mile when the tree canopy opened up above a small clearing. Graham parked his quad and removed his helmet. "This is my happy place. Surrounded by hundreds of acres of woods. No neighbors. No lights, no noise, just peace and quiet. It's starting to get chilly, though, so let's get a fire going."

Chapter Twenty-Eight

They walked through the brush picking up sticks of various sizes that had fallen to the ground. In the center of the clearing was an area of exposed dirt covered in ash, remnants from one of the many fires held here this year already. Graham built the fire up quickly and put his chair down close enough to feel the heat but far enough to not melt his shoes. Bryce joined his friend and handed Graham the cooler from his quad. "Yours has Diet Coke, I figured it was the lesser of two beverage evils for you. Mine has beer, sorry," said Graham.

"I get it. Thank you; this is so peaceful. It's a great place to sit and think."

"And talk. Okay, Chapman, hit me with it. What's going on?"

Bryce started at the beginning. He talked about Kent Carpenter's first visit and the subsequent return visit where he died shortly after arriving to the hospital. The trip to the Bahamas that had started out so perfectly. He shared the story of their trip to Thunderball Grotto and the events with Tony. The plane flight with Colton Hix to Nassau. The legal battles that stemmed from that, and the CEO ultimately threatening his job. He didn't skip details on his personal struggles and told Graham about how his bladder probably saved his life last night. He truly had no recollection of his suicidal thoughts and had been trying to psychoanalyze himself to see how much of that was real versus alcohol induced.

"Wow, man, I didn't realize it was this bad. Do you think you need to go somewhere for professional psychiatric help? This is serious stuff, my friend."

"I asked myself that today too. Ultimately, I said no. I had a moment of weakness and irrational thought and actions brought on by situational depression and alcohol intoxication. I was drunkicidal. Thankfully, I'm alive and well today. I'm going to see a counselor by myself and I'm hoping Val will go with me to couples counseling. I need to get better so that we can get better."

Graham leaned over and added more wood to the fire, sending a stream of hot embers up into the air. "You sound like you're saying all the right things, Bryce. I believe you know what's wrong in your personal life and relationship, and you have a plan to fix it. But what are you going to do about the patient who died and the legal issues in the Bahamas? How are you going to get the CEO off your back?"

Bryce had been thinking about these questions for days but had been unable to come up with a definitive solution. "It's all so complicated." He picked up a stick and rearranged the coals, sending a wave of heat emanating from the fire. "For the CEO, I need to prove that his son started all of it. The only reason he's threatening me is that he thinks I caused the injury to his son. If I can convince him that it was Tony's fault, I should be clear of both him and the assault charge."

"How are you going to convince him of that?" asked Graham.

"I wish I knew. I lost the video of the scene when my camera fell off as I climbed into the plane. All of Tony's friends are telling the same story and the only people to support me are the charter captain and Valerie. Guess who the CEO is going to believe?"

"Okay, well let's come back to that. What about the lawsuit? You think it's bogus?"

"I think something happened that we don't know about. Some outside force acted on the patient to make him get so sick so quickly. Nothing else makes sense. I think he was murdered."

"Woah, that's quite a statement. Is that really the only thing that can explain it?"

"I guess some extremely unlikely series of events could have happened, but easiest solution is that he was intentionally made sick. So, yeah, I guess murder is the correct term. The other problem is our coroner is an idiot and said because the patient died of Pseudomonas and his father had cystic fibrosis, then obviously he did also. He said I should have checked an X-ray. I'm telling you, the guy felt sick for under two hours when I saw him, and he died two days later."

"Why didn't he come back in sooner?"

"I have no idea. We tell everyone to return for any new or worsening symptoms, but it's up to them to do it. I think the inertia of his disease was so great he was probably going to die no matter what either of us did. We just didn't know it at the time."

"So let's start poking holes in the narrative. Did your patient have CF?" said Graham.

"I can't be certain, but I highly doubt it. He was in his thirties and had never been seen for pulmonary complaints that I could find, and had a normal pulmonary exam at the first visit."

"That's a genetic mutation, right? Can you test his DNA to see if he had it?"

"I'm impressed, Graham. You're an ortho doc but still remember some clinical medicine. I promise to not tell any of your colleagues. I'd hate for them to make fun of you," joked Bryce.

"Hey, we're not just bench presses and protein shakes. We still have to worry about the stuff around the bones, too."

"Well, if I had any of his DNA, I'd test for it. He was cremated, though, and the lab didn't keep any samples since we never ordered anything other than the respiratory culture."

"What about the autopsy? They always keep samples on record for years, I think."

"That's another problem. The coroner did not feel the need to do an autopsy. They felt it was a simple case of a cystic fibrosis patient getting pneumonia and dying. What's suspicious about that?"

"Sounds like you need a new coroner. I'll write a check whenever you announce your candidacy. Did he have any kids? Can you test them?"

"Probably, but that would take time and a court order to compel a sample to be taken. And even then, it's possible he didn't pass the gene on to them since it's recessive. A person needs to have two copies of the gene to have the disease. If he was a carrier, who only had one copy, he may not have passed it to his kids. There is one possibility though. He had testicular cancer and only had one testicle when he died."

"Ah... and you want to go find that lost testicle? Sort of an Indiana Jones thing? Raiders of the Lost Nut?"

Bryce couldn't help but laugh. "I wouldn't pay a dime to watch that. No, apparently patients are encouraged to leave a semen sample prior to surgery in case something happens and both testicles are removed or the other damaged during chemotherapy or radiation. It's possible there is a DNA sample on file somewhere in the city. I just need to find it."

"Huh. I've had some pretty interesting conversations out here, Bryce, but this is the first time I've talked about trying to procure another man's semen. Shouldn't there be banjos playing in the background?"

"Hilarious. I think it's a reasonable shot. The problem is we can't just go ask for the sample, and I don't have time to use the courts to access–" said Bryce, trailing off the sentence and looking at Graham.

"What? Why are you looking at me like that?"

"I need your help."

"With what?" asked Graham, drawing his head back and squinting his eyes a bit.

"You know exactly what. I need to steal some semen."

Graham jumped out of his chair and pointed at Bryce. "You're not allowed to say stuff like that around the campfire when it's just two dudes in the woods, man. Now we gotta do something manly. Grab your rifle."

"What are we going to shoot? It's dark out, I won't be able to see anything."

"Remember, I told you I brought some surprises? That's how we're going to see."

Graham walked to his ATV and removed a hard-plastic case. He unlatched it and removed a piece of closed-cell foam padding, revealing two futuristic looking pieces of equipment.

"What are those?" asked Bryce.

"A set of thermal binoculars and a night vision monocle. The thermal binoculars are just fun to play with. You can see the heat coming off decomposing wood. Footprints of mice as they run through the woods. You may see a coyote or deer as well. The night vision is for the infrared laser mounted on your rifle."

"These will pick up the heat signature from a mouse footprint?" asked Bryce in a tone of wonder.

"Yeah, it shows up even better if the mouse has a fever." Graham lifted the night vision monocle and clicked it into a latch on the front of his helmet. He pulled it down and into position, looking through the lens at the surrounding woods.

"There's a raccoon about fifty yards that way," he said, pointing off to the right. Bryce powered on the thermal binoculars and scanned that direction, easily seeing the glowing white outline of a raccoon as it walked slowly between the trees. He was surprised to see faint, white circles behind the raccoon, fading as the animal walked further away and the area cooled.

"This is pretty sweet. What do you do with these?"

"Hunt coyotes mainly. We could use them on hogs if my wife ever let me go on a trip. Look to your left; do you see a steel torso target about a hundred yards out?"

Bryce turned and saw the target suspended from a tree by a chain. "Yes, I see it."

"Okay, that's what we're going to be shooting. Grab your rifle and put on this helmet."

Graham helped Bryce setup the equipment. He inserted two tiny plastic ear plugs that Graham handed him. "Are these going to be enough? They're tiny."

"Another great innovation. They filter out about twelve decibels at normal background volume but block more sound with louder noises like a gunshot."

"You have a lot of really cool stuff. I bet some of this could be used to steal semen," said Bryce.

"Dude, just shut up and shoot," said Graham as he opened another beer.

Bryce depressed the pressure switch on the laser mounted along the barrel of his rifle, and then looked through the night vision monocle. He could see the beam project out like a long finger. Whatever the laser pointed at, a skilled shooter could send a bullet through a fraction of a second later. Bryce was not a skilled shooter, a fact confirmed by several missed shots. Shooting with a laser sight is not as easy as it seems. There is a lot of technique and skill involved in a proper trigger pull to achieve accuracy.

"Hey, slow down. Gently squeeze the trigger until it fires. Don't anticipate the gun firing, and don't jerk the trigger. Then, once you've fired, keep the trigger depressed for a few seconds and let the energy dissipate before slowly releasing the trigger until you feel it reset. Then you can take the next shot." Bryce did as his friend suggested and was rewarded with a loud metallic PING. "Great shot!" said Graham.

Bryce proceeded to hit the target ten times in a row, and then the bolt stayed back and the chamber remained as empty as the magazine. "You're a quick learner, Bryce. I think you're ready for the final surprise. Get over here."

Bryce set the rifle down on his ATV and walked over to Graham. He saw his friend holding a small box, the sort of thing that would normally hold facial tissue. Graham held out a Sharpie along with a few scraps of paper for Bryce who took them with a curious look on his face. "What is this for?"

"I learned this at a church camp back in high school. You're going to write down the problems you're facing. Specifics. Name names. Then you're going to put them in this box and you'll use your rifle to send them straight to hell."

Bryce figured it couldn't hurt, so he sat in his chair and started writing. Graham silently drank his beer and tended to the fire. He pretended to not see the tears streaming down his friend's face. "Okay, all done," said Bryce after a few minutes.

"Great, fold them up and toss them in here." Bryce complied and then watched Graham walk down by the target they had been shooting at. He looked around for a bit and then put the box down at the base of a dead tree and then walked back. "Now that you can hit the broad side of a barn, let's see if you can hit the broad side of a box. I only want you to load one round in the gun at a time, okay?"

"Okay, sure." Bryce fed one round into the magazine and slammed it into the rifle. He thumbed the bolt catch and the spring released, moving the bolt carrier into position and bringing a round with it. "Just shoot the box?" asked Bryce.

"And send your problems straight to hell," replied Graham.

Bryce took a deep breath and then exhaled. He centered the laser beam on the box and started to slowly squeeze the trigger. What happened next could be described as a Rube Goldberg machine of awesomeness. A fraction of a second after Bryce pulled the trigger, the box and the tree it was sitting in front of disintegrated in a bright flash of light. The light and noise startled him and he nearly dropped the rifle. When he recovered, he looked at his target and could find no evidence it was ever there. The tree was laying on its side and smoking, completely severed at the base.

"What the hell was that?" yelled Bryce.

"Closure my friend. That was five pounds of ammonium nitrate mixed with aluminum powder, detonated with the energy from your well-placed shot. Now, let's go back to the house and rest up. You've got to go kick a lot of these things in the ass tomorrow. And of course I'll help you steal semen, just don't quote me on that."

Bryce walked back toward his ATV and placed the rifle back in its mount. He looked back at the tree and the hole where the box used to be. He pulled his arms outward and back, flexing the muscles in his back against his jacket. "I thought writing your feelings on paper was just some touchy-feely nonsense. But I feel so powerful right now. Like I can blow up anything that gets in my way. Thank you, Graham. I'm going to head back to Indy in the morning and kick some ass."

"I know you will; you're Bryce Chapman," replied Graham, enunciating the name by revving the engine of his ATV.

Chapter Twenty-Nine

The drive back home seemed to take forever. Bryce was eager to start attacking his problems and didn't have the patience for slow traffic on the busy interstate. He thought back about the incident in medical school. The one that nearly made him quit medicine and never look back. It was during his fourth year while he was on an internal medicine rotation, part of a team caring for patients in the hospital. The team consisted of a medicine senior resident, an intern, and a medical student. The attending physician was at home overnight but available for consultation.

The team had admitted an elderly male patient for a COPD exacerbation, and he was doing well with their treatments, improving every day. The day before he was to go home, he choked while eating dinner and vomited, sucking a large amount of stomach contents into his lungs. This led to rapid deterioration and the need to be on a ventilator.

As a student interested in emergency medicine, Bryce had performed many advanced procedures already and was eager to intubate the patient. He was outranked by the internal medicine intern and was obliged to stand by and watch while the patient was sedated and a breathing tube passed into the trachea. The intern was not confident in his technique and struggled for a few minutes before finally passing the tube. Bryce commented that it seemed too deep as he could not hear good breath sounds on the left side of the chest. He was concerned the tube had entered the right mainstem bronchus, providing air to only one lung. He was overruled by the intern and senior resident who both felt the breath sounds were good enough and were busy celebrating the intern's first successful intubation.

As a consolation prize, Bryce was allowed to place the central line, a large IV catheter usually placed into the neck, chest, or groin to allow direct central venous access for strong medications. It was a procedure he had done several times, and he even used an ultrasound to visualize the anatomy in real time while performing the procedure. The medical residents had not seen ultrasound used for a central line before and were nervous about the new technique.

The intern was tasked with ordering an X-ray after the procedures and the team separated now that the patient had stabilized on the ventilator. Unfortunately, he forgot and never ordered the X-ray. An hour later, the nurse noted vital signs beginning to deteriorate and activated the code blue alarm. The team raced to the beside to find their patient without a pulse and unable to be bagged due to high pressure.

It was then they realized no X-ray had been done after the intubation and central line. The team removed the breathing tube and tried to bag the patient, hoping there was a blockage in the tube from food particles. It did not work, and they still could not ventilate the patient.

Bryce had pulled a 14-gauge IV out of his white coat pocket and stabbed it into the patient's right chest without seeking approval from the residents. There was an immediate rush of air as the popped lung was allowed to decompress.

With reduced pressure in the chest, the team was able to push air into the lungs again, blood could return back to the heart, and the patient's heart started beating again. Briefly. Unfortunately, the patient ended up dying the next day.

The internal medicine residents presented the events to their attending the next morning and placed the blame on Bryce and his central line. He felt attacked, inadequate. Like a failure. He was told he had killed a patient by puncturing the lung with his central line needle. For the first few days after the event, he actually believed it and had wanted to quit medical school. Every patient he saw reminded him of that man and he wondered if he was going to harm them too. He didn't understand how his procedure had hit the lung since he was so far away from it and watched the needle in real time as it entered the vein directly. If he couldn't perform procedures without complications, and not even understand how the complication happened, did he have any business being a physician? How many people would he kill?

Graham Kelly hated to see his friend go through this. He was planning a career in orthopedics and knew all invasive procedures carried risks. He also knew ultrasound was a great way to place a central line, and that the neck vein Bryce used carried a very low risk of puncturing the lung. Graham discussed the situation with an anesthesiologist between cases on his orthopedic rotation and was given an alternative theory. The anesthesiologist felt it was likely an improperly placed breathing tube that led to the popped lung. If the ventilator is trying to deliver two lungs worth of air to one lung, it will cause significantly increased pressure and the risk of rupture causing an air leak into the chest. Exactly what killed Bryce's patient.

Graham tracked Bryce down in the hospital and shared the new theory. They pulled up a recent chest CT on the patient and saw severe emphysema with many dilated air sacs, just poised to rupture. Sending twice the expected volume of air into an already diseased lung could absolutely cause the lung to pop and pressure to build in the chest, killing the patient.

This new information changed Bryce's outlook instantly. Instead of broken and humiliated, he was armed and angry. He kept the idea to himself, until he was asked to speak at the M&M meeting. There he presented the alternative theory and used documentation from the respiratory therapist about how far in the tube had been secured as his evidence. He showed the CT scan and the pre-existing weak spots in the lung. A popped lung is a known complication of central line attempts when the needle accidentally touches the lung and punctures it. But it is very unusual when the jugular vein is used, especially when performed using ultrasound guidance to visualize the needle enter the blood vessel. He provided literature to show the safety of the central line insertion technique he used. He brought up the fact that both the intern and resident failed to order the X-ray to confirm placement of the tube and evaluate the central line positioning.

By the time he was done, he had changed the narrative and earned the respect of nearly everyone in the room. Everyone except the two residents who had been present that night. Graham Kelly had helped saved Bryce's reputation, his self-confidence, and his medical career. And last night, he was kind enough to do it again.

Chapter Thirty

Alani Kahele rarely entered the emergency department. Her kingdom resided in the hospital's lab. She knew every machine, every beep, and every click that happened. The ED was loud, disorganized, and often outright scary. There was always a reason to avoid being physically present in the ED. But not today. She came today to try to help a doctor who had always been kind when they talked on the phone. Usually, when a doctor called the lab it was because a test was delayed, or a result was unexpected and they wanted clarification. Dr. Chapman called for those same reasons but managed to be pleasant and respectful on the phone. He understood delays and systemic problems were just part of the game, and he didn't take it personally. It was a sad commentary when someone acting polite stands out from the crowd.

She smiled when she saw him walk out of a patient room. "Hi, Alani! How's my Hawaiian lab guru doing today?"

"Hi, Dr. Chapman; I'm fine, thanks. I wanted to talk to you today about a bacterial culture that was sent on your patient a few weeks ago."

"I send a lot of those. Who are we talking about?"

"His name was Kent Carpenter. The culture was actually sent by Dr. Sharpe, but I saw you took care of him on the first visit."

"What an odd case. I'm actually getting sued over that visit. It makes no sense to me. They say he had cystic fibrosis, but I can't find anything in his chart about it and he had never been here for any pulmonary reason."

"It's strange for me too. The culture grew out Pseudomonas aeruginosa."

"I heard, that certainly fits with cystic fibrosis, but none of the rest of it does."

"What's more intriguing than the bacteria species is the resistance pattern. It was resistant to every antibiotic we usually test for."

"Woah, multi-drug resistant Pseudomonas? Where did he pick that up from?" MDR Pseudomonas was an institutional organism. The sort of beast that evolves after years of exposure to powerful antibiotics in the hospital setting. The super bug we've been warned about since Alexander Fleming discovered penicillin. The reason coughs, colds, bronchitis, and many other mild illnesses are not to be treated with antibiotics. This is one of the many harmful realities of antibiotic overuse.

"That's a great question. We have only had this with one other patient in our facility. She is vent dependent and here about every other week."

"Eleanor?" asked Bryce.

"None other. Eleanor Livingstone. She causes us so much work when the samples come down. Infection control makes us disinfect everything that came in contact with the sample. Takes us forever to clean it all."

"Trust me, they are on us too. We have to be fully gowned up before she gets here, disposable stethoscopes, the whole nine yards."

"So how did this bacteria jump from Eleanor to Kent?" Alani asked.

"That's what I need to find out. You have been a huge help. Thank you." Bryce was starting to feel better. Coincidences can happen, but not something like this. This seemed intentional. Intentional meant a resolution was not imminent, but it also meant he didn't screw up and cause a patient to die.

"Hey, hang on. I don't believe we've met yet," said Dr. Peter Thrasher, rising from his workstation. He combed his left hand through his blond hair and extended his right out to greet Alani. "Peter Thrasher, ER doc."

"Hi, nice to meet you. I'm Alani from the lab. You probably won't see much of me since I hang out in the lab, but we'll probably chat on the phone," she said.

"Oh, I don't know. I wouldn't mind seeing you more. Maybe I'll stop by in person rather than call when I need something," he said with a smile.

Alani flashed a nervous smile and turned away. "It's really easier to reach me by phone. I'm never in the same place very long. Nice to meet you." With that, she turned and walked away quickly.

"Go easy on her, I'm pretty sure she's dating someone already," said Bryce.

"But not married?" asked Peter as he stretched his arms behind his back. A loud snap from behind Peter Thrasher caused both men to turn around. His scribe, Emily, had just shut her laptop forcibly and was walking away.

"What's with her?" asked Bryce.

"We dated for a while, but it didn't work out. I think she may still be upset about it."

"Oh man, when did you guys break up?"

Peter locked his fingers together and extended his elbows, flexing his triceps. "Yesterday."

Bryce shook his head. "I thought you just moved here for this job? Did she move here with you?"

"Sure did. But I decided new city, new job, new start, you know?"

"But same scribe?" said Bryce.

"Of course. She's a fantastic scribe," he said with a grin.

Chapter Thirty-One

Bryce parked his car in the public library parking lot. He had considered viable locations to call sperm banks from without revealing his identity with caller ID, and the public library seemed the most logical.

He looked at the piece of paper with three names and numbers on it. He had assembled the list on his phone sitting in the hospital parking lot after his shift. Three didn't sound like a large number, but considering it represented the options for semen storage in town, it really was remarkable.

Bryce walked into the library and found a reference desk with a phone and no librarian on duty. He picked up the phone and dialed the number of the first company on his list. The call was answered on the second ring. "Hello, thank you for calling Henderson Biotech. How can I help you?" asked the voice on the line.

"Yes, hi. I'm moving out of state and want to know the procedure to collect my sample and transfer it to my new location."

"Okay, sir, I can help you with that. We have a standard process for transfer and a form you need to fill out. The transfer itself is done through a commercial carrier using overnight delivery. What's your name?"

Bryce swallowed hard and looked around to make sure no one was interested in his call. "Kent Carpenter," he said.

He heard keystrokes in the background and a muffled groan of confusion. "I'm not finding you on record here. Can you confirm how you spell your name?"

Bryce drew a line through the number on the paper but played along to finish the call without raising suspicion. "Oh, I'm sorry. I'm sure you're spelling it correctly. I must have called the wrong facility. Sorry to have wasted your time." The receptionist ended the call pleasantly and moved on with her day.

Bryce moved down the list and had the same conversation with the next facility. The last name on the list had appeared the most promising. Cryo Tech. Bryce got through his opening line and was prepared for disappointment when the voice on the other end replied. "Yes, Mr. Carpenter, I see your sample in our system. It's been with us for three years now. Do you have the name of the facility you'd like it transferred to? I can start filling the form out and have it ready when you arrive."

Bryce held back his desire to leap into the air and scream. He was in a library, after all. "Actually, I don't have a place selected yet. I was hoping to learn the process for transfer. I'll call you back when I have that information."

"Very well. We're here when you're ready. Have a nice day."

Bryce replaced the phone in the cradle and circled the name several times on the paper. He had found the sample. He pulled out his cell phone and sent a quick text to Graham.

Semen location identified. More info to follow.

He walked out of the library happier than he'd been in days.

Chapter Thirty-Two

Bryce had been ignoring the legal situation in the Bahamas since Val left. This was completely outside his comfort zone, and he had hoped to tackle it with her assistance. Now he realized he needed to do it on his own.

He reread the letter from the judge in the Bahamas twice and then did an internet search for attorneys in Nassau. His browser displayed dozens of ads for attorneys in Nassau County, New York. The results reminded Bryce he'd read that the United States has more attorneys than the rest of the world combined. He added in the term "Bahamas" to his search and tried again.

The first result looked promising. A criminal defense attorney who was born and raised in Nassau. Samuel Russell. His website had several pictures of smiling clients walking out of the court room. Bryce clicked on the fees section of the site and groaned. Three hundred dollars an hour. He searched through several more attorneys and found rates as low as seventy-five dollars an hour. He considered the options and decided it was worth paying more. If Samuel Russell could charge those rates and stay in business, he must be worth it.

Bryce picked up his phone and dialed the number. After talking with the administrative assistant for a few minutes he was given an appointment for later in the day to discuss the case with the attorney. She explained it would take some time to pull the arrest warrant and obtain the background material. Bryce heard the words but felt the three hundred dollars an hour rate begin to add up. He provided his email address to receive the letter of engagement, background of the charges, and retainer contract. Five thousand dollars just to get started. Bryce sighed. He took difficult prerequisite classes, then four years of medical school, three years of residency, and now worked to save lives for less money than a criminal defense attorney gets to sit in an office.

He looked around the house and realized no one had done dishes in over a week, yet the sink wasn't full. It was another reminder of how lonely his life had become. He stood up and started cleaning the kitchen with plans to progress to the rest of the house. Order out of chaos.

A few hours later, his phone rang with an incoming call from the Bahamas. He answered quickly and was greeted by a deep and confident sounding voice.

"Hello, this is Samuel Russell. I'm trying to reach Dr. Bryce Chapman."

"Yes, this is Bryce. Thanks for calling me back. Did you get the information I sent in?"

"I did receive it, yes. I'm sorry you are facing this situation. It's an unfortunate thing that our nation's laws do not make accommodation for actions such as yours. I spoke to the judge, and you don't have a lot of time before they begin the extradition process. I intend to file a motion to delay giving us more time to prepare a defense. I assume you do not wish to be brought to a Bahamian jail if you can avoid it?"

"No, I would prefer not to. Look, all I did was defend my wife. She was being attacked by a group of drunken men and

I allowed her to get away. Then they turned on me. I was lucky his punch missed as it would have taken my head off. I pushed him away with my leg, the rest of it was just bad luck."

"That does sound defensible. I must say, it's a unique situation that two Americans are the opposing parties in a Bahamian criminal matter. Usually, I represent locals who have gotten themselves into trouble."

"Do you think I can beat this?" asked Bryce.

"Yes, I do. But I'm sorry to say it's going to take a lot of time and money. The plaintiff's father is well known in the Bahamas and his attorneys have already filed several affidavits with the court in this case. We're not just up against the prosecutor, we're up against the corporate attorneys for a multi-billion-dollar company."

Bryce liked to hear the term "we" in the attorney's speech. He felt like he had a teammate and was no longer facing this alone. Suddenly three hundred dollars an hour seemed like a bargain.

"Well, we need to win. I can't spend time in a prison in the Bahamas. I'll lose my job and possibly my medical license. Not to mention the further disruption to my family."

"I'm going to enjoy working with you, Dr. Chapman. Most of my clients are straight-up guilty. I believe you to be innocent of intent in this matter and it will be a pleasure fighting for you. I love John Grisham books and I'll be the small-town attorney who chews up the fancy, big-city law firm and emerges victorious at the end."

"I sure hope so. Let me know if you need anything else from me."

"Very well. My team will get started immediately. Have a good day."

Bryce ended the call and looked around. The dishes were done, the floor was vacuumed, and the laundry was started. A plan was forming to address the legal matter in the Bahamas. Order from chaos.

Chapter Thirty-Three

Bryce parked in front of Cryo Tech but did not exit his car immediately. He slowly looked over the exterior of the building, looking for cameras and other security features. Finding none, he exited the car and walked toward the front door.

He reached for the door to pull it open but jumped back as the door opened quickly from the inside. Bryce nearly ran into a man exiting the building. Their eyes met for a moment and Bryce noted a "New Customer Welcome Kit" in his hand. Both men muttered awkwardly and passed by, no longer meeting each other's gaze.

The lobby was small but modern. Engineered wooden flooring provided an echo of footsteps and as he approached the front window. Bryce could not see an alarm pad near the front door and did not notice a sticker on the door warning of a monitoring system. "Good morning, sir. How can I help you?" asked the friendly secretary from behind a window.

"Hi, I'm looking for a facility to store a sample for fertility purposes. I came across your company on the internet, but I couldn't find much information on your storage techniques. Is it possible to get more information or a tour of the facility? My wife and I take this very seriously."

"Absolutely, sir, that's a very common request. We understand you are trusting us with the future of your family. Please wait a moment while I go find someone to give you a tour." She stood up from her chair and disappeared around a corner.

Bryce didn't have to wait long. A door opened and a professionally-dressed woman stepped through, welcoming him with a smile. "Good morning, I'm Nicole. I understand you'd like to hear more about our services?"

"That's correct. I was hoping for a tour of your storage equipment and a quick overview of the process for specimen handling," said Bryce.

"Okay, great. Follow me," she said, holding the door open. "Our facility follows all appropriate FDA guidelines for handling medical specimens. We are HIPAA compliant and take your privacy very seriously." They continued down a short, carpeted corridor. "We understand that this is a very serious relationship, one that can literally affect all your future generations." She pointed to a small room with an examination table similar to a doctor's office. "Here is our in-house donation room, if you need to use our facility; otherwise, we can provide you with a home collection kit. We do recommend providing several samples to increase future fertility success."

"What are your fees for storage?" asked Bryce.

"Right, there are several different fees. We charge an initial processing fee that includes sample collection, testing, and initial freezing. That's two hundred and fifty dollars. We also recommend testing for infectious disease such as hepatitis, syphilis, and HIV. We can perform those for you, or you can bring us documentation of negative results. After the initial processing fee, there is a two-hundred dollar annual fee for storage."

Bryce was now generally curious about the process of storage and later use of the specimen. "Is there a limit on how long a sample can be stored? Does the effectiveness change over time?"

"No, there is not. You're only limited by how long you wish to continue paying the storage fee. Once frozen, sperm can remain viable indefinitely. The process of freezing and thawing is where the damage occurs, so we only do that once per sample. Usually over fifty percent of the sperm remain viable after thawing, no matter how long the sample was frozen. There is a two-hundred dollar thaw charge assessed at the time of use."

"That's very interesting," he said. "So if we wanted to do in vitro fertilization, I should store a sample for each attempt we may need?"

"That's correct," she replied.

Bryce did some quick math. Ten rounds of IVF from frozen samples would cost at least five thousand dollars for the semen side alone. A huge expense for a couple trying to start a family. "That makes sense. Can I see the storage equipment?"

"Sure, right this way." She led him around a corner to a wider corridor with a metal door centered along the rear wall. A two-foot square window in the door gave a glimpse of the equipment inside.

She reached an arm out and turned the handle, opening the door. Bryce noted the lack of a key or access code to gain entry. The room had a different feel than the rest of the office. This was a clean room. Immaculate, stainless-steel counters. Warm LED lighting. The gentle hum of expensive freezers.

"This is our storage and processing room. We keep the specimens labeled in these freezers and try to spread a patient's samples into different freezers for redundancy purposes. In the extremely unlikely event of equipment failure, we don't want to lose what is so precious to you. In fact, we have a full diesel generator for backup power, and we don't stock the freezers to more than fifty percent capacity. We have twenty-four-hour monitoring of the freezer temperature and are alerted if the temperature rises more than ten degrees."

"Fifty percent capacity. Is that in case you lose a machine you have adequate space to move the samples to another one?" asked Bryce.

"Exactly," she said.

"I'll be honest, you have a very impressive setup," said Bryce. "This truly is a top-notch facility, and the fees seem reasonable and a worthwhile investment in my family. I'll talk to my wife and we'll let you know our decision." Bryce scanned every wall as he was escorted to the front reception area. He noted a rear entry door but did not see an alarm panel near it. *Perfect.* Nicole waved as he exited the front door and walked towards his car.

Chapter Thirty-Four

"Dr. Chapman, you're an internet sensation!" The words came from a nurse walking into the department to start her shift.

"What are talking about?" he asked.

"A video just got posted of you saving the life of some guy on vacation."

"What? How is there video of that?"

"It said someone found a waterproof action camera while snorkeling and it's got footage of the whole thing. Was it on your head or something? That's the view it gives of you guys doing CPR."

"Are you serious? I lost the camera while climbing onto a plane. Who found it?"

"I have no idea, but the video is amazing. I watched it three times. You're such a great doctor!"

Bryce jogged back to his desk. He had to tell Val about this. He grabbed his phone to call her and saw she had tried to call him a few minutes earlier. He touched her number and the call connected on the first ring.

"Have you seen it?" she asked.

"No, I just heard about it. Have you?"

"Yes, I watched the whole thing. I wanted to vomit watching you give mouth to mouth, but I looked awesome dragging Tony back to the boat and doing chest compressions. And about chests, why was the camera focused on mine so much during the video?"

"Okay, you caught me. But have you ever seen someone do chest compressions in a bikini? It's sorta hard not to watch. Seriously though, do you know what this means? We can prove that Tony started it and get this assault charge thrown out. I can also talk to the CEO and likely get him off my back about my job. This is fantastic." Bryce was elated, he wanted to hug his wife and his kids. Their separation from him felt infinitely wide at the moment.

"I'm not so sure. The video started when we were on the boat and looking around for Tony. It didn't show any of the time we were in the cave."

"What? Why not? That's the evidence that we need," Bryce said. "Are there any other videos linked to it? Like maybe you just saw part two?"

"I looked; I couldn't find anything else." He sat down like a popped balloon. Another moment of excitement turned into disappointment; he couldn't find words worth speaking. "Bryce, I'm as disappointed as you are. And I don't mean to make it worse, but do you remember what else was on that camera? Something a bit more intimate?"

He had forgotten. When the camera vanished, he had assumed all the video was lost forever. "Great, you finally agreed to keep the camera running in the bedroom and now someone has the memory card and is posting files on the internet? Wonderful. What can we do about it?"

"I don't know, but I'm pissed. I'm going to look into it. I may fly down there and start punching people until I find out who has it."

"Val, our family doesn't need any more assault charges in the Bahamas. Have you thought about when you might be coming home?"

"It's all I think about, Bryce. The kids keep asking when we're going home. I just don't know if home is where I'm at now, or back in Indiana. I do love you, but I need more time to think. Everything seems stacked against us."

"I know, but all of it is external to us. Our relationship. You and me. My drinking is the only thing that wasn't. I haven't had a drop since I went up to Graham's house. I'm a changed man."

"I'll believe you're a changing man, not sure I can believe you've changed yet. You were not treating me or the kids well at all. Maybe it was all alcohol, maybe depression from what is going on, or maybe it's more than that. Keep working on you, I'll keep working on me, and we can both work on us. Let's talk again tomorrow."

"Okay, babe; tell the kids I said hi. I'll call you in the morning. Love you."

Bryce stood up to go see a patient when his phone vibrated. He glanced at the screen. Three new text messages, from three different people. All about the video. "Paula, if anyone calls for me, tell them I'm not working today, would you?"

"Shall... I lie for you?" she sang to the tune of "Little Drummer Boy."

"Yes, please." Her reply brought a much-needed smile to his face.

Bryce's shift ended at 10:00 p.m. He was out of the hospital thirty minutes later and drove straight to Cryo Tech to check on the building again, and then he went home.

***

The next morning, Bryce was up early for a quick turn-around to a day shift starting at 10:00 a.m. He looked at the tracking board and saw a six-year-old had just been placed in a trauma room. Usually, a child in these rooms meant either a severe respiratory complaint or an injury to an arm or leg with deformity. Maybe a seizure or an ingestion. He quickly walked to the trauma room to assess the patient.

As he neared the trauma bay, he could hear the screams of a child in pain paired with the anxious words of a mother in distress. Bryce pulled the curtain back to see an adorable blond-haired girl laying in the bed with a large splint on her right forearm. The child's mother was leaning over the bed, holding her head, and trying unsuccessfully to calm her down.

"Ma'am, I'm Dr. Chapman; what happened today?"

The mother turned and wiped the tears from her eyes. "It was such a beautiful day outside. We decided it was perfect to try another bike riding lesson. She didn't want to, but I--" her voice broke as sobs of guilt washed over her.

"It's okay, that's why we call them accidents," said Bryce with a reassuring hand on the mother's shoulder. He turned to the child. "Sweetie, what's your name?" He knew what it was from the tracking board and arm band, but he knew kids liked to say their own name.

"It's Mattie. Are you going to give me a shot?"

"Hi. Mattie, I'm Bryce. We're going to give you medicine to help this feel better. It's a squirt of water up your nose and then we're going to take a picture of your arm, okay? You will feel a lot better soon." He didn't answer her question yet; no sense making her any more nervous and fearful.

He placed an order for intranasal fentanyl, an extremely potent narcotic that had unfortunately led to a massive uptick in recreational narcotic overdoses recently. Drug suppliers add it to anything they can think of to increase the effect and thus the price of their illicit goods. But when used appropriately in a controlled environment, it is a wonderful pain medication. Especially when it can be delivered via an atomizer squirted into the nostril to an anxious child fearful of needles.

Two minutes after receiving the dose she was much calmer, as was her mother. Bryce questioned whether the nurse gave some to the mother as her demeanor had improved after watching her daughter's pain reduced. He examined the arm and confirmed the skin was intact, it was not an open fracture. The child's sensation, motor function, and pulses were also intact. There was a small laceration on her arm near the tricep that would require stitches but was straight and should heal with minimal scaring. He called X-ray to obtain images quickly and stayed at the bedside to review them on the computer screen attached to the portable X-ray machine. Emergency medicine was often delivered at a rapid pace, and that could be quickened even more when a child was suffering. The other patients with minor complaints could wait a few more minutes to be evaluated.

Bryce saw the first picture of the forearm and noted both the radius and ulna were not only fractured, but they were angulated and would need to be aligned better for pain control and proper healing. "Mom, she did break both bones in her forearm, and I will need to manipulate them into better alignment before she goes home tonight." He paused to make sure the mother was following what he was saying. "We'll give her ketamine, which is a great sedative for children. I'll use a fluoroscope as a live X-ray to make sure we get the bones set the best we can. She'll be sedated for about an hour but then you should be able to take her home in a splint and sling to follow-up with orthopedics. While she's sedated, I'll also repair the laceration on her arm."

"I broke my arm?" slurred Mattie as she looked at her left arm, clearly altered from the dose of Fentanyl. It usually wasn't a truth serum like midazolam, but some people were light weights. Like six-year-old girls.

"Yes, Mattie, but this one," said Bryce, pointing to her other arm. God bless whoever got FDA approval for intranasal fentanyl.

"Are you going to fix it?" asked Mattie as she looked at Bryce through half-open eyes.

"Yes, I'm going to do my best, Mattie."

"Good. I'm glad you're my doctor. When something's hurt or broken, you know how to fix it. And you're going to fix it."

"That's right, Mattie-cakes. He has trained his whole life to be able to help people and fix things. It's going to be okay."

The conversation pierced Bryce like a scalpel. The metaphor reached inside him like a surgeon and found the part of his soul that was broken, defeated. Wrapped its hand around the diseased part. Suddenly the injured child was his daughter. The mother his wife. The arm the summation of battles he was facing.

He started to ask the nurse to administer the Ketamine, but the sentence never materialized. His voice cracked on the first word, and he realized his eyes had teared up. He coughed and excused himself, "I'm going to get a pair of gloves, and we'll get her fixed right up."

Bryce walked to the staff bathroom and emptied his bladder. As long as he had a free moment it was never the wrong thing to do. He washed his hands and stared at himself in the mirror. Had his daughter said those same words in her prayers at night? Did his wife think those words while she tucked them in? Does his son still want to grow up to be like him? He walked back to Mattie's room and saw the entire team was assembled.

"Doc, you couldn't find a pair of gloves?" asked the nurse as her eyes went from his empty hands to the rack of gloves mounted on the wall. Bryce smiled at her. They had worked together for five years. He knew she had caught the crack in his voice earlier and that he simply needed a moment to compose himself. They had seen each other break down enough after difficult experiences in the ER to read each other's emotions. Every nurse and doctor in an ER have. If they say they haven't, then they're probably still on orientation. The ER team does not break down in the moment, but when the adrenaline has worn off, and the immediacy of the event has passed, even the strongest occasionally succumb to the flood of emotion that follows. It's hard to stay human if you don't.

"Nope, but I see we have some in the room here now. I'll just use these," he said with a wink. "Okay team, let's get Mattie fixed." The procedure went perfectly. After the nurse administered the injection of Ketamine, Bryce was able to reduce the fractures, confirm anatomic alignment with the fluoroscope, help his physician assistant splint the fractures and repair the laceration. All while having a small-talk conversation with the mother. "When she wakes up and satisfies our sedation protocols, she'll be able to go home. Bring her back in ten days and we'll get those sutures out." Bryce removed his gloves and walked towards the exit.

"Thank you so much, Doctor. Can you remind me what your name is? I want to let the hospital know what a great job you did with Mattie."

Bryce stopped and turned around. The sudden twist sent his ID badge swinging around in the air. He pulled it out on the retractable lanyard and held it for her to see. "Doctor Bryce Chapman." His voice carried a confidence that hadn't been there in weeks. He and his family were hurting and broken. He has trained his whole life to learn how to help people and fix things. He was going to find a way to fix everything. Damn right he was. He glanced one more time at Mattie, still happily sedated and breathing easily. *Thanks, kid, I owe you one.*

Chapter Thirty-Five

Bryce finished the shift uneventfully and was ready to leave at six o'clock. Normally, he would go directly home after a shift, but today he had other plans. First, he stopped in the supply room and pocketed a plastic tube. *What's a little office theft if it might actually save your employer millions of dollars in a lawsuit?*

He left the hospital and headed for Kent Carpenter's apartment complex. He was greeted with a "CLOSED" sign hung on the manager's door. Bryce sighed. It is difficult to complete chores when you work during the day shift, but at least sleeping is easier. He backed out of the lot and drove home with plans to return in the morning.

***

"Can I help you?" said the elderly apartment manager with a distinct eastern European accent.

"My name is Bryce Chapman; I was friends with Kent Carpenter."

"Ah yes, sad thing, sad thing," said the landlord with a shake of his head. "Young guy, ex-wife, two kids, and no one takes his stuff. Make me deal with it."

"Well, I had loaned him some things I was hoping to get back. What are you planning to do with his belongings?"

"Hah! Garbage. It is all garbage. Never seen an adult live like that. Only nice thing was his laptop, but ex-wife got rid of that. Know what she do? Fill the bathtub and throw it in. Left it there all day."

"Why would she do that?"

"You think I ask her? To me it seems like she was drowning bad memory."

"Do you still have any of his belongings? I really would like to get back what I had loaned him."

"Yes, yes. I keep everything for a few months and then donate what I can and throw rest away. I keep things like this in an empty unit I cannot rent. 14C. Come, I take you." The landlord reached into the top drawer of his desk and removed a set of keys. He grabbed his jacket and led Bryce out the door. They walked a few minutes until they reached the last building in the complex.

He pointed to the door marked 14C. "Careful. Mold problem in this building. People getting sick so I can't rent it. Also cannot seem to find source of mold." He handed the key to Bryce. "You lock up when done and bring key back to me."

Bryce unlocked the door and walked in. The one-bedroom apartment was small and utilitarian. The carpet felt as thin as his scrub pants. A musty odor hung in the air, likely the mold the landlord seemed plagued by. He walked to the far corner of the room where a pile of belongings was stacked clumsily. Pink clothes, boxes of bathroom supplies, and high-heeled shoes lay among the items. Not exactly what he expected to find in the apartment of a single man. As he walked around the pile, he found a piece of paper with the owner's name on it. A woman's name. Not Kent Carpenter. He headed further into the apartment.

The kitchen was missing every appliance, likely salvaged for use in a unit that was occupied. Just past the empty bathroom was a closed door. He turned the knob and entered the unit's only bedroom.

His eyes tracked to the pile of belongings in the corner. Stuck to the front of a plastic tote was a piece of paper with the words "Kent Carpenter". Bingo. After his eyes reported their sensory input, it was his nose's turn to check in. A strong smell of tortilla chips greeted him and reminded Bryce he had not yet eaten breakfast.

He realized had no idea what he was looking for. He was confident that Kent did not die of natural causes. No healthy person would have such a rapidly progressive pneumonia from an institutional organism without help from an outside party. But who? How?

He scanned the belongings, looking for something that might carry a clue as to what happened to Kent, something that might carry DNA, or at least a bag of tortilla chips to snack on. Bryce searched every pile and found nothing helpful. The only thing left was the plastic tote that displayed the sign. He opened the lid and was met with a strong smell of tortilla chips. *Better than nothing.* Looking inside though he saw no chips, only a CPAP machine along with tubing and other supplies. He pulled it out to examine it closer, careful not to touch the face mask or any other part that may contain secretions in case DNA could be extracted to prove Kent did not have cystic fibrosis. He pulled open the water reservoir that added humidity to the machine and pushed it away quickly. The smell was overpowering. After taking a breath he leaned over and peered inside.

A thick goo was attached to the walls of the container. Bryce had seen the TV commercials advertising devices that clean CPAP machines and tubing to prevent exactly this from happening. Clearly Kent did not use one of these devices. Bryce pondered the size of the reservoir and compared it to the humidifier he used at home when his kids were sick. The volume of water the CPAP held could be not more than a day or two of water. How could the bacteria grow so much, and Kent not see it when he refilled it? Even if it did grow on its own, why was it such a drug-resistant institutional organism? It should be a typical skin bacteria, or maybe something from the water supply. Not a multi-drug resistant hospital-acquired infection.

He reached into his pocket and removed the plastic tube he had taken from the hospital supply room. He twisted the cap off and removed a cotton-tipped swab. Bryce reached in and collected a sample of the goo and placed the sample back in the tube, ensuring he buried the cotton tip into the culture medium at the bottom.

He put the machine back together and grabbed the lid to close it. Just before shutting the lid, he saw something strange on the side of the water reservoir. He pulled it back out again and held up the container to the light. Along one side was a small hole in the plastic. The edges were rounded up like a crater, as if something hot had been pushed against the side and melted a hole in it. A plug of silicon was inside the hole now, squishy and air tight.

Bryce decided to steal another item today and placed the CPAP machine in his backpack. He grabbed the tubing, the power supply, and anything else he could find that might have gone with the machine. Something wasn't right, but he didn't know what it was. He needed to get the culture tube to Alani and suddenly felt the need to wash his hands. In bleach.

***

Bryce drove directly to the hospital from Kent's apartment, using an entrance on the far side of the hospital to avoid contact with his emergency department colleagues. He walked in the entrance and took a moment to orient himself. Emergency physicians are not used to being outside of the ER and he was a bit confused where to go. "Sir, can I help you?" asked an elderly lady standing next to him.

"What? Oh, I'm trying to find the lab," said Bryce, turning to face the woman. He recognized her uniform, identifying her as a volunteer at the hospital.

"Well, you're very close, my dear. Just down that hallway, turn left," said the volunteer with a voice that reminded him of his grandmother.

Bryce thanked the woman and headed toward the lab, now that he knew where it was. He used his badge and opened the door displaying a "STAFF ONLY" sign. The silence of the hallway was replaced by mechanical hums, the whirring of centrifuges, and chatter among the lab technicians.

"Dr. Chapman, to what do we owe the honor of your visit?"

Bryce smiled at Alani and walked over to her station. "I brought you a sample I was hoping you could culture for me. But be careful, I have a feeling it's going to be something nasty." He set his backpack on the counter and put on a pair of nitrile gloves. He retrieved the culture tube and showed it to Alani. "I took it from someone's CPAP machine. Here's what it looks like." He pulled out the water reservoir from Kent's CPAP machine and flipped open the lid.

"Oh, that smells awful. Put that under the hood," said Alani, covering her nose with her hand.

Bryce walked over to the negative pressure isolation hood and put the reservoir on the stainless surface. The hood was connected to a ventilation system that pulled air into the chamber and eventually pushing it outside. This allowed the techs to work with noxious fumes without being exposed to them as the air flow carried it away.

"I recognize that smell, but I still want to culture it. I'll do aerobic and anaerobic cultures just to make sure we don't miss anything," said Alani as she stuck several cotton-tipped applicators into the slime coating the walls of the chamber. "No offense, but I want to obtain my own culture of it. I should have preliminary results for you by tomorrow."

"Wow, that's pretty fast. I thought it took longer to grow and identify a specimen," said Bryce.

"We use chemical and genetic testing now to get a quick idea of what it might be. The confirmatory culture and sensitivities to antibiotics does add another day or two to the process."

"Okay, thanks for the help. Let me know when you have something." He put the device back in his backpack, removed his gloves, and headed out to his car.

Chapter Thirty-Six

Bryce's shift in the department was one of the busier ones he could remember. Patients were in beds in the hallways, consultants were upset at the number of admissions, and he hadn't taken a moment for himself in four hours. During a momentary pause in the action, he slipped into the supply room and dialed his friend Graham Kelly. "Bryce, how you doing, buddy?"

"Rushed. I'm at the hospital and we're getting slammed. I'm ready for your help in obtaining some DNA if you're still up for it. I know the place and the right time. Are you free this week?"

"Not today; I could be down there tomorrow. Would that work?"

"Sure, I work during the day but I'm off at six o'clock. We'll need to be at the place by eleven, and probably a little early just in case the cleaning lady gets there ahead of schedule. There's a back door with a keypad that she uses to get in."

"Perfect. Mouse prints?" asked Graham.

"I sure hope so. Maybe we'll get lucky, and she'll have a fever too."

"Right. See you then. I'll call you when I'm close," said Graham.

***

"Bryce, I'm ten minutes out; are you ready to do this?"

"Yes, but I can't believe it's actually going to happen. I've never broken into a building before."

"So that's the unusual thing about this for you? The breaking into a building? Because for me, the odd thing is stealing another dude's semen. I guess we've all walked different paths since med school."

"Just shut up and get here. Did you bring the stuff?"

"Of course I did. I am better equipped than our troops in Afghanistan."

They met at a Walmart several miles from the building. Graham pulled up next to Bryce and gently set a duffel bag in the back seat of his friend's vehicle. Bryce had spent several nights watching the building and learned when the cleaning crew arrived. It was always just a single person and they entered from the rear door using a digital access code. It took about an hour to clean the building and then the worker exited the back door and threw a bag of garbage in the dumpster. Every weekday. Usually around 11:00 p.m.

They parked Bryce's SUV across the street from the rear entrance of the building. Far enough away to not arouse suspicion, but close enough for surveillance to be effective. "When she punches in the code, I'll watch with my spotting scope. You said she's right-handed?"

"Yes, that's why I parked here. You should have a clear view since she stands on the left side of the keypad."

"Perfect. And you said there's no alarm system in place?"

"I have been in there and even took a tour, but I didn't see any panels. I was trying to be discreet, though; I could have missed something."

"Well, let's hope not. I'd rather not be caught stealing semen. That's the sort of thing that's tough to live down in the orthopedic world."

***

At 11:03 p.m. a Honda Civic drove up and parked near the rear door. The trunk popped open, and the driver exited the vehicle. "What did I tell you? 11:00 p.m.; one person," said Bryce proudly.

Graham picked up his spotting scope and rested it on the steering wheel. He had a perfect view of the keypad. The driver pulled several cleaning items from the trunk and put them down by the entrance to the building. She turned and started gesturing at the car as if mad at it.

"What's she doing? I could see her by the door and now she's not in my view," he said while peering into the scope.

"She appears to be yelling at her car. Maybe she locked her keys in it?"

Graham backed away from the scope in time to see the passenger door open and a second person exit the vehicle. He looked at Bryce with raised eyebrows, "Always one person?"

The second person was much shorter than the driver, and they moved much quicker. They ran to the door and stood directly in front of the keypad. The driver walked up and leaned over as if to speak to the second person. Graham peered through the scope and had a perfect view of the back of a head. There was no time to move, and they were not going to be able to watch the code get entered. A child's right hand extended through a jacket sleeve and slowly pushed the buttons to unlock the door. The left hand held what appeared to be a stuffed animal, maybe a horse. The driver opened the door, pulled the cleaning equipment through, and the door shut behind them.

"No!" said Bryce as he struck his palm against the dash. He did not have time to keep doing this. The hospital was going to settle on the malpractice case any day and he needed answers now. He needed to convince them that something else happened to his patient other than medical malpractice.

"Quit yelling and throw me that duffel bag, quickly," ordered Graham.

Bryce reached into the back seat and handed it to Graham, who had put down the spotting scope. He ripped the zipper open and lifted out an expensive looking pair of binoculars. He pressed the power button and held them up to his face.

"Four, eight, one, six," he said.

"What? That's the code? How did you do that?" asked Bryce incredulously.

"Well, it's at least most of the code. There may have been a number before it, but I couldn't tell. The seven was lit up a little but I don't know if that's because it was the first number touched or if it was accidentally touched when the four and eight were pushed." He turned to look at Bryce. "Mouse prints."

"With a fever," replied Bryce.

"Yep. This pair cost eight thousand dollars. But try hog hunting at night without them. They are easily worth it. I try to not mention these things because it may get back to my wife."

"I should have gone into ortho," lamented Bryce.

"You said she normally takes an hour, but with her child helping, should we give her about forty-five minutes?"

"Are you serious? Double that. If a project takes me an hour alone, I plan at least ninety minutes if my children help." They pulled out of the parking space and found a nearby bar that was still serving food.

Chapter Thirty-Seven

After two beers and a dozen wings, it was time to check the building again. They drove by once, confirming the parking lot was empty. Graham parked in the same spot, grabbed his duffel bag, and headed toward the door. "What do you think? Try the four- or five-digit code?" he asked Bryce.

"Let's try the four first." He reached out with a gloved hand and pushed the numbers deliberately. Four, eight, one, six. Nothing. He hit asterisk then the pound sign. Nothing. After a few seconds, a light beeped red three times and then stopped.

"Must need the seven." Seven, four, eight, one, six. Nothing. He hit the asterisk and a metallic click signaled the code was accepted and the door was now unlocked.

"Guess I didn't pay attention to whether the asterisk was glowing or not," said Graham. Graham pulled the door open, and they both hustled through, pulling it closed behind them. A quick beeping sound had started as soon as the door was open. "Only one person? No alarm system?" Graham said as he traced the sound to an alarm panel behind a shelf. They likely had what remained of sixty seconds to enter the alarm code or this was going to be a failed nocturnal mission, with no specimen to show for it.

Graham pulled the cover down on the alarm and looked at Bryce. "Four or five digits?"

"They probably have different codes for each person who needs to access the building so they can track who is coming and going. Try the same code as the door."

Seven, four, eight, one, six. A quick double tone sounded, and the alarm panel showed it was deactivated. They breathed a sigh of relief and turned toward the hallway. "The storage room is down here. They use liquid nitrogen to keep the samples at -196 Celsius."

"Oh, I'm glad you learned something during your reconnaissance, not that it helps us," laughed Graham.

"Hey, we're almost done. Just behind this door." Bryce reached out to open the door but stopped when the handle didn't turn. *Locked!* Graham put a hand to his forehead and rubbed the frustration off his face. "Okay, let's look around. The key has to be somewhere." They split up and started looking everywhere for a set of keys. Office drawers, behind cabinets, on top of shelves. Nothing. The only thing they found was a white plush stuffed unicorn on a chair in the waiting room. "Hi, little guy. Want to watch some super criminals in action?" Bryce picked it up and brought it back and sat it on a table near the back door.

"Well, what now? Do you want me to shoot the lock off? I have a .50 caliber handgun in the car. That should do the trick."

Bryce looked at Graham, not sure if he was being serious or not. "No, I think we can find a different way in. He looked up at the drop ceiling tiles and wondered what was above them. Much of the security that's visible is actually only the appearance of real security. Bryce pulled a chair over to the door and stood on it, reaching above his head to move a ceiling tile out of the way. "There you go, our first break. There's a large flexible duct running through a hole in the drywall. The contractor cut the hole larger than necessary, and I think one of us can fit through there if we move the duct."

Bryce looked at Graham's shoulders, easily six inches wider than his. "Okay, I'll do it."

"I saw a ladder in the mechanical room; be right back," Graham said. He placed the ladder under the opening and reached into his bag. "If the other side of the door handle is key access only, you'll need a way to get back up into the ceiling from inside the room without a ladder. That could be tricky. Let me make something for you." He took the length of 550-pound paracord and tied a few knots attempting to make a loop for a foot hold but they kept acting as slip knots.

Bryce took the paracord and quickly tied a series of bowline knots about eighteen inches apart. "You're clearly not a sailor, Graham. If you can't tie a knot, just tie a lot, right?"

"Okay, mister boy scout. Want to race on placing sutures twelve inches deep in someone's fat thigh? Don't forget some mittens; it might be cold in that freezer," said Graham as he handed Bryce a set of gloves from his bag.

Bryce climbed the ladder into the ceiling, disconnected the HVAC duct, and pushed it through the hole. He tossed the paracord through and then crawled halfway through. The ceiling would not support his weight, so he had to balance on the wall until ready to descend into the room.

He ran the paracord through rounded steel supports on the ceiling, hoping the curve would act as a pulley. He moved a ceiling tile inside the room and dropped the paracord with knots down inside. He grabbed the ceiling support and swung his legs over the hole, letting go when centered over the opening. "I'm in!" yelled Bryce after getting back on his feet. He looked around and found the deep freezer. Fortunately there was no electronic lock in place. Bryce put the gloves on and opened the freezer, hoping to find alphabetized samples; instead, he found hundreds of vials with numeric codes. No names. "Hey, these are stored by ID number, not name. We need to know his patient ID," yelled Bryce, loud enough for Graham to hear.

"Reconnaissance strikes out again. That ends the inning folks. Please drive home safely. Let me go try to find something." Graham walked into what looked like the administrative office. He found a filing cabinet labeled "backup files". That sounded promising. He pulled the top drawer only to find it locked. He smacked the side of the cabinet in frustration, noting how much the thin metal flexed when he did. He pulled a knife from his pocket and flipped the blade open. He pushed the blade into the gap between the frame and the drawer until it made contact with the internal lock mechanism. He pulled down on the blade, prying the metal surfaces apart until he had enough clearance to open the drawer. "I've got it!" he yelled. Inside the drawer was a file called "Patient IDs". It contained dozens of pages with columns of names and ID numbers. Unfortunately, it was ordered by ID and not name. On page twelve he found was he was looking for. He put the paper back and closed the drawer. "ID 138921: Kent Carpenter (drawer four, D32)," he yelled to Bryce.

Bryce pulled out the fourth drawer and found three vials resting inside D32. Each had ID number 138921 printed on the side. He selected one and laid it on the counter. He closed the freezer, removed the gloves, and dropped the vial into the glove. -196 Celsius was not something he wanted to hold in his hand or keep in his pocket. He tucked the gloves in his shirt and walked towards the rope, mission accomplished.

Graham heard a noise and turned toward the rear door. It sounded like car tires pulling into a parking space. He paused to listen and whispered for Bryce to hold still.

Chapter Thirty-Eight

A car door slammed and Graham was moving in an instant. He grabbed the ladder, threw the rope up into the ceiling, turned the lights off and rounded the corner of the hallway as he heard the door access panel beeping with each press of a button. "I asked you if you had everything, and you said yes. Now go find your unicorn."

The woman walked toward the alarm panel and stepped back in surprise when she found that it was unarmed. "Sorry, Mommy, I know right where I left it."

Bryce heard the conversation from behind the door. He had turned out the light and crouched as low as he could. Time slowed to a crawl as he tried to control his breathing and not make a sound.

"Mommy, I left my unicorn in the front. I know it. But now she was sitting back here on a table." Bryce's stomach clenched.

"Silly child, you probably just forgot," said the mother as she grabbed the child's hand and walked toward the back door. She paused when her eyes caught white flecks of material on the ground in front of the storage room door. She had just vacuumed this area an hour ago. Her eyes drifted upward and saw a ceiling tile out of place, with a rope leading through a hole in the wall. "Come on, baby, let's go home. There's no one here who could have moved your unicorn. I'll prove it next time we clean."

Graham heard the door slam shut and the car engine start. Gravel crunched as the car backed up and then a louder crunch as the engine provided a bit more power than the tires were ready for. "We need to get out of here now!" said Graham.

"Yeah, I don't like what she said. She had to have known someone was in here. Get that rope down and help pull me up."

Graham replaced the ladder and pulled down the paracord. He wrapped it around his hands and stepped on the end as an anchor as Bryce grabbed the loops and began to climb. He crawled through the hole and reattached the ductwork. He dropped his legs through the ceiling and climbed down the ladder after replacing the ceiling tile. Graham jogged to the storage room to replace the ladder and they met at the back door.

Bryce entered the alarm code, and they exited the building at a jog. No line of squad cars, no shouts from armed police to drop the semen. Bryce hit the remote start on his keys and tossed them to Graham. "You drive; there's something I need to do."

Graham pressed the accelerator hard and pulled the SUV onto the deserted road, heading for Walmart. As he turned onto the interstate, two police cars were exiting with full lights and sirens. "Looks like we just made it. I hope it helps you figure this mess out, my friend," said Graham with a tone of sincerity.

Bryce reached into his glove and removed the stolen sample. It had warmed considerably, and he no longer felt that holding it posed a risk of frostbite. Spinning it around in his fingers, he noted it to be a small plastic Eppendorf tube with identification labels on it. He pulled a similar tube from his pocket and flipped open the lid.

"What are you doing?" asked Graham as he glanced sideways towards Bryce.

"I need to drop this off at the post office tonight. I'm overnighting it to a lab who can do the testing in a few days. I didn't want to mail them the original tube with Kent's name so I'm moving the sample to a new tube before shipping it." Bryce opened the sample lid and saw it had thawed enough to ooze sideways when he leaned the tube over. He held both tubes together in front of his face and slowly raised his left hand to pour it into the new tube.

"This would be a bad time to hit a bump, wouldn't it?" said Graham.

"Don't you dare," replied Bryce in a monotone voice as he focused on transferring the sample. He snapped the lid closed and dropped it into a small cardboard box that held a miniature foam cooler. He reached into the backseat and grabbed his own cooler, opened the lid, and filled the void in the box with dry ice pellets. He then shut the lid and taped it tight.

Graham drove to the post office, and Bryce dropped the package into the collection box reserved for overnight letters and packages. "Now we wait. Should have results in two or three days. Thanks again for your help," said Bryce.

"Absolutely. I'm glad it worked out, for both of our sakes. I'll head to my car and then I need to roll back home. It's been good hanging with you. Let's do it more often, but under better circumstances."

Chapter Thirty-Nine

Bryce sorted through the mail that had come in the last few days. He had not checked the box because the kids usually raced to see who would bring the mail in. When he got home last night, he noticed the mailbox wasn't shut all the way due to it being completely full.

Inside the stack of envelopes was a letter addressed to him, written in ink. A personal touch. It also bore no return address but the postmark said Raleigh, NC. Bryce ripped the end of the envelope and slid out a single piece of paper, folded into thirds.

Doctor Chapman:

I have your camera and the videos. There are some very interesting scenes on the memory card. I'm sure the internet would find them even more interesting than the partial video of your rescue mission. If you don't want your wife to be the next sex tape star on PornHub, I am going to need $500,000. When I receive your funds,

I will mail the memory card to you.

Bahama_man500k@gmail.com

Bryce closed his eyes and tried to control his breathing. Receiving a blackmail demand of half a million dollars to protect his wife's honor was not what he needed right now. Not only did he not have half a million laying around, he had no idea who had sent it. His mind raced trying to make sense of this new problem when his phone rang and snapped his attention back.

***

"Chapman," said Bryce into his phone.

"Hi, doctor, it's Alani from the lab. I got the results on the sample you brought me."

"Excellent, thanks for calling so quickly. What did you find?"

"It's Pseudomonas aeruginosa like we suspected. Whenever I smell a bacteria culture and suddenly have a desire for guacamole, it's usually Pseudomonas."

"Can you explain a bit more? I hate to use my imagination to determine what you mean by that," said Bryce.

"Sure. Pseudomonas has a classic smell; it reminds people of tortillas."

"Now that you say that, I thought the room smelled like tortilla chips the other day. You're telling me that smell means I brought you Pseudomonas?"

"Yes, and not just any strain. The resistance patterns on this are awful. This is the same bacteria that we always culture from Eleanor Livingstone." Bryce had expected this, but to hear the words from someone else brought a wave of uncertainty over him. Suddenly his belief that Kent was murdered became less of a hope, and more of a fact. He had to tell Tom about this.

"Thank you for calling me; this helps a lot."

"You're welcome. Let me know if you every need anything from the lab again."

The last call was still showing on his screen when Bryce used the voice command to call Tom Sharpe.

"Hey, Bryce; what's up? I was just thinking about you between balls."

"Excuse me? What were you picturing me between?"

Bryce waited as the prolonged laughter began to slow down. "No, no, no. I'm at the driving range hitting some golf balls and was wondering how you were doing. That came out wrong."

"Sure it did, Tom. I've known you long enough to know you did that on purpose," said Bryce, eliciting more laughter. "I got some news about Kent. I talked to his landlord and was able to get his CPAP machine from his apartment complex before they threw it all away. The water bath had an impressive biofilm growing in the container. I took it to the hospital lab and guess what it grew out?"

"Multi-drug resistant Pseudomonas?" asked Tom, the laughter replaced with a serious tone.

"Indeed. The exact susceptibility profile as the culture from your visit with Kent. And also the exact bacteria we culture from Eleanor."

"Interesting. So how did that bacteria wind up in Kent's CPAP water container? Did they know each other?"

"Not that I know of. She's been bed-bound for years and only goes between her home and this hospital."

"Well, how did it get there then? Are you thinking someone spiked the water bath with the bacteria and then Kent breathed it in all night before coming to see you?"

"That's exactly what I'm thinking. I even found a hole melted in the side and patched. This was murder Tom. But I have no idea who did it," said Bryce.

"That sucks."

"Yes, it does. I'm still thinking about the connection though. Something will turn up, I hope."

"Okay, I hope so. Keep me in the loop. If this truly was murder then we were both seriously screwed over, not to mention the patient."

"Tell me about it. Okay, I'll leave you to your balls. Just wanted to share the news about the culture. Talk to you later." Bryce ended the call and stared at his phone, pondering his next move. He was confident Kent was murdered, and somewhat confident he knew who did it. He lacked the how and the why. Unfortunately, these missing questions and the circumstantial evidence were unlikely to be enough for the police to begin an investigation into a closed death. Bryce needed a confession. He tossed the phone onto the couch and stared across his empty family room. He leaned forward on the couch with his head in his hands and said softly, "Valerie, I wish you were here right now."

***

Bryce was on his way home and stopped at a red light when his phone buzzed in the front pocket of his scrub top. He reached in and slipped it out around the seat belt chest strap and glanced at the caller ID. He did not recognize the number, but it indicated the caller was in the Bahamas. *The arrest warrant and pending assault charges!*

He threw the phone on the passenger seat and smashed his palm against the steering wheel. His horn responded with an appropriate honk, drawing a raised finger from the car in front of him. He raised both hands up with palms forward in an apologetic stance. As the light changed, his phone beeped and signaled a voicemail was waiting for him. He chose to keep driving and deal with that when he was out of the car. Anger behind the wheel brought enough patients to the ER, no sense listening to it before he got home.

Bryce parked in the garage and sat down at the kitchen island. No one screamed and ran up to give him a hug. No one smelling of perfume smiled and wrapped her arms around him.

He pulled out his phone and looked at the list of voicemails, wishing he could have a beer before listening to it. But those days were past him. You don't get stronger by using crutches when you don't have to. He pressed the screen and put the phone to his ear.

Chapter Forty

Bryce finished listening to the voicemail and immediately hit redial. It hadn't been about the pending charges; it was actually Captain Kyle with an update.

"This is Kyle."

"Hey Kyle, this is Bryce Chapman calling you back. Good to hear from you."

"You too," replied the captain. "How are you handling the internet fame?"

Bryce shook his head. "It's terrible. You'd be shocked how many of my patients have seen it and ask me about it. I just wish they had released the whole video. There's nothing on it showing who actually started the situation in the first place. And I'm being blackmailed over it. I got a letter from whoever has the video, offering to sell it to me for half a million dollars."

"Yeah, Valerie told me about that. Don't you just hate people sometimes?" said Kyle.

Bryce paused for a moment. Valerie had been talking to their captain? Why hadn't she told him about that? The last time he knew they spoke was when the captain took her back to their villa after the rescue. Where's that beer? "Oh, I didn't know you two had spoken," said Bryce, trying to gather information.

"She called me a few days ago when the video was released. Said she was considering coming down here and trying to find out who found the video so she could punch them in the face."

Bryce smiled, relieved. That did sound like her. "She told me the same thing actually."

"I told her to wait a bit and let me look into it. There are certainly private boats here but also a lot of charter captains too. My hope was the camera was found by a group on a paid trip. I posted in a social media group of captains in the Bahamas, and wouldn't you know it, someone said they had a client find a GoPro camera around the grotto a week after your trip. He even sent me their contact information."

Bryce sat in stunned silence. His luck was starting to change. Sure, his team was down big late in the game, but until the final whistle blows there's always a chance. And the other team just fumbled the ball near their own end zone. "That's incredible. Can you send it to me?"

"I'm not sure about that, I need to know you're going to do the right thing with the information before I agree to give it to you," replied Kyle.

"Are you kidding? That prick is extorting money from me and assisting in the destruction of my family and my career. I'm going to go kick his ass," answered Bryce, his voice loud and angry.

"That's exactly what I meant when I said *do the right thing with it,* buddy," laughed Kyle. "I'll text it you. Let me know if I can be of any more help."

Bryce thanked the captain and ended the call. Moments later, an image arrived via text message showing an address written on a piece of paper. Durham, North Carolina. He picked up his phone and scrolled quickly through the list of contacts. When he found Tom Sharpe, he punched the screen to make the call, put it on speaker, and set the phone on the counter. He paced around with excitement, waiting for his partner to answer.

"Hey, Bryce; what's up?" asked a sleepy Tom Sharpe.

"Oh sorry, were you sleeping? I didn't check the schedule before I called you."

"It's fine. Our sleep schedules are so crazy; besides, I'm off for a few days, so I'll sleep later. What do you need?"

"You're off for a few days? Perfect. Want to go on a road trip with me tomorrow?"

"A road trip? Where? Why?" asked Tom, his fatigue fading as his curiosity rose.

"To Durham, North Carolina. I know who has the video from our trip to the Bahamas. I'm going to go down there and get it back."

"What? How do you know who has it?"

"I'll tell you when we're in the car. You may need to bring that scalpel you cut apart the donut with just in case he doesn't want to hand it over politely," said Bryce.

"I'm still a little hot over that whole situation. You need me to be your enforcer? Okay, fine. Let's do it," said Tom. "When do we leave?"

"I need to get a few things ready, but can we leave around nine o'clock tomorrow morning? I want to be there right around sunset."

"Okay, I'll be at your place before nine. My wife's going to kill me," said Tom as he ended the call.

***

His next call was to Valerie. "Hey Bryce, I wondered if you were going to call today. The kids are already asleep," she said.

"That's too bad. Did you guys have a good day?"

"We did, but they are really getting tired of being here. I told them I'd take them to Disney World to break things up a bit. I didn't realize it's a six-hour drive. How big is this freaking state?"

"Listen, I got some news. Captain Kyle called and said he thinks he knows who found the camera. It's in North Carolina. Tom Sharpe and I are going to drive down there in the morning. It's possible that by this time tomorrow I'll have the video back in our possession. Then I can show the CEO it was Tony who started it and see if I can get him to drop the charges."

"How do you know that this person found your camera and not a different one? You may be getting a little too far ahead of yourself again."

"I'll figure it out, I promise. Plus, I have a good hunch. The extortion letter came from Durham and that's where this kid lives. This is the next step in fixing what is broken. To getting our lives back on track."

"What's the guy's name?" asked Val.

"Stetson Murray."

"Stetson? You're joking."

"That's the name Captain Kyle gave me. Said he was the one who chartered the trip and found a camera."

"He sounds like some Ivy League trust fund kid. Let me know how it goes. Be careful, Bryce, and don't get into any more trouble, please."

Tom showed up at 8:45 a.m. with a large container of hot coffee and a bag of snacks. "I wanted to make a mixed tape for the trip, but my wife said we only have CDs," he said.

"No problem at all, I plan to crank some high-intensity stuff from my workout playlist the whole way. I bought a case of BANG and some IV supplies in case we get sleepy," said Bryce. Tom gave Bryce a sideways glance. "I'm joking, relax."

They climbed into his black GMC Yukon and pulled out of the driveway. Tom waited a few hours to pass before pressing Bryce on what the plan was. "So tell me, what are you planning to do when we get there? How do you know this guy actually has it?" asked Tom.

Bryce had spent considerable time pondering this exact question. What are the odds that the extortion letter came from the same city where someone else also randomly found a GoPro in the same place where he lost one? He figured it had to be less than one in a million. Was that low enough to be confident in kicking someone's ass? Bryce didn't think so. Action was not something an ER doctor feared. It was action applied inappropriately that concerned him, or lack of action, when it was necessary.

"I am very confident, but not one hundred percent. I'm at least 99.9 percent sure this is the guy. I sent him an email last night asking to speak in person before I sent half a million dollars. I asked for a number I could call to speak with him and that I needed to hear back by noon. That's in an hour."

"What if he doesn't answer?"

"We'll just have to think of something else, then."

Bryce was getting more and more anxious as the miles went by and the clock ticked on. He received an emailed response at 4:00 p.m. "He said he won't talk on the phone, but we can do a voice chat in Discord. He gave me a username to request the call. It's the same one he signed the letter with. What the hell is Discord?"

Tom replied, "My kids use it when they're playing Fortnite. It's a chat room app that supports voice calls and messaging. Very anonymous."

Bryce pulled off at the next exit and parked at the closest gas station. He downloaded the app on his phone and registered an account. He found the user named Bahama_man500k and saw the button to click to initiate a voice chat. "What do I say to him?" asked Bryce.

"See if you can make him prove he has the whole video. Anyone could play the rescue footage, make him play something that wasn't released online already. And see if you can tell if he's at home."

"How do I do that?"

"I don't know; just see where it goes. Don't tell him you know where he lives and are an hour away from kicking his door down."

He clicked the voice chat button and waited for a connection. Three minutes went by and no response. He was about to move the car into the drive-through line of the fast food restaurant next door and order food when his phone beeped and the hushed static of open two-way communication started. "Hello," said the voice on the line. "Is this the hero ER doctor? My proud benefactor?"

Bryce tried to control the anger welling up inside him. His hands gripped the steering wheel and he squeezed, his forearm muscles flexing. The voice sounded like it belonged to a younger person. Maybe high school or college aged. Not at all who he was picturing, and this put him off balance a bit. "Yes, this is Bryce. Who is this?"

Laughter filled the car from the phone speaker. "You know you don't get to know that answer. I'm the guy you're going to pay half a million dollars to in order to get your precious memory card back. Do you have my money?"

"Half a million dollars is a lot to come up with in a short amount of time. I am prepared to pay it, but I need assurance that this is the end of it. I don't want to get an email from you a year from now asking for more money. And how do I know you actually have it?"

"I figured you would want proof. I have my favorite video pulled up right now. Let me turn up my speakers for you." Suddenly, the car was filled with the sounds of romance. Loud, playful, intoxicated romance. Bryce and Val's voices were easily recognizable. He could picture exactly what they were doing as the audio played on. He glanced at Tom, who quickly looked away.

"Can you tell me what that move is called? It's not something I've seen before. And the–"

"Okay, okay. You made your point. How do you want me to get you the money?"

"I want it in Bitcoin. I'll send the wallet address to this Discord account."

"How do I send half a million dollars in Bitcoin? I only learned what it was a few months ago."

"Dude, you're an ER doctor. Figure it out. I'll publish this video on PornHub in a week if I haven't received the money. Later, Doc." A strange sound came through the line and then the call ended.

Chapter Forty-One

His phone vibrated and showed a new Discord message. It was a long alphanumeric string of characters, likely the Bitcoin wallet address. Whatever that meant.

Bryce looked over at Tom. "Sorry you had to hear that. Valerie and I had some fun on our trip to Exuma."

Tom exploded in laughter. "Yeah, I'd say you did. I'm sorry for laughing, but I just can't figure out how to feel about you, Bryce. On the one hand, you are so unlucky, and it seems like the deck is constantly stacked against you, and then the next moment I'm disturbingly jealous."

"Well, don't get too jealous yet. Wait until this is all over. The way it's going, you may be doing my eulogy soon enough. This kid seems like he's in college. And, honestly, I bet he's at home."

"I agree. He could have taken the call on his phone like you did, but he had the video queued up and adjusted his speakers, which sounds like he was using a desktop," said Tom.

"I thought the same thing. But what was the noise at the end? It was like he was starting to sneeze."

"Could it have been a laugh? I can't say. It didn't sound like his voice, though."

"Maybe there's more than one person home? That might complicate things. What if his parents are there? Have you checked it out online?" asked Tom.

Bryce shook his head no and was too upset with himself to voice a response. In his eagerness to get the drive back, he hadn't done the most basic research. "Well, let's take a look," said Tom, pulling out his phone. He entered the address and pulled up a map view of the area. It was three blocks away from the Duke University campus. Switching to satellite view, he saw a two-story home in what appeared to be a well-established neighborhood. There were mature trees lining the street, and each driveway held several cars. Actually, an excessive number of cars per home than he expected to see. "I think this neighborhood is filled with Duke students," said Tom. "Every house has at least three cars in the driveway or in front of the home. This one even has half a dozen lawn chairs in the front yard. We're dealing with some Duke college prick. I guarantee it."

"Great, I absolutely hate Duke fans. Have you seen their ridiculous towel taunts during basketball games?" said Bryce. "Let me give Val a call; she wanted to know when we were close."

Valerie answered on the first ring. "Do you have it yet? Are you okay?" she asked, her voice revealed her fear for her husband.

"No, we're just outside the city. Just wanted to let you know we made it here okay. How are you guys?" asked Bryce.

"We're fine. I have some news though. I stalked this guy on social media and you'll never guess what I found about his trip to the Bahamas," she said.

"What?"

"Absolutely nothing." Bryce stayed quiet, not sure how to respond. "He literally posted nothing about the trip. Scrolling through his feed, he posts several times a day, and usually some picture to make him look like a titan of something. But then he goes to Exuma and posts nothing? I thought that was strange, so I searched the feeds of his friends and found several pictures of him on the trip, including one with him holding a GoPro covered in sargassum. This has to be him."

Bryce looked at Tom and relayed what Valerie told him. "But why didn't he post any pics of himself? He posts all the time," asked Bryce.

"I bet he did, but then went back and deleted them once he decided to use the videos as blackmail," she said.

"Ah, that makes sense. But he didn't think to ask his friends to erase their pics of him. Thanks for the update. We'll have this over in less than an hour. I'll call you back. Love you." He swiped to end the call and put the phone back into the cradle, suction cupped to the windshield. He looked at his friend and said, "Are you ready, buddy?"

Tom didn't speak; instead, he took two fingers and rubbed them horizontally beneath each eye as if applying war paint. Bryce nodded and pressed the gas pedal. *No turning back now.*

Chapter Forty-Two

"There it is; the white one with two cars in the driveway," said Bryce, slowing down as they drove past the address Captain Kyle had sent.

"Keep going a bit and find a place to park where we can see the house," said Tom.

Bryce pulled the car into an open space on the curb two houses down and put it in park. They were finally here, but now what? The house was a small two-story with a covered porch and a window over the front door. There was a faint glow coming from the window, but no light was on in the room.

"The biggest concern I have is doing this to the wrong guy. Or we barge in and he's not home. What do we do then?" asked Bryce.

"Ask Val to send you a picture of him she found, and then we'll find a way to get him to the front door for visual confirmation before we go in."

"How are we going to do that?"

"It's dinnertime in a college town. Let's order him a few pizzas," said Tom. He reached into his bag and pulled out a cell phone that was secured inside a plastic clamshell package. He struggled for a few minutes and then got the package open, dropping the phone into his lap. After powering it on and entering an activation code, he made a call to the local Papa John's. Two pizzas and a four-pack of craft beer. And hurry. He paid using a prepaid VISA gift card and left a generous tip, explaining this was a gift delivery, and asked the driver to say it was from a secret admirer.

Bryce watched his friend in amazement. "How did you know to get a new phone and an anonymous payment source? That's brilliant."

"I read a lot of novels. Authors always try to impress their readers with sneaky spy-craft sorts of things."

"Well, I like it. So when he answers the door to get the pizza, we can make sure it's him, and then we move?"

"Exactly. We should know in twenty-five minutes, or my prepaid card better get the price of the pizza refunded back onto it, according to their commercial."

"Why four beers? They're not going to have time to drink them before we get in there."

Tom smiled at Bryce. "They had better not."

While Tom was ordering pizza, Bryce had texted Valerie and requested a copy of a picture of Stetson Murray. She replied quickly with a zoomed in photo of his face. He was a good-looking kid, strong jaw, wavy blond hair. But a smirk on his face that was just begging to be smeared off with a fist.

***

The pizza delivery arrived just under thirty minutes after Tom placed the order. They watched as the driver brought the order up the sidewalk and knocked on the door. A few seconds after the knock, the upstairs window lit up bright yellow as if a light switch had been flipped on. Five seconds later the front door opened, and Stetson stepped onto the porch. They could see him pause and consider the scene before him. They couldn't hear anything but saw the driver make a few hand motions and hold the order up in the air. Stetson pumped his fist in the air and took the order from the driver with a big smile on his face. The driver jogged back to his car and headed down the street, off to deliver joy to the next good girl or boy.

"Let's roll," said Bryce, opening the door. Tom followed quickly, bringing his backpack with him.

Bryce looked up and down the street and didn't see anyone paying attention to them. He knew they were probably being recorded by fifteen home security cameras and doorbell cams, but with any luck, this would be the end of the nightmare. No police involved. No further communication.

They reached the front porch at the same time. Bryce's stomach was in knots, his hands tingling with nervous anticipation. Tom looked over noticed the tremor in Bryce's hand. "Relax, it's not a neonatal intubation. We're just going to kick some ass for the right reason. You're defending your wife. You have the moral high ground here. If you didn't, I'd still be at home. Let's get this over with." He reached forward and knocked loudly on the front door.

They heard footsteps, and then the door opened. Good-looking kid, strong jaw, wavy blond hair. Stetson Murray. Stetson paused when he opened the door. He expected it to be the delivery driver again and was a bit confused as he stared at the two men. "Can I help you?" he asked. Then he stared at Bryce for a few seconds and asked, "Do I know you? You look familiar."

"Yes, you've seen me before, but usually not with clothes on, you dickhead." Bryce stepped into the home as he finished the insult. His arms shot out together, shoving Stetson backward and knocking him to the ground. Tom entered quickly and locked the front door. They looked around and saw no one else. There was a table in front of the couch, adorned with two pizzas and a pack of four beers.

Bryce closed the distance before Stetson could recover and get to his feet. He drew his leg back, feigning a kick to the head, and Stetson curled into a fetal position, rolling away from the blow he thought was about to come. "Oh, not so tough when you're face to face, huh?" said Bryce, lowering his leg back to the ground. "Give us what we came for and you won't be touched. Where's the memory card?"

Stetson pulled his hands down from his face and turned back toward Bryce. His eyes were huge, hands trembling. He tried to speak, but no words came out. "Get up or get a foot in your ass," said Tom, walking towards Stetson.

That was all the encouragement he needed, and he quickly rose to his feet. "It's upstairs; let me go get it," said Stetson as he walked between Tom and Bryce.

"No, I think we'll all go get it. Me first," said Bryce, starting up the stairs. "Let me guess, your room is the one in front?"

"Yes, how'd you know?" asked Stetson.

"We know everything about you," lied Bryce. Tom suppressed his smile and instead smacked Stetson in the back of the head. "Move."

The trio ascended the stairs and turned right at the top, walking back toward the front of the house.

They entered a bedroom that looked like it belonged to a college kid. Dirty clothes on the floor, empty beer cans and food wrappers, and a desk in front of the window. On the desk was a computer.

"There it is," said Stetson, pointing to the USB port on the front of the case. Attached to the port was a card reader that held a MicroSD card. "It's in that card reader. The same card that was in the camera. Just take it and get out of here."

"Gladly. But I'd like to confirm it's the correct one first. Open up the files and show me one." Stetson sat down at the computer with his back to the bedroom door and used the mouse to bring up the file manager screen. He navigated to the USB card and saw a list of video files. He clicked on a random filename and a new window opened, showing a familiar beach scene from Exuma. Bryce nodded and confirmed it was real. He leaned down and removed the card reader and put it in his pocket.

Stetson turned around in the chair and looked back at Tom and Bryce. "There; it's done. Will you leave now?" As he finished talking, his eyes opened wider, and his gaze deviated to look at something to Bryce's right. At the same time, the sound of footsteps echoed behind the trio.

"Bryce!" yelled Tom as he saw a flash of movement in the hallway. Stetson's roommate. They had forgotten to check the rest of the house, as they were too focused on getting the memory card.

Bryce rotated to his left and took a step forward. As he spun, he saw someone charging full speed at the space he used to occupy. Momentum is a great thing when lined up for a tackle, but it's a terrible thing when the person you're aiming at moves out of the way. Then inertia takes over and continues the charge into the void. Bryce sidestepped the attack and shoved the person in the back, throwing him forward even faster. He smashed into Stetson sitting in the chair and continued until his head crashed into the computer monitor, cracking the LED screen. He rolled off the desk and laid on the ground, stunned but awake.

Bryce bent down to examine his assailant and found no obvious wounds. He told Stetson his friend may have a concussion and to not let him do anything that might injure his head for a few weeks until he was feeling normal again. The only response he got was a nod from Stetson and a groan from the pile of flesh crumpled on the floor. He reached down and started disconnecting the cables from the computer.

"Hey, what are you doing?" asked Stetson.

"Do you really think I trust you to not have copied the files onto your computer? I'll be taking this with me also," said Bryce.

"You can't do that. My projects are on there. I need them for school!" implored Stetson.

"Seriously? Maybe you should have used a different computer to blackmail me with then. Tell you what, once I've scanned the machine for copies and made sure there's no online backup, I'll send you the hard drive back. For two Bitcoin, of course."

"What? That's eighty thousand dollars!" yelled Stetson.

Tom had walked around the bedroom during the exchange and found something on the dresser. "Hey Bryce, looks like Stetson here is into cocaine. Or is that powdered sugar on this mirror?" Let me get a picture of that. Tom grabbed the mirror and turned around, showing Stetson in the background with his friend on the floor. He took a few pictures and then sat the mirror down again. He picked up a half-empty beer and poured it over the cocaine. "This is a nasty habit. I bet Daddy doesn't know about it, does he?

Tell you what, if there's ever any trouble with my friend and his videos again, we'll send your parents a copy of these pics, okay? If your parents are okay with it, we'll just forward them to your employer. The tables have turned, Stetson. Stop being an ass and just be kind to people. Get off drugs, son."

Bryce walked backward out of the room. Once Tom exited, they shut the door and hurried down the stairs. Bryce opened the front door and walked toward the car. He wanted to run, but figured that might draw attention. Something felt wrong, so he turned around and saw he was alone. Where was Tom? Panic set in as Bryce imagined his friend entangled in all sorts of peril. Some hidden second roommate emerging to attack him, or worse. He spun around and went back toward the front door and nearly ran into Tom as he exited the house. His arms were full of pizza boxes and a four-pack of beer. He was grinning as he said, "Move it; let's get out of here."

They climbed into the car, and Bryce pulled out of the parking space. He hit the accelerator and the powerful V8 engine quickly got them up to speed.

"I can't believe that worked!" said Bryce, barely able to contain his excitement.

"What do you mean? We're bad asses, my friend. Now enjoy the spoils of war with me." Tom handed Bryce a beer and a piece of pizza.

"Not sure I should drink that while driving."

"Is it any worse than drinking a few beers and then driving? I'd argue it's safer, actually." Tom got quiet and began shoving slice after slice into his mouth.

Bryce got quiet and reflective. Things were certainly improving. He was in possession of the video footage that should prove he didn't start the fight. With luck, that would fix the assault charge in the Bahamas. He hoped it would also get the CEO off his back and help restore his job security. Plus, it would give Valerie relief that their video wouldn't be released publicly. All in all, it was the most successful trip he'd ever taken.

Valerie. Suddenly, he missed her more than ever. He put down his unopened beer and grabbed his phone. Looking at a website while driving isn't great, but he figured it's probably better than drinking while driving. Especially when he'd promised Valerie he wouldn't drink anymore.

He did a few quick searches, and his excitement built back up. He pulled up the map and entered a new location. Tom heard the digital voice announce they would arrive in fifteen minutes. He lifted his eyebrows and looked over at Bryce. "Need a potty break?"

"Yes, but that's not where we're going. How upset would you be if I asked you to drive home alone?"

Tom sighed. "Bryce, I'm this far into things with you already. I guess it's not too much to ask, but you're getting me a hotel tonight. And I keep the rest of the pizza and beer."

"Deal," confirmed Bryce.

Chapter Forty-Three

Bryce pulled into the Raleigh-Durham airport and followed the signs for departures. He parked in an open spot against the curb and exited the car, meeting Tom on the sidewalk. "You're a great friend. Thank you for doing this for me," said Bryce as he held out a hand to Tom.

Tom swatted the handshake aside moved in for a massive bear hug, lifting Bryce a few inches off the ground. "We are brothers in arms Bryce. Handshakes are for introducing yourself to a stranger. We're family now. I'll have the car back at your place tomorrow. What do you want me to do with the computer?"

"Can you put it in my kitchen? I'll text you the garage code soon."

"Sure thing. Can you do me one last favor for helping you out today?"

"Anything. What is it?"

"When you hug Valerie tonight, promise her you'll never let her go again. I can't be the only one to help bail you out of the situations you seem to find yourself in. I need her help with you."

"You have my word. Let me know what I owe you for the hotel," said Bryce.

"The hotel won't be too bad. It's the room service and pay-per-view that's going to eat you alive," replied Tom while stepping into the driver's seat. He honked twice quickly, shifted into drive, and pulled away, leaving Bryce alone at the curb. A traveler without luggage or a carry-on. He didn't need any. The only things in his life that mattered were already at his destination.

Bryce headed into the airport and secured a ticket on the non-stop flight to Panama City Beach, Florida. It was the closest he could get to Destin tonight. His phone told him it would take just over an hour to drive the rest of the way. He cleared security and boarded the plane with ten minutes to spare before the gate closed. Just enough time to book a one-way rental car. He was finishing a text to Val when the stewardess came through and scolded him for using his phone while the plane was pushing back from the gate.

He had just under three hours to think about what to say to Val when he showed up. Two hours in a plane and one in a car. In his text, he had asked to talk with her around 9:30 p.m. to give her an update on what had happened. He left out the part that he would be there in person.

***

As soon as the plane rolled to a stop at the gate and the pilot sounded the tone signaling seat belts were no longer required, Bryce hopped up and hurried to the front of the plane, eager to be the first off. He ignored the annoyed looks of his fellow passengers who couldn't possibly understand the events that led him to be so excited to get off the plane and into his rental car. He jogged through the terminal and was in his rental car fifteen minutes later. The lack of luggage and a self-serve kiosk at the rental car company helped speed him along his journey like favorable winds upon the sea.

Bryce picked up his phone and selected the number for Tom Sharpe. "Hey, Bryce. Where are you?" asked Tom.

"I'm in the rental car driving to Destin. I should be there in forty-five minutes. What hotel did you end up at?"

"I found a Conrad just outside of Greensboro. I figured I'd put some miles between myself and Raleigh. I backed into the space to make it harder for anyone to notice a license plate, just in case."

"You're always thinking," said Bryce with admiration. "I think Stetson has learned a lesson and I can't imagine we'll hear from him again. I don't need anything, just wanted to hear you were hunkered down and resting somewhere instead of trying to drive all the way home. Now I can stop worrying about you."

"Okay, drive safe. Tell Val I said hi."

Bryce agreed and ended the call. He pulled up the number for the Conrad Hotel Tom was staying at and called the front desk. He talked to the night attendant for a few minutes before reading off his credit card information. It turned out the employee was new and eager to help bring more money into the business. He promised to deliver the gift promptly

Fifteen minutes later, Bryce's phone received a picture of Tom smiling while holding a plate of chocolate-covered strawberries and a bottle of champagne. Attached to the bottle was a note that read, 'From your secret admirer.'"

Bryce laughed to himself as he pictured the hotel employee taking that note to Tom. He deserved every drop of that champagne. Everyone has friends, but how many have a friend who will do what Tom did today? He considered himself lucky for the people in his life and looked forward to arriving in Destin to add a few more back in. His phone predicted fifteen minutes left on the drive. He rolled the windows down and inhaled the warm salty air. He sang a killer duet with fellow bad boy Tom Petty as they both lamented breaking the heart of a good girl.

Bryce decided he had time for one more phone call.

"Hey, buddy, how you doing?" asked Graham Kelly.

"Fantastic," replied Bryce. "Best I've been in a year. I'm actually in Florida, headed to Val's parents to try to get her to come back home with me."

"Good for you," said Graham, emphasizing the first word loudly. "I've been thinking about you guys a lot. By the way, nice job on saving that guy in the Bahamas. We watched the video, and my entire operating room team is in awe of you. I downplayed it, of course, but people love a happy ending, I guess."

"Speaking of the video, I have the rest of the footage now that shows how the scene unfolded. I think I can use it to clear up a lot of the mess that's arisen from that day. I wanted to again say thank you for helping me out. I feel like a different person. I hope Val feels that way too because I'll be there in five minutes."

"Well, stop talking to me then and figure out what you're going to say to her. Good luck, buddy. You got this."

Chapter Forty-Four

Bryce texted Val's mother and asked that she take her out on the back porch for a glass of wine. He explained he was in the area and wanted to see her. A few minutes later, he received an excited reply saying that they were in position.

Their house sat directly on the gulf and had a beautiful porch that ran the length of the back of the house. For flood reasons, the house was built on ten-foot stilts, which also conveniently put the porch height above the dune and allowed unobstructed views of the water. A long wooden walkway led from the porch, over the dune, and out onto the sand.

Bryce parked the car on a side street two blocks away and walked through an empty lot onto the beach. He could see Val's parent's home with its distinctive roof line. Silhouetted against the light shining through a sliding glass door were two women. Valerie and her mother.

Bryce wanted to run the rest of the way, but instead, he paused. He considered everything they'd been through these last few weeks since the trip to the Bahamas. Everything had changed. His job, his relationship with his wife, himself. He was ready to begin the next stage in their journey together. That silhouette was definitely Val, but lacking features in the dark. It was just an outline. Bryce promised himself he would relearn everything about her. Every detail. It was time to be the husband and father his family deserved.

Bryce bent down and removed his shoes and socks. He rolled his pants up to keep them out of the sand and continued walking toward the home. He came to the staircase at the end of the boardwalk and knew from prior trips that Val still couldn't see him. He sent her a text saying he'll talk with her in a few and waited until she glanced down at her phone. Val said something to her mother, who stood and walked over to her. She leaned down and gave her daughter a hug and then went back inside. Val picked up her phone, the screen lighting her face and blocking her night vision.

Bryce took the stairs two at a time and strode confidently toward her. She heard footsteps and looked up from her phone when he was twenty feet away. "Bryce? What? How did you get here?" she asked as she put her phone down and stood up.

He met her next to the table and wrapped her in his arms. He inhaled her scent and felt her heartbeat against his chest.

"I missed you. When we finished in Raleigh, I just had to see you, so I hopped on a plane and came down here. Tom's driving my car back home tomorrow."

"You just missed my mom; she'll be excited to see you. The kids are already asleep."

"Your mom knew I was coming," he said, smiling. He pointed to the second glass of wine, still full and untouched. "I think she even poured me a glass." Val turned her head slightly and backed away from the hug a bit.

"Don't worry. It was just a nice gesture. I still haven't had a drop. That's your second glass."

She leaned back in and squeezed him hard. She had missed him dearly. "It's so nice to see you. The kids will be thrilled. But I already promised them we'd go to Disney World in the morning. I was planning to leave right after breakfast."

"Well then, let's take them to Disney World. I can't think of a better place to spend a few days with my family. I'm supposed to work in two days, though; let me try to get it covered."

They separated and sat down next to each other. Bryce reached into his pocket and held up the memory card like a trophy. He told her the story of what happened in Raleigh. She was scared to hear he was nearly tackled from behind but laughed hysterically when Bryce painted the picture of Tom running out holding pizza and beer.

"Those poor kids. They had no idea who they were up against," she said as she took the card from his fingers and looked it over before looking directly at him. "It's good to have you back. But tell me, where are you at with your other behaviors? I can't pretend all of that didn't happen."

"I know you can't. As I said, I haven't had a drop since the day you left. I got pretty depressed that night and ended up going to see Graham the next day. We toured his land on ATVs, did some shooting, sat by a fire in the woods, and talked everything out. I'm not where I want to be yet, but I'm not where I used to be. I'm planning to see the counselor at our church for a reality check and some ongoing help. I have no pride left anymore. I'll do whatever I need to do in order to get our family back together."

Valerie stood and then eased herself down onto Bryce's lap. "After Disney, let's all head home together." Bryce said a silent prayer of thanks and answered her with a tight squeeze.

The next few days went by quickly for the Chapman family. Peter Thrasher was happy to pick up the extra shifts and allow Bryce some extra time with his family. Disney World worked its magic, and everyone was in a good mood as they drove back home to Indiana. Valerie and Bryce were getting along well, and the kids were thriving in the healthy environment.

"We're home!" yelled Noah from the back seat. Valerie turned around and looked at her kids.

"Did you guys miss the house?" They both nodded eagerly. "Mommy did too. Let's go play outside when we get the car unpacked, okay?"

Bryce put his hand on her knee and gave it a gentle squeeze. "I missed all of you guys. I get to go on the next vacation, right?"

Noah and Hannah answered in unison, "Yes!"

"I work early in the morning, so I'll be gone when they wake up. I'll get the car unloaded and everything put away tonight," said Bryce.

While heading back to the car, he checked his email on his phone. A new one had just arrived from Polygenetic Diagnostics. *The DNA results from Kent!* Bryce clicked the email and scanned the text quickly, looking for something formatted as a lab result. When he got to the bottom, he still hadn't found it, but saw an attached PDF document, which he clicked immediately.

Patient: Bryce Chapman Test ordered: Cystic Fibrosis Screen Results: CFTR mutation positive

Bryce felt a stab of pain in his midsection when his eyes scanned the top lines of the results page. He had researched cystic fibrosis diagnosis and knew CFTR meant cystic fibrosis transmembrane conductance regulator, the site of the genetic mutation that causes CF. He thrust the phone back in his pocket and started grabbing suitcases. It didn't make sense. Kent had no symptoms of CF and, even then, he should not have gotten that sick so quickly. Bryce walked inside and kicked the door to the house open out of frustration, causing it to smash into the doorstop.

"Hey, you okay?" called Valerie.

"Just bringing in all this damn stuff from the car," he said.

"Well, be careful; no need to destroy the house. Take more trips and carry less each time."

Bryce couldn't hold back the sigh. "Thanks, I appreciate being told how to unload a car." Valerie frowned and stared back at him. "I'm sorry, it's not your fault. I just got the test results on Kent, and it said he did have the cystic fibrosis mutation. Now it looks like I'm going to be successfully sued and ended up missing something that got my patient killed."

"Oh no, how is that possible? You were convinced he didn't have that disease."

"Here, look for yourself," said Bryce, as he unlocked his phone and handed it to Valerie.

She scanned the screen slowly, reading every word. When she got to the bottom, she cocked her head at an angle and spoke slowly. "Bryce, I didn't take much biology in college, but I do remember a bit of it. Doesn't heterozygous mean someone only has one copy of a gene?"

"Yes, that's correct." He looked up from the kitchen floor with wide eyes. "Does the result say heterozygous?" he asked quickly.

"It sure does. I thought to have cystic fibrosis, a person had to have the mutation in both copies of their gene. One from the mother and one from the father?"

"You're exactly right. It's a recessive disease. Show me where it says that in the result," said Bryce as he quickly moved behind Val. His eyes scanned the entire message this time, and his attitude changed instantly.

"Woah! Put me down, you animal," said Val as Bryce's hug lifted her off the ground. "If you didn't use your man eyes to read the email the first time, you could have saved yourself the grief, and our doorstop wouldn't be so sore either."

"I owe you one, again. Thanks, Val. I'd be lost without you."

She turned around and kissed him on the lips. "Yep. And don't you forget it."

Chapter Forty-Five

The next morning Bryce awoke to the alarm on his phone. He felt the weight of Val's arm on his chest and didn't want to move, but the volume of the alarm was rising, and it was going to wake her up soon. He reached over slowly and silenced it with his right hand.

He gently moved Val's arm off his chest and rolled onto his side to watch her sleep for a few minutes before sliding out of bed and getting ready for work. He peeked at the kids sleeping in their beds and then headed to the garage.

***

The EMS radio beeped a loud tone indicating an incoming call. The triage nurse answered and put the call over the speaker. "We're five minutes out with a chronic ventilator patient. She is thirty-nine and has a tracheostomy and G-tube. We got called out for fever and low oxygen. If you don't have any questions, we'll see you at triage."

The staff sitting around the physician work area looked at each other and smiled. "Eleanor, it has to be." Two doctors and a PA both said, "Not it," just before Bryce walked around the corner and took a seat.

"Bryce, looks like you're it," said the physician assistant.

"What are you talking about?"

"EMS called; they're bringing in a thirty-nine-year-old woman with a trache–"

"Not it," said Bryce quickly. The rest of the team laughed and informed him he was too late. "That's fine; she's an easy admission. I'll go see her." He grabbed his stethoscope and walked back toward their resuscitation rooms.

The EMS crew arrived right on time. Eleanor was as described, looking ill even for her. "Hey, doc, we're having a hard time bagging her. I think she may have a mucous plug on her trache tube but I couldn't dislodge it with saline," said Clay. "I tried a suction catheter without success and figured we'd just get her to you."

"You did the right thing. We probably need to change the entire tracheostomy tube. I looked in her chart and this one has been in for over six weeks. They're supposed to be changed at least once a month." Bryce asked the respiratory therapist to get another tracheostomy tube and prepare for the exchange. Eleanor had the tracheostomy for so many years the tract from her skin to trachea was well established and it should be an easy exchange.

"Eleanor, we're going to change your tube," he said while leaning toward her ear. I know it's not comfortable, but it will help you breathe a lot better." The respiratory therapist handed Bryce a lubricated tube and elevated the patient's bed to position her appropriately. She removed the Velcro strap that held the tube in place and signaled to Bryce that everything was ready.

Bryce held the new tube next to her neck and said, "Ok, here we go." He used his left hand to slide the old tube out. This induced a coughing spasm that sent small droplets across the room. The stoma was wide open, and she was moving air well now. Bryce turned the new tube ninety degrees and inserted it into the hole, rotating it down as he advanced it into her neck. The respiratory therapist quickly secured the tube with a new strap and hooked her up to the ventilator.

Bryce breathed a sigh of relief. Changing a tracheostomy tube is not something emergency physicians do often, and if something goes wrong, it can get bad in a hurry. He looked at the old tube and saw a large green ball of slime attached to the bottom of it. This ball obscured well over half of the size of the tube. He held it up and showed the others in the room. "No wonder she couldn't breathe. This biofilm was covering half of her airway. I'll throw this out in our biohazard area. Everyone, make sure to wash your hands and stethoscopes well; she's got multi-drug resistant Pseudomonas."

"Yeah, we know. I bring her to you guys all the time. I'm probably covered in it by now," said Clay, the paramedic who transported her.

Bryce stopped and turned back toward Clay. Why didn't he think of this sooner? He limited his search for the connection between Kent and Eleanor to people at the hospital. He should have added pre-hospital contacts as well. "How many times do you think you've transported her?" he asked.

"Hell, I don't know, probably at least twenty times," said Clay. "She lives half a mile from our fire house. If we're not out on another run, we're the ones dispatch sends to pick her up. I could find my way through her house in the dark."

Bryce was thinking fast. EMS often enters the home of patients they transport. This would give Clay access to the person, the layout of the home, and who knows what else he could find out about them.

Making a quick decision, he took the tube and dropped it into a biohazard bag and walked toward the dirty utility room. He returned quickly and tracked down the EMS crew before they went out for another run. "Clay, are you free to help us out around the house? I need an extra set of hands with some chores, and my wife will be busy with the kids."

"Sure, I'm actually off for the next few days. What do you need help with?"

"Fantastic! We are redoing the back porch, and I need help cleaning gutters, power washing the pool house, and carrying a bunch of landscaping stone."

"Oh, so I'm gonna be your pack mule?" he grinned back.

"Well, you're always bragging about setting the record on the fire department's qualifying fitness test. I figured if I needed some stuff moved or ladders climbed, you'd be the one to ask."

Clay stood up taller upon hearing the praise. "Absolutely, Doc. When do you want me over?"

"How about noon tomorrow? I'll have the hard seltzers nice and cold for you."

"Sounds perfect, except that candy-ass drink better be for you and your wife, not me. I'm a Corona guy. And if I'm going up a ladder, I'm going to need fresh cut limes as well." Bryce agreed to the terms, and they parted ways.

He spent the time between his next patients reviewing the chart of Kent Carpenter again. He looked at the femur fracture visit and checked which EMS crew transported to the hospital. *It was Clay!* The date of the visit was about three months before the visit Bryce saw him for a cough. He checked the dates of Eleanor's visits and saw Clay had transported her four days prior to that. *Got ya. Well, maybe.*

***

He sat down at his workstation and broadened a search through the hospital medical records for patients who were transported by Medic 93 in the last six months. He eliminated anyone under eighteen and over sixty and was left with a list of nearly a hundred people. Bryce printed a list of names and began searching the state death registry to check on their status. Sixty minutes later, he finished running the list and reviewed his notes. According to the Social Security actuarial tables, an eighteen-year-old has a 0.036% chance of dying in a year. A fifty-nine-year-old has a 0.644% chance of dying in a year. Bryce did some quick math in his head and realized in a healthy population, less than one person on this list of a hundred should have died in the last year. He counted seven that had died, including Kent Carpenter.

An exception to the HIPAA privacy law allows chart audit review for patient safety. Bryce called Ash on his cell phone to get permission. "Hey, Ash, it's Bryce. Do me a favor, would you? I'd like to chair our task force on investigating young unexpected deaths in our community. Would that be okay? I'd need to review the charts of some of our past patients here in the department."

"What task force? We don't have one of those," said Ash, confused.

"Sure we do, you just created it. I'm happy to lead it, I'll give you a preliminary finding on whether there are more deaths in our patient population than would be expected based on national trends. That may suggest foul play involved and possibly a murderer in our community."

"Ah, now I see. Sorry, I wasn't following. Yes, please do that. Let me know what you find," said Ash.

"Roger. I think we're on to something here. Talk to you later." Bryce ended the call and scooted forward in his chair, fixed his posture, and set to work on the next stage of his investigation.

Chapter Forty-Six

Bryce went back to the state's death registry and checked the cause of death on each patient from the list he compiled. Out of the seven names, two had died of cancer. He scratched them off the list. He knew what happened to Kent Carpenter, so he scratched that name off as well. Four names to go.

The next was a thirty-year-old woman who died from blunt force trauma. He found several visits for broken bones and facial injuries, reportedly from falling down the stairs or other unlikely acts of clumsiness in the months leading up to her death. There was no hospital record for this, so he searched the internet instead. He found a news article that detailed the arrest of her alleged murderer, live-in boyfriend David Lewis, age thirty-five. Bryce stopped and reread that name. David Lewis.

He turned and looked at the paper containing the list of patients who had died. There it was. David Lewis. The woman was killed in January, but David's death date was nearly a month before this. *How is that possible?* A surge of adrenaline rushed through his body, bringing with it a slight tremor and goosebumps on his arms.

Bryce looked at the date she was transported to the hospital with a head injury. November 26th. Thanksgiving Day.

He pulled up the EMS run sheet and did not see Clay's name on it, but his partner's name was. The EMS report documented concern for domestic violence and stated the patient denied it and begged them to not get the police involved.

He opened the state's record on the death of David Lewis and found he died due to a fall from a tree. A quick internet search revealed David had gone to the woods to rescue an injured owl after a tip from a concerned hiker. His body was found the next day near a broken tree limb in a very remote section of a state park. His death was ruled an accident due to blunt head trauma from a fall. The coroner report documented the phone call came from the public library but that was the only unusual finding. It was felt to not be important, and the death was ruled accidental. The local Audubon Society had started an annual award in his honor. Canary Creek Apartments, where he had lived, even renamed their playground after him.

Bryce again felt a chill run down his back. Canary Creek Apartments? Where had he seen that before? He was aware of the complex; it was the largest one in town and a few miles from the hospital. He pulled up the woman's chart again and looked at the demographics page. Her address was 762 Canary Creek Lane, Apartment C. David's address was listed as 1410 Canary Creek Court, Apartment A. How could he be a live-in boyfriend if he lived in a different apartment?

Bryce did another internet search for "David Lewis Canary Creek Apartments." He clicked on a white pages site that sold personal information for a fee. There were two different listings for David Lewis with a Canary Creek Apartment address. They were the same age but had different family members and prior addresses listed.

Bryce let out a groan. There were two David Lewis's in that apartment complex. Both aged thirty-five. One an abuser, one an animal lover. One a murderer, one murdered. One case of mistaken identity. Two people dead as a result. He immediately realized why the call from the public library was relevant. *That damn coroner. Creating a murderer's paradise.*

He quickly finished the list of deaths and found none of the rest suspicious for outside influence. It didn't matter; he had what he needed. All that mattered now was what he was going to do with the information.

***

Bryce made a few stops on the way home. First to the supply closet in the hospital microbiology department. Then to the hardware store for a halogen light, and finally a store selling everything a new parent could need. Instead of going home after this, he drove to the public library, which was closed for the night, and parked in the closest spot to the door. He sat quietly and thought about what he should do. Should he go to the police and ask them to investigate Clay for two murders? It would begin a long road that was not guaranteed to end in a proper resolution. Clay had been careful, except for the mistaken identity. Bryce considered the pain that he suffered because of Clay's actions. Loud sirens and flashing lights interrupted his thoughts. He looked up and saw a large garage door open across the street and then a fire truck and ambulance pull out of the fire station. Medic 93 off to save another life. Starting from directly across the street from the public library. The perfect place to make an anonymous phone call about a fake injured owl.

Bryce put the car in reverse and headed home. *I've made my decision.*

He brought his purchases to the mechanical room in the basement and set to work. First, he opened the box from the baby store and removed an automatic rocking bassinet. He placed a glass jar inside it and wedged it in place with a few blankets. Next, he pulled out a one-liter bottle acquired from the hospital lab and poured the contents into the jar. He turned on the halogen lamp and clipped it to the PVC pipe leading out of his sump pit, just far enough away to keep the jar around ninety-eight degrees Fahrenheit. Culturing bacteria is an exact science, so he placed his wireless meat thermometer next to the jar and confirmed he was receiving data on his app.

He turned on the bassinet and watched it gently swing back and forth, sloshing the culture media inside the glass jar. The sight reminded him of the summer he spent in a research lab before his first year of medical school. That lab had hundreds of thousands of dollars of equipment to culture and work with bacteria. Bryce felt proud of his one-hundred-and-fifty-dollar setup.

He reached into his jacket and removed a fresh set of gloves, and slid his hands inside them. Once protected, he reached deeper into his pocket and pulled out a biohazard bag. There was a large red symbol on the bag, marking it as possibly infectious. Bryce let out a nervous laugh. There was nothing *possible* about what was inside. He opened the bag and removed a tracheostomy tube, partially blocked with a large ball of mucus. He gently placed the tube in the jar and swished it around before dropping it to the bottom. He gave a quick glance at his watch to note the time and then stepped out of the mechanical room, locking the door behind him. He washed his hands while wearing the gloves, and then tossed them in the garbage and washed his hands again.

Bryce checked the app on his phone and saw the thermometer read ninety-seven degrees. Close enough. Half his patients claimed their normal body temperature was ninety-seven anyway, hoping to convince him the 98.6°F was actually a fever.

He climbed the stairs out of the basement and tried to ignore the increasing volume of his conscience yelling at him. He walked upstairs and shut the door to the basement behind him. "Val, keep the kids out of the mechanical room. Something isn't right with a wire on the sump pump. I'll get it fixed this weekend."

"Oh darn, we were planning to do a puzzle down there next to the furnace tonight," she replied, her voice dripping with sarcasm.

Bryce smiled at her, happy to have her humor back in his life. "Listen, tomorrow a friend from work is coming over and we're going to work on the pool outbuilding and make your flower garden. Any chance you could take the kids somewhere for the day?"

"I suppose we can find somewhere to go. I hear Florida is nice this time of year." Bryce couldn't let that one go. He scurried around the kitchen island after Val who managed to stay a few steps ahead the entire time. "I'm just kidding," she said between laughs. She slowed down and spun around to embrace him in a strong hug.

"Next time you go to Florida, I'm coming wi–" he said before his words were silenced by Val's lips.

"Yes, you're coming with me," she finished.

Chapter Forty-Seven

"Niles Proffit please," said Bryce into his phone.

"I'm sorry. He's not available right now. May I take a message for you?" The voice articulated each word precisely, not even a hint of disinterest. It made him wonder what the training and salary for a billionaire's secretary was. Advanced degree?

"Yes, tell him Dr. Bryce Chapman would like to speak to him about a private matter. Please let him know it is urgent, and the timing is important. He can reach out to me on this number."

"Oh, Dr. Chapman. I was instructed to let Mr. Proffit know if you called. Please hold the line."

Bryce stood and paced the room, waiting for a response. No one ever slew a dragon sitting down. The situation had changed since he last spoke with Niles. He had video evidence showing Tony was not the victim of this ordeal. It proved he was operating a boat while intoxicated, caused an accident while under the influence, and provoked the fight that led to his facial injury and ultimate drowning.

Bryce hated confrontation, but it was the only way to get this behind him. He did not seek out confrontation, but refused to avoid it at the expense of his family and career. Some things are worth being uncomfortable for a bit.

"Sir, Mr. Proffit is available to speak with you now. I will transfer you back. Have a great day," said the secretary with a positive inflection in her voice. Another task completed with perfection.

He heard several short beeps and then the voice of Niles Proffit came through. "Dr. Chapman, I didn't expect to hear from you today. What is this regarding?"

"Sir, last time we spoke you told me you believed you had sufficient evidence to convince a jury that I assaulted your son and caused his injuries."

"That's correct. In fact, I spoke with our attorneys today and will be submitting Tony's affidavit to the prosecutor this week."

"Before you submit that, you need to watch a video. It is the rest of the footage recovered from my camera the day of the accident. It clearly shows who the aggressor was and documents several crimes committed by your son."

"Be careful, Doctor, those are very serious allegations to make against my family. I don't need to remind you who pays your check," said Niles in an openly hostile tone.

"I'm fully aware who I work for, sir, and it's my family, not you. Ultimately, we are all self-employed. I lease my services out to you. It is you who is my client, not the other way around. That being said, I enjoy my job, my colleagues, and the hospital where I currently work. My goal in reaching out to you today is to clear up the confusion and restore the security I have always felt in my current position. Now, are you willing to watch this video, or do I need to defend myself using the court of public opinion? The rescue video is still one of the top downloaded videos on the internet right now. This prequel footage would surely be of interest also. I am choosing to show it to you first out of respect to you as my employer, despite your threats to me."

Niles was curious now. He was not used to being spoken to in such a manner. This ER doctor had a set of balls on him, but so do most people when backed into a corner. The question was whether there was merit to his claim or not. Squashing a grape isn't worth it if the juice splatter ruins your expensive clothing."Okay, you have my interest. How can I view the footage?"

"I have it on my computer now. I'll send you a private key to remotely view my desktop as I play the video," said Bryce.

Niles typed in the key as Bryce read it out. The computer beeped to signal the incoming screen share request and Bryce accepted it. Niles confirmed he can see Bryce's screen. "Okay, here we go. I'll stop it when it gets to the publicly released footage."

Bryce clicked play, and the video began. The camera jiggled as it was put on Bryce's head and then panned around, recording in the direction he faced. Shortly after the video started the camera jostled and yells could be heard. The camera panned toward a second boat that had struck Bryce's from behind. Tony's intoxicated voice was loud enough to be heard all the way in Niles' office. Bryce sat silently as the video played on. He fidgeted in his chair and felt his palms begin to sweat. He knew what scene came next.

The video showed Valerie in the sunbeam posing for a picture before the men surrounded her. Their inappropriate comments were muffled by the waterproof case, but clear enough for Niles to understand what was said. He watched Val dive under water to escape the advance and watched his son chase after her. He watched Bryce's hand stop Tony from following her and heard him calmly ask for this to end.

Tony's arm pulled back, setting up for a massive right hook. The camera angle showed how close the punch actually was. Bryce hadn't realized how close he had come to a broken face.

The camera tilted toward the water and caught movement under the water as Bryce's leg came forward in a kicking motion. The camera panned to the ceiling as Bryce extended backward to deliver the blow and turn for the exit. Bryce clicked the mouse to pause the video.

"Sir, that is the majority of what you haven't viewed before. The next scene shows Tony unconscious under the water, stuck to the rock because of his swimsuit. Do you want to see that? It may be hard to see your son in that situation."

"I appreciate your concern. This video has given me a lot to think about. I think I should watch a bit more before I decide what to do. Go ahead and play it."

Bryce left clicked on the video and it continued. The scene shifted from the grotto to the boat, and then back into the water as Bryce dove in to look for Tony. The view was obscured as Valerie swam past Bryce and got to Tony first. It showed her struggling to free Tony and then Bryce using brute force to rip him free.

Goose bumps formed on Bryce's arms as he watched the scene unfold. When that segment of the video finished, Bryce pressed stop, and Niles sat quietly for a few moments." Dr. Chapman, this video tells a much different story than what my son and his friends have shared with me. It is hard to imagine my son lying to me as dramatically as you are claiming he has. Give me some time to talk to him and his friends again and I will be in touch. I appreciate you coming to me privately with this."

"Okay, please let me know as soon as you can. This has been extremely hard on my family." Bryce ended the call and leaned back in his chair; eyes closed. "How hard is it to just put an end to it?" he whispered.

Chapter Forty-Eight

The doorbell rang at 11:55 a.m. "I got it!" yelled Noah as he raced his sister to the front door.

"Kids, wait to see who it is first. Remember, we don't open the door if we don't know who it is," said Val as she followed them to the door. She looked through and saw an attractive man wearing a sleeveless shirt, exposing chiseled arms covered in tattoos. *Well, I don't know you, but you must be at the right house.* "Good morning," she said pleasantly, the words ending in higher pitch in a mix of a statement and question.

"Hi, ma'am, I'm Clay from the hospital; I'm here to help the doc with some things around the house."

"Oh right, come on in. He's just getting out of the shower. The kids and I are headed to my sister's house, so it'll just be the two of you."

"Well, I'm sorry to hear that," he said, smiling at her. After a pause, he added with a wink, "I just adore children."

She stepped aside to allow him to enter the home. She led him through the tiled entryway into the kitchen and offered him a cup of coffee. It had "World's Best Dad" written on the side. "Clay, thanks for coming," said Bryce from behind them. "Let me show you what the plans are for the day. It's right out back."

Bryce pulled the sliding door to the left and stepped onto the elevated deck off the back of the kitchen. The deck overlooked a large rectangular pool with a slide and diving board. Sunk into the deck sat an inviting eight-person hot tub. "Hey, why have you guys never hosted a pool party for the entire emergency department? This setup is perfect," Clay said.

"I would like to, but I keep getting push back from—" Bryce looked back toward the kitchen.

"Yeah, I get it. But does she know guys like me would be strutting around in Speedos?"

Bryce laughed, "Somehow I never thought to use that argument."

He led Clay to a building on the far side of the pool. Last year, they had a pool house constructed that held a bath- room, small kitchen with a bar, and storage closet. Valerie hated having dozens of guests walking through the house wet, searching for a bathroom.

"When we built this, we chose engineered wood siding, thinking it would be easier to maintain. But this northern facing wall got covered in mildew. We need to power wash that using a cleaning agent and clean all the gutters. I also bought a gutter protection system that we can install, so I don't need your help again next year."

"Right on. What about the blocks? I saw a pallet of them in the driveway."

"Oh yeah. We need to dig out a channel for those along the south edge of this building and then stack them up. She wants to add a flower garden."

"Okay, where's the wheelbarrow?" Bryce looked back at Clay with a blank stare. "Do you not have a wheelbarrow?"

"No, sorry. I hire most of this sort of thing out and never felt the need. Guess we'll be the pack mules today."

"You're killing me, Doc. Did you at least get my Corona?"

Bryce pointed to a cooler resting in the shade. "There's two six-packs and a few limes cut and ready to go."

"That's what I'm talking about. I got off work at 9:00 a.m.; time to drink!" Clay walked over and picked up two Coronas, popping the caps off and wedging a lime in the top of each. Placing a thumb over each bottle, he inverted them slowly until the lime floated to the bottom.

"Thank you, but I need to wait a bit before I start," said Bryce.

"Suit yourself. These were both for me, anyway." He took a long pull on a bottle and set them both in the shade. They walked toward the driveway and started carrying blocks toward the building. It was an exhausting job. Each block weighed thirty pounds. Each trip moved three blocks, with Clay pointing out he was doing twice the work every chance he got.

"I'm going to stack a few on this side to work as a platform to powerwash easier," said Bryce. He made three short stacks spaced out about the length of his arm, holding the pressure washer wand. Clay finished the first beer and started on the second. "Hey, when we're done here, mind if I sleep by your pool? The beer is going down pretty easy, and I have many more needing my attention."

"What kind of guy would I be if I said no?" asked Bryce. "But you should know the sprinklers turn on at 10:00 p.m."

"You'd be a better guy if you wouldn't make me drink alone," said Clay.

"Boys, we're leaving. We'll be back by dinner," said Val, poking her head out the kitchen sliding door.

"Okay, have a good time. Tell your sister I said hi, and please apologize to her again for stealing all the good genes from your mom."

"I'm telling you, she really doesn't think that joke is funny anymore." She shut the door and a few minutes later they heard the garage door open and her car back out of the driveway.

"Okay, hand me a beer," said Bryce.

"That's what I'm talking about," shouted Clay as he jogged over to the cooler, grabbing two more Coronas.

"I haven't drunk in a few weeks, not sure what my tolerance is right now," said Bryce.

"Don't worry; it's me going up the ladder, not you. And I'm a professional. Drink up!" said Clay, clinking his bottle together with Bryce. Clay took a long pull from his bottle and Bryce appeared to do the same and then held it next to his chair and poured beer into the mulch.

They worked quickly, each accomplishing their tasks independently. Clay cleaned the gutters in under an hour and even rinsed them with a hose. Bryce dug the channel for the retaining wall and get out the pressure washer before attaching the hose to it.

"Why don't we take a break for a few?" Clay agreed, and they each grabbed a chair by the cooler. Bryce refreshed their drinks. "I really appreciate you coming out here to help me today. It's been a rough few weeks. Have you heard what's been going on?"

"I watched a video online where you did mouth to mouth on a guy with a bloody face. I'm pretty hardcore, but I would never do that," said Clay. "I also heard you got in some sort of trouble over that?"

"Yep, but that's hopefully just about worked out. It turns out the person who published the video held onto the part that showed the truth and chose not to publish it. They had heard about the criminal charge and tried to sell the video to me. Publishing the video was just guerrilla marketing. They wanted me to buy my innocence and my wife's dignity."

"What does your wife's dignity have to do with it?"

"We also shot some video of a more intimate nature. That was also on the card," said Bryce.

"That's cold brother. That's the kind of move that pisses me off. I'm afraid I'd have to do something about that."

"But what can I do?" asked Bryce as he seemed to finish his third beer.

Clay stood up and handed him a fresh one. "These are the last two, Doc. Four for you, eight for me. You sure I can sleep by your pool when we're done?"

"Absolutely. Heck, I may join you."

"That's fine, but I'm the big spoon. It's just my personality," said Clay with a wink. "But seriously, you should do something to that guy for trying to screw you over. You can't have your life destroyed by someone and just sit back and take it."

Bryce pondered that statement as he swung the bottle up to his lips. Gravity pulled the beer to his lips, chased by the lime wedge that smacked into his lips. "What can I do, though? I'm here, he's not. I'm a doctor, I help people. It's what I'm called to do."

Clay leaned forward; his face devoid of emotion. "Doc, I was in the military. Our job was to help protect this country and its citizens. All three hundred thirty million of them. Most of us are great people. Some of us outright bastards. Sometimes we have to do it by killing people. Does that make us bad?"

"I guess it depends whose side you're on," he replied. "What if the action taken ultimately led to something else bad down the road?"

"Yeah, that happened from time to time, but we trained for it. You just need to improvise. The important thing," Clay said while finishing the last of his beer, "is that you never second guess your decision. What's done is done. You can't change what happened, but you can change the effects of what happened. It's in the past. Plan for your future. Worry is for fools; action leads to change." He set the bottle down hard for emphasis.

"Damn right," said Bryce. He had spent the last few weeks worrying about the future with no idea what actions to take. These last few days had given him a sense of purpose and the energy to work the plan. "Have you met our new temporary doc, Peter Thrasher?" asked Bryce.

Clay burst out laughing. "That meat head? Yeah, I brought him a few patients the other day. Sure thinks he's good looking. He actually hit on my female EMT. He seems like he stepped out of a trashy romance novel, but I like him, honestly. He reminds me of myself when I was a bit younger. Why do you ask?"

"Just curious about what you thought. You meet a lot of ER docs. I like how he handles himself in the ER and the patients love him. We're thinking about offering him a full-time position."

"I bet he knows plenty of positions and would be interested in sharing his knowledge with your nurses, but I doubt any of them are full time," Clay said as he let loose with another deep laugh.

Bryce laughed and set his bottle down. "Let's finish up," he said. "Just a bit more pressure washing and the rest of the gutter guard system, then we can pass out for a few hours before Val and the kids get home."

Chapter Forty-Nine

Clay stood up and walked over to the gutter guard supplies on next to the building. The pressure washer was parked there as well. "Hey, can you add some more of that mildew treatment to the soap reservoir for me? I'm going to go take a leak," said Bryce. Clay looked around and found the nearly full bottle of mildew remover. He scanned the directions to see how much to add, but the text was smaller than his alcohol consumption. Looking at the mildew buildup on the siding, he figured it was going to take more than recommended, anyway. He poured nearly the whole contents into the reservoir and then emptied his bladder behind the building.

"Hey, we have security cameras out here. You can't just whip it out like that," laughed Bryce.

"Well, I hope it's high definition; little Clay deserves to be viewed in the best way possible." After he finished, they both returned to their tasks. Clay went up the ladder to install the gutter shields, and Bryce walked to the pressure washer.

He grabbed the pull cord and yanked his arm back, starting the pressure washer on the first pull. The four-stroke engine drowning out any chance of conversation. Bryce loved this machine as it created beauty out of chaos, like some sort of magic eraser of filth. He slowly worked his way to the left along the wall toward Clay, erasing a year of mildew and moss with each wave of his arm. The 2700psi water stream restoring the building to its former glory.

He reached the first stack of block and climbed up, stretching to reach the eave and clean along the roofline. "Hey, you're soaking me with back spray," yelled Clay, having to shout to be heard.

"Sorry, let me move and change the direction I'm spraying," replied Bryce. He took a step to the left in order to direct the wand to the right and away from Clay, but instead of the ground, his foot planted firmly on air and he fell off the stack of blocks. His body fell sideways, accelerating toward the hard concrete. His arms spread out behind him to attempt to break the fall, but he didn't drop the sprayer wand.

A loud scream erupted as Bryce landed hard on his back. He released the wand and rolled over to see what caused Clay to scream out in surprise. A large laceration extended from Clay's right shoulder, curving across his back and ending at his left hip. The pressure washer stream had cut through Clay's clothing and skin like a ragged sword. The wound was deep, and blood flowed quickly from the length of it, exiting out the bottom like a maple tree cut for sap. Clay's knees buckled and jumped off the ladder, landing on weak legs and rolling to the side. Blood mixed with the water on the ground and quickly spread to cover the pool deck.

"Dude! I'm so sorry," said Bryce. He ran to get a towel and pressed it firmly against the wound. "We need to get you to the hospital. That wound looks awful."

Clay couldn't talk. To do so would mean he had to take a break from screaming and moaning in pain.

Bryce called 9-1-1 on his phone and requested an ambulance, instructing them to come around to the back of the house with their stretcher. "Hang on, let me kill the engine," said Bryce. He reached over and switched off the engine, its silence exposing the whimpers of pain coming from Clay.

"I can't believe that happened. I am so sorry."

"Just keep holding pressure on it. Is the wound deep?"

When Bryce pushed the towel onto the wound, he could see the ridge of Clay's scapula, and the top edge of his pelvic bone. "Yeah, man, it is." He didn't think Clay needed to know exactly how deep it was at this point. Within minutes, they could hear sirens as the ambulance approached the home. "You know what that sound is?" asked Clay.

"It's the ambulance," replied Bryce, fighting off a wave of nausea at realizing what he had done.

"No, it's the Fentanyl delivery service coming to take my pain away."

The paramedics jogged around to the back of the house, pushing their stretcher ahead of them. As they neared Clay, they stopped short, the pressure washer blocking their path. Bryce jumped up and grabbed the washer, and threw it to the side to make room for them. A second and a half after he let it go, he heard a splash. He turned and saw the washer sitting at the bottom of his pool.

"Clay? Is that you? What happened?" asked the first paramedic to arrive. "You look like you lost a fight with William Wallace." He knelt down next to Clay and began to quickly assess the wound. He placed a blood pressure cuff on Clay's arm and documented a quick set of vitals while his partner inserted an IV catheter in his other arm.

"Yeah, feels like it too. Doc nailed me with a pressure washer. Drop that line in, hit me with the Fentanyl, and get me to the ER."

They helped Clay to his feet and onto their gurney. They packed the wound with gauze and laid him back, hoping the weight of his body would help hold pressure on the wound. Now that the IV was inserted, they hung a liter of Lactated Ringer's solution and left the stopcock wide open. The paramedic reached for his medication bag and retrieved a pre-filled syringe.

"I'm coming with you, guys; let me grab some clothes and I'll meet you in the ambulance," said Bryce. He put his hand on Clay's leg and said, "Again, I'm so sorry about all of this." Clay nodded and leaned his head back, closing his eyes as the Fentanyl coursed through his veins.

Chapter Fifty

"Dr. Sharpe, you need to hear this," said Jackie Sirico, approaching Tom from behind.

"What's up, Jackie?"

"Your buddy Chapman is bringing in a patient with a pressure washer injury."

"Bryce? Why is he bringing someone in? Is he driving them in his car?"

"He's riding in the ambulance. It happened at his house."

Tom's stomach rolled over as a feeling of dread washed over him. Was it Valerie? One of their kids? He had been so happy when Bryce shared the news his wife and kids had come back from Florida. Now this?

"OK, let's start in trauma. How old is the patient?"

"Forty-three," said Jackie.

Forty-three. Tom exhaled deeply. It wasn't the kids. But Valerie? She wasn't in her forties, was she? If so, she sure carried it well. "Is it a female?"

"I didn't hear. They'll be here in a few. Do you want me to page it out as a trauma?"

"No, let me take a look at them first. Thanks."

"Hey Peter, come with me on this one." Thrasher jumped up and jogged around the corner after Tom. His scribe Emily following closely behind with her laptop in hand. "Emily, I'll do the note on this; you can leave the laptop here," said Tom.

"Okay, thanks. It's just a habit to bring it wherever I go. It'll be nice to be in a room simply to learn rather than to take notes."

They walked toward the trauma room, unsure of what they were going to find. Pressure washer injuries are often to extremities and are much worse than the outward wound would suggest. The high-pressure injects air and liquid deep into the tissue planes of the body. An injury to a finger could push material up into the forearm. They were a surgeon's nightmare to clean, especially if a solvent or oil was injected.

The doors opened and paramedics rolled through with their patient on a gurney. Tom recognized Clay immediately, but not the look of excruciating pain he had on his face. Clay was always smiling or stoic; this wasn't good. The blood-soaked sheets suggested the wound was large and must be on his back, as no wound was yet visible.

The paramedics quickly gave their report as the entire team worked in unison to transfer Clay onto the ER bed. He was lifted into the air and transferred over to the bed. Blood dripped through the sheet and covered the side of the bed.

"Clay, I'm going to look at your wound. Do you prefer which way we roll you?" said Tom.

"Doc, I don't care. Just do it fast and drug me up," said Clay.

"Okay, team, let's roll him to the left. There's more blood on the right, so I think we'll see the wound better on that side." He walked to the right side of the bed, opposite three nurses who prepared to roll him on his side. Peter took the position at the top of the bed and held Clay's head in a neutral position while the team log rolled him. Clay screamed as the team pulled him onto his left hip to allow Dr. Sharpe to examine the wound. Tom turned on the overhead exam light and focused on Clay's back. Several people in the room gasped at what they saw. There was a large wound traveling from his left shoulder blade, angling across the spine and down to the right buttock. Several areas of bright white shone through from the depth of the wound; one along the midline and one near the right hip. Blood was pulsating out of two places, shooting nearly a foot through the air. Tom filled each hand with gauze bandages and pressed them firmly against the bleeding vessels to slow the blood loss.

"Get me two hemostats and a suture kit. 3-0 Vicryl. Clay, I need to control two bleeders. You're going to feel me put in a few stitches, sorry, buddy."

The equipment arrived at the bedside in moments, and Tom clamped the hemostats over the two bleeding vessels. He then quickly placed sutures around the vessels and tied them off, stopping the brisk hemorrhage. He chose to leave the sutures long rather than cut them so the trauma surgeon could tell where the bleeding vessels were. *The surgeon can cut them later.* Clay moaned during the procedure but didn't move. He knew enough to hold still so the doctor could perform the procedure quicker.

"Let's roll him back. Clay, you have a large wound on your back. I can see the bones of your spine in two places and your right pelvic bone is exposed. Can you feel your toes and move them okay? Can you feel your groin?" Clay wiggled his toes and nodded.

"Good, your spinal cord is working. I hope this is just a superficial wound and no significant damage to the deeper structures. I'll order pain medication, antibiotics, and con-tact the surgeon to get you fixed in the operating room. When is the last time you had something to eat or drink?"

"I had eight beers; finished the last one thirty minutes ago."

"Eight? Why so many?" asked Dr. Sharpe.

"Because that pansy Chapman could only handle four." He started to laugh, but this movement brought on a fresh wave of pain. "Well, maybe if I hadn't given him so many, I wouldn't be here in this bed right now."

"Hey, I'm no pansy. You're the one demanding pain medicine for a cut." The words came from Bryce, who had quietly entered the trauma room.

"Bryce, what happened?" asked Tom.

"Clay was helping me knock out some chores around the pool today. We took a break, and the beer tasted fantastic. He kept pounding them and pushing me to drink more. When we got back to work, I tripped over something while using a power washer and slashed him with the spray. I guess I just reflexively held on to the sprayer when I was falling. I feel awful. How does the wound look?"

"Peter, can you pack the wound for me while I talk to Bryce and get some more details?"

"Can do. Emily, can you bring me gauze and a bottle of saline?" said Peter, all sense of joking was cast aside. It was time to work.

Tom pulled his friend to the corner of the room and spoke in a quiet voice. "It's pretty bad. I can see his spine and right ilium. I think his spinal cord is okay. I'm hopeful this is just a deep flesh wound, but it's going to need closure in the operating room. I can't give him enough Lidocaine to close that; it would be a toxic dose. I'm going to call Elisa and see if she'll take him to the operating room to explore the wound better and repair it under general anesthesia. She's on call for trauma today."

Tom picked up the phone and dialed the number for Elisa Morales' phone. The call lasted less than a minute and seemed pleasant. Bryce was impressed. "Said she'll be down in a few. The OR is on standby, and we should have him up in ten minutes. I'm going to step out and order the antibiotics."

Bryce walked over to Clay's bed and sat down in a chair next to it. He reached out and put a hand on Clay's shoulder. "Is there anyone you want me to call to let them know you're here?"

"No thanks. It's just me and the fire station. And I'm sure they all know I'm here by now. Listen man, things happen. I enjoyed hanging with you today, Doc. Well, until you went Luke Skywalker on my ass."

Bryce smiled at the mental image. "I think Luke would have been more graceful; besides, the light saber would have cauterized the wound instantly. I'll check on you after they get you fixed in the OR, okay?" Clay nodded and closed his eyes, trying to block out the pain and regain some dignity in front of the people he'd worked with for years.

Dr. Elisa Morales kept her word and arrived in the ER quickly. She examined the wound and agreed it would be best evaluated in the operating room, where an anesthesiologist could provide a painless environment for Clay. She walked over to Bryce, Peter, and Tom. "Look, I'll take him to the OR, but I'm not sure we should close the wound entirely. Injection wounds have a very high risk of infection. I may need to put a vacuum bandage on and leave it open for a while. We can do a multi-stage repair with delayed closure once we've proven there is no significant infection."

"Thanks, Elisa; glad to have you on call today. Please do what you can to help fix him up," said Bryce.

"I'll say one thing about you guys; you sure keep my OR schedule full." Her team swarmed the room and soon Clay was wheeled out of the emergency department toward the bank of elevators that led to the operating rooms.

Chapter Fifty-One

Bryce had intended to wait in the surgery waiting room for an update on Clay, but the increasing number of fire and EMS arriving to support Clay had led to too many uncomfortable glances and conversations. He retreated back to the office in the ER and pondered the events of the last few days. His family was back together. The CEO may actually be coming around to seeing Bryce as a true hero, rather than someone who assaulted his son. That would clear the criminal charges in the Bahamas also. The memory card and its files are back in his possession. He now knew what happened to Kent, and it wasn't an error in his medical judgment. Each of those events were difficult enough, but Clay's injury was weighing harder on him. This was a direct result of his actions.

Bryce stayed at the hospital until Clay was out of the operating room so he could hear a report from Elisa directly. She texted him after the case and he met her in the surgery lounge. "I looked for you in the waiting room but it was full of firemen and paramedics. That was a nasty wound, Bryce. Took me forever to clean it up."

"No offense, but I feel worse for Clay than I do for you. Were you able to close it, or did you leave it open?"

"A bit of both. I closed the ends of it but left the middle open to drain with a wound vac. There is such a high risk of infection with these pressure washer injuries. He lost a lot of blood but I'm trying to avoid a transfusion. It will depend on how much he oozes in the next few days."

"Is he still on the ventilator?" asked Bryce.

"No, we were able to wean him off of it in the recovery unit. The question is whether his pain will be too much to deal with or whether he'll need to be sedated while he heals a bit more. At least with the wound vac we won't need to do dressing changes." She paused for a few moments before continuing. "This is a pretty unusual wound, Bryce. How did you manage to slash his entire back?"

"I know. I keep playing it over in my head. When I fell my arms flailed out and my hand squeezed down on the wand. It was a reflex to try to hold onto something. I feel so bad for him. Do you think he's going to be okay?"

"It's too early to tell. If I had made that wound in the operating room, yes. But with a high-pressure injection injury, I just don't know. I'll keep you updated on his condition." Elisa turned and walked away slowly, tired from a long day in the operating room.

Bryce walked to the elevator bank and considered the options. His car and home were down two floors. Clay's ICU room was up a floor. He leaned in and pressed the up button. He wanted to check on Clay before leaving the hospital. The ICU is arranged in a large rectangle, with storage and other rooms in the center. Bryce stopped in front of Clay's room and looked through the glass door. He saw a nurse checking on multiple IV medications including fluids, antibiotics, sedatives, and pain medication. *It sure looks easier to order those than administer them.*

Staring at Clay in bed brought a surge of emotion as he was again faced with an injury he caused another person. Nausea built in his midsection as he recalled the wound immediately after the injury. He pictured the exposed muscle and bone, the screams of pain. Then he considered what the past few weeks have been like in his own life. Of Kent Carpenter's last moments. Of David Lewis and the life he never got to finish.

I'm not who I was years ago. That kid in medical school who was too afraid to stick up for himself in the moment has grown up. Bryce raised his right hand and placed his palm on the glass window. He lowered his head and spoke quietly, "I will stop at nothing to defend myself and my family against those who threaten us. Whether directly or indirectly. If you come at my patients, you're coming at me."

A few rooms down the hall, another ICU nurse leaned over and poked her colleague in the arm. "Look, Dr. Chapman is praying over the patient he injured. What a nice man." Bryce finished speaking and turned around to head home, knowing the hardest part was still to come. Once Clay could talk.

***

Valerie and Bryce tucked the kids into bed, then retreated to their own.

"Have you heard any updates about Clay?" asked Valerie, as she pulled the sheets back.

"Elisa updated me before leaving the hospital. The surgery went well, but the wound was very long and deep. She wasn't able to close it entirely. She's hoping to have it fully closed in a week once the swelling goes down and any infection is under control."

"That's just awful. The poor guy. I still don't understand what happened," she said.

"It was just a freak accident. I can't believe it myself," said Bryce, shaking his head.

Valerie looked at him for a moment before continuing. "Bryce, I heard that you two had been drinking before it happened. You promised me that you weren't going to drink anymore. That's part of the reason the kids and I came home."

Bryce grabbed her hand and looked her in the eye. "I swear to you I wasn't drinking. I poured mine out on the ground. Clay was the only one who drank anything that day. I just slipped off the blocks."

"Why would you pretend to drink in front of him? Why not just have water or a Coke?"

Bryce adjusted himself in bed and looked away briefly. "I didn't want him to feel bad about drinking alone," he said. "I didn't want him to know that I had sworn off alcohol and that it was a problem for me. I was embarrassed."

"Okay, I guess that makes sense," she said. "But why did you want the kids and I to leave while you two worked? We could have been inside, leaving you guys alone." She stopped talking for a few seconds and climbed out of bed before pacing the room slowly. "But then we would have been home when the accident happened. I hate to ask this, but did you plan the accident?"

Bryce looked away again. He hated lying to Valerie. She had stuck with him through medical school, residency, two children, the beginning of his career, and the recent events. She deserved to know the truth. And she was no fool. She graduated from college with a degree in mechanical engineering. She was going to figure it out, anyway.

"What would you think of me if I told you that perhaps it wasn't entirely an accident?"

"I would want to know why you did it. That's a serious wound to inflict on someone. Before Tony, I've never even known you to get in a fight, let alone slash someone open with a pressure washer. What really happened?"

Bryce sighed and leaned back against the headboard. "Clay killed the patient I saw right before our vacation. The guy whose family is suing me for malpractice. He somehow spiked the CPAP water bath with a nasty bacteria and the guy breathed it into his lungs all night. I saw him two hours after he woke up, but his lungs were already full of bacteria at that point. I didn't recognize how sick he was because that's not how natural illnesses progress. I wasn't expecting to see a murder victim before he died. I also found out Clay likely killed another person. It seems like he tries to provide justice for the universe by going after people who did bad things. The second person, though, he screwed up and killed someone with the same name, but not who he thought it was. I slashed Clay to repay him for the pain and suffering he caused us by the malpractice suit and for the murder of my patient."

"The second person? What do you mean?" she asked.

"I found another death that is too coincidental to not have been Clay's fault. That was the final straw for me. He had to be stopped."

"But what if he dies? Won't you be guilty of murder?"

"I see it as self defense and defense of others. He picks these victims from the interactions he has with them in his role as paramedic. He learns things about them that are private, and sometimes he decides it's best if society isn't exposed to them anymore. He transports a lot of our patients. This was going to happen again. He would kill another of my patients. Or Tom's patients. Or any of my partners. Or someone random to cover his tracks. Something had to be done."

Valerie paced back and forth in their bedroom while she considered what Bryce had revealed. "Who are you... Dexter?" she asked.

"No, I am the one who took down Dexter," replied Bryce. "I'm the good guy here. I saved lives by injuring Clay."

"Or took another one if he dies."

"He won't. Unless he chooses to. Trust me; I have a plan."

Valerie stopped walking and stared at Bryce. She shook her head. "Your plans have not turned out well these last few weeks. I hate to bring that up, but it's true."

"That's because outside forces acted on them and created issues. This time I am that outside force. I'm in control. His reign of terror is over. My plan is solid."

"So what about Clay? Now that you sliced him, how can you go to the police about what he did? They will immediately see the motive in what you did and likely arrest you. How are you going to shake the lawsuit if you can't tell them Clay did it?"

"I know, it's tricky. I've been thinking about this a long time. I'm still working out the details on that, but I have a plan. You just need to trust me."

"What I need is a drink. I'll be right back." She left the room and returned a few minutes later with a generous pour of red wine, only to find Bryce sound asleep.

"Well, you must be confident in your plan if you can fall asleep that quickly, Chapman," she said. She climbed into bed next to her husband. "Don't worry; I'll get us through this too. I made myself your wife, but you just made me an accomplice." She took a large drink of wine and shook her head. "Lord help us if your plan doesn't work."

Chapter Fifty-Two

"Are you ready?" asked Dr. Ashford Tate.

"No, but let's go," replied Bryce.

"This is ridiculous," said Elisa.

Tom Sharpe sighed and shook his head.

They had met outside the hospital administrative conference room and walked into the room together.

The hospital attorney stood and greeted them as they entered. Lorena McCarthy stayed seated but offered a warm smile to the doctors.

"Gentleman, and lady, thank you for coming today. I setup this meeting to inform you we have filed suit against the hospital and Drs. Chapman, Morales, and Sharpe. As you know, nothing moves quickly in the world of medical malpractice. I expect several months involving hundreds of billable hours to prepare our case." She smiled at the mention of billable hours.

Bryce caught Ash smiling back at her and kicked him in the shin. "You realize that we intend to show that this patient was murdered, correct? The harm he experienced was not caused by our hospital or our physicians. You're missing that pillar of a malpractice claim. The harm was not caused by our parties." The words from the hospital attorney sounded great to Bryce's ears.

Lorena shook her head. "It's possible to have multiple harms in a particular situation. Kent Carpenter was let down by everyone around him. The mysterious murderer you keep mentioning, and also the doctors he came to for help. Rather than receive help while apparently being murdered, he was discharged immediately so the doctor could fly to the Bahamas. Then he returned nearly dead and was cut in half by your surgeon. I'm not sure what is sadder; the fact no one helped him, or that he is unable to be a supportive father to his children." She paused a beat and resumed with her accent on full display. "Perhaps we'll let the jury decide."

"Okay, I'm done listening to this," said Elisa Morales as she pushed her chair back and stood up. "Sometimes people just die. We do everything we can to stop that from happening, but it's a reality. Humans are not electronics with perfectly functioning systems and easy diagnostics. People like you make a living off those of us who spend our lives trying to keep people on this side of the grass. You are parasites on the body of society. You cause exponentially more harm downstream than any momentary benefit you provide your client with a verdict. You're driving up the cost of health care and causing physicians to burn out, satisfying the administrative rules established to fight back against your lawsuits. Goodbye."

Tom Sharpe clapped loudly several times and then followed her out of the room. Bryce looked over at Ash, who raised his eyebrows and shoulders at the same time. Bryce nodded, and they stood in unison.

"See you in a few months for the deposition," said Lorena as the two doctors exited the room.

The group reconvened in the corridor outside the administrative offices. "I hate that woman," said Tom Sharpe, pacing back and forth.

"She's part of the system, just doing her job for the patients," offered Ash.

"Fine then, I hate the system. Or the patients. Hell, I hate everyone right now."

"Right there with you, Tom. I'm going to grab some food before my next case. Let's keep in touch boys and try to stay close. This is going to go on for a while, I fear." Elisa turned and walked down the hallway.

She made it about twenty feet away before stopping and turning around. "Bryce, aren't you going to ask me how Clay is doing?"

"I stopped by to see him after the surgery while he was still sedated. He looked rough. I didn't want to hear bad news, so I figured I'd see how he was doing tomorrow.

"Well, he is certainly in rough shape, but if we can stay ahead of the infection, I think he'll make it. It's going to be a long road to recovery with an extended stay in a rehabilitation facility, I'm afraid."

"Living at a nursing home is going to be tough on a guy like Clay," said Bryce.

"Yeah, but it beats being dead," said Elisa as she turned and walked around the corner.

***

"Hi, this is Bryce," said Chapman, holding the phone to his ear. He was sitting on a barstool near the center island in their kitchen.

"Hello, Niles Proffit calling. Do you have a moment to speak with me?"

"Yes, sir. Hang on just a sec." Bryce hit the mute button and double checked it was truly on mute. He looked across the kitchen at his wife, who had taken a break from preparing dinner. "Val, this is Niles Proffit, the head guy, Tony's dad."

"Yeah, I know who he is. The same guy trying to fire you and who is pressing charges against you? The guy who nearly drove you to alcoholism and suicide? Got it," she replied coolly. *Suicide? She read the email!* Bryce's confidence vanished in a heartbeat and a sickening feeling of dread was more than willing to fill the void. He stared back at her, speechless. She gestured at him with a nine-inch knife. "Well, talk to the man before he hangs up on you."

Bryce had forgotten about the call. He hit the mute button again and put the phone back to his ear.

"Okay, sorry about that."

"No problem at all. Listen, Tony's rehabilitation is coming along very well. He is now walking with full strength and his mental acuity improves every week."

"That's wonderful news. I'm very happy for you both," said Bryce sincerely. *Now maybe you can stop harassing the guy who saved your pretentious son's life?*

"As are we. Now that his cognitive abilities have improved, I've been able to speak with him more directly about the events that happened down at Staniel Cay." Bryce nodded as if Niles could see his reaction on the phone. "He was still very adamant that you started the altercation, and he was simply defending himself. When—"

"Sir, that is just not true. You need to talk to the captain who was there, Kyle Lafayette. Talk to Tony's friends," implored Bryce.

"Please let me finish. I was going to say that when he stuck to his story, I mentioned I had watched a video that told a different story. I did speak with your charter captain who confirmed your version of the events. While I love my son, he often drinks to excess and causes trouble for himself and others. I pressed him harder and even threatened to cut off my financial support if he did not tell me exactly what happened. The real version. Ultimately, he admitted that the entire situation was his fault. I spoke with his friends, who also corroborated the story."

"So where does this leave us, then?" asked Bryce.

"First, I want to apologize to you. You heroically saved my son's life, even after he harassed your wife and attempted to hit you. Then I didn't believe you, threatened your job, and tried to have you put in jail. Despite all of that you still showed up to work in my hospital, provided our patients excellent care, and have been respectful in our interactions. My family and my corporation owe you a debt of gratitude."

"Apology accepted. Does this mean you are dropping the charges in the Bahamas and my job is secure?" asked Bryce as he quickly stood up from the stool. Val mouthed the word "what" and looked at him with wide eyes. She put the knife down and washed her hands.

"Yes, absolutely. I have the name of your attorney on the island. I will call and pay your outstanding fees and request he release your retainer. This entire situation has put a stain on my family that I'd rather not expose for public review. I would appreciate if you kept the video in the grotto private."

"Of course, I want it to go away also. Thank you for covering those expenses for us."

"Now, don't be afraid to take credit for your heroics down there. That is a joyous thing and should be celebrated. What can I do to repay you for saving my son?"

Bryce's mind raced, thinking of what he wanted. He felt like an explorer who just freed a genie from a bottle and was granted three wishes. He looked at Val, who gave him a confused look. He turned around and saw the kids playing quietly in the family room. "Sir, to be honest," his voice cracking with emotion. "I have everything I need already. But if you want to do something, we could use another nurse or two per shift in the ER. Our staffing situation is getting to the point of becoming dangerous. We don't have enough staff to care for the patients in the department in a safe manner. Our nurses are burning out and blaming themselves when something happens because of inadequate resources."

"Done. I will make a call once we finish here. Dr. Chapman, you have my utmost respect. Thank you again."

"You are welcome. Oh, one more thing," added Bryce quickly. "When I was doing CPR on Tony, he had a lot of blood and secretions that got in my mouth. I still have five months left on my post-exposure testing for HIV and Hep C. Would it be possible for Tony to get tested? If I know he's negative, then I can stop worrying."

"He has an appointment for therapy this afternoon. I'll make sure he stops in the lab and gets that done. I will forward the results to you as soon as they come in."

"Perfect. Sir, thank you so much. This has taken an enormous weight off of me. I thoroughly enjoy working at Washington Memorial and look forward to many more years of practice."

"Wonderful. Take care, Dr. Chapman." The call ended and Bryce stared at his phone until it went back to the home screen. He stared at it in disbelief.

"So? Are you going to tell me what he said, or do I need to cut it out of you?" asked Val, picking up the knife.

Bryce walked around the island and pulled her in tightly. After several slow breaths, he sighed and said, "They're going to drop the charges. My job is safe. Tony is getting tested today for Hep C and HIV and we should know by the end of the week. It's over Val, we made it." A shudder ran through his body as the built-up emotions tried to escape through his tear ducts. His man card stepped in and stopped the waterworks from the beginning.

"Hey kids, come in here for a sec," yelled Val towards the kids in the other room. A quick series of hard footsteps echoed through the house as the kids raced each other to the kitchen. Noah jumped and planted his feet, sliding the last few feet on his socks. Hannah lagged a few paces behind. Bryce caught him like the wall at a hockey rink. He knelt down and hugged both kids at once. Valerie leaned over from the opposite side of them and completed the group hug. "Guys, we have great news. The stuff that has been happening that has made Mommy and Daddy stressed and sad is almost all gone now.

Noah looked up at his dad with a grin as wide as his face. "Good, we like happy Dad a lot more than grumpy Dad."

Val and Bryce laughed together and gave the kids a tight hug. The fire in Bryce's soul returned and burned hot enough to incinerate his man card, allowing tears of joy to flow freely. He wasn't concerned about the card. Once the rest results came back, he planned to get another one from Valerie in a very dramatic fashion.

"Yes," said Bryce. "It's almost over."

Chapter Fifty-Three

"I can't believe it," said Jackie Sirico as she hung up the phone.

Several nurses turned and looked at her to continue. "What? Who was that on the phone?"

"That was the chief nursing officer. She called to tell me the hospital is adding two additional nurses on each shift starting Monday. I can hire eight more nurses and offer everyone incentive bonuses until the positions are filled." The nurses cheered the news and then immediately began texting their significant others to inform them of the bonus opportunity. "I have been asking for this for years. Why did they suddenly give it to me?" she asked.

"Who cares, Jackie? Just be happy they are giving us what we need. Nice job! We know you've been trying to get us more help for a long time."

Jackie nodded and looked at the floor, her eyes filling with tears. "I just want us to be ready to help anyone, no matter when or what they need. To support my nurses. I can't believe they listened to me. This calls for a celebration. We're all going to the bar after shift, my treat!" A second round of cheering followed quickly.

Dr. Thrasher heard the commotion and came over to the group. "What are you guys so excited about?"

"The hospital is giving us two more nurses for each shift. Our critical staffing shortages are about to get a lot better," said Jackie.

"That's great to hear. I know my life is always better with more nurses around," he added with a wink. Every nurse in ear shot rolled their eyes, except Stacy, a newly hired nurse standing at the end of the counter. She sent back a slightly raised shoulder, a head cocked to the side, and a smile as big as Thrasher's biceps. This brought another quick wink before he turned continued on toward a patient room.

Chapter Fifty-Four

Bryce pushed the button to summon the elevator. This was the second time he had visited Clay since he was admitted. The first time was immediately after surgery when Clay was still sedated from the anesthesia. Bryce wanted to make sure he had survived. Today was a personal visit, but not social in any way. He fingered the manila folder under his arm. Bryce was confident enough of Clay's guilt to slash him with a pressure washer, but was he confident enough for the next step?

"Hey Dr. Chapman, what are you doing outside the ER?" The question was innocent enough. Asked by a janitor as he pushed a cart past the elevators.

Bryce stiffened at the question and clutched the folder close to his chest. "Hah, well, I have to go to meetings once in a while. I never knew this hospital had more than one floor until I was here for a few years," he joked.

The janitor continued on, an unsung hero in the battle against contamination and hospital-acquired infections. The elevator dinged, and the doors opened. He put his hand into his pocket and clutched the item buried deeply within. With any luck, one of his two remaining problems was about to be solved.

***

"Hey, hey, that's my assailant! Nurse!" Clay got out before a coughing spasm overtook him. The coughing jolted his body, which caused extreme pain through his incisions. He winced and then smiled at Bryce. "Thanks for coming up."

"Sure thing, my friend. How are you feeling?"

"Like someone slashed my ass open with a pressure washer. They say the infection is getting worse, and my pain is not improving much. How are you doing?"

"Not good, not good," Bryce said as he shook his head. He pulled a chair up next to Clay's bed and sat down. His reply was directed both at Clay's statement and his question. "I talked to your surgeon, and she said the incision looked good, but she's concerned about the infection progressing. They have you on powerful, broad-spectrum antibiotics, so hopefully things will improve soon. The disease got a head start on the treatment."

"Yeah, they told me that, too. Honestly, I'm nervous. I should be getting better by now. They said they cleaned me out, but with high-pressure injuries, it's impossible to get everything. The wound culture has grown something, but they don't know what it is yet. Hear that sucking sound? It's not you, it's my wound vac. I have a big sponge across my back and ass sucking fluid out of me all day long. I should be out in the truck doing paramedic stuff; instead, I'm stuck here trying not to die."

Bryce leaned back in the chair and crossed his right leg over his left. He reached into the cooler and grabbed a Diet Coke. "Mind if I drink in front of you?" he asked Clay.

"You know what happened last time you did that," he replied sarcastically.

"To be fair, you were the one who kept bringing me more beer. And you owe me a new pressure washer. If you had fallen the other way, I wouldn't have had to toss it in the pool to make way for your friends to get to you."

"Can we just call it even? I don't think I will be able to work for quite some time. May even have to go onto disability for a while, damn it. I don't want disability; I want action. Excitement. To make a difference."

"Tell me about what keeps you going. You're a very capable guy who could make a lot more money doing something else; why do you still do it?".

Clay inhaled and leaned back into his pillow. A deep question like that takes some consideration before responding. "Trust me, I find myself asking that same question every few months. Then I go on a run, and it completely renews my love for being a paramedic. It is such an intense feeling to be the one in charge when a patient is trying to die. You know that."

"Intense and terrifying," nodded Bryce.

"Yeah, it's both. You're right. But I love being the one who can make a difference between life and death. My actions, or inactions, can lead to a life saved or a life lost. I'm like the guy standing at the train switch, deciding whether the train goes on the right track to safety or the wrong one toward the 'Bridge Out' sign."

"Your inactions? What do you mean?" asked Bryce.

"What if I don't recognize something that's wrong? What if I miss the IV? What if I can't secure the airway?"

"Oh, I thought you meant you could withhold a treatment if you wanted to."

"Well, I could, but that would be pretty harsh. That would border on murder."

"True. I know I get attached to some ER patients. Does that ever happen to you?"

"Absolutely. In both a good way and bad way," replied Clay.

"What do you mean? What is a bad attachment?"

"Like I can't stop thinking about them. We make runs on domestic violence all the time. I see things about how some people live that would make you vomit. Not everyone has a chance to hide their shame before they dial 9-1-1."

"No, I guess they don't. Do you mind sharing some examples?"

Clay pointed at a cup of ice sitting on the bedside table. "Hand me that cup and we can begin story time." Bryce handed the cup over and raised his can as they toasted to Clay's health.

"It's just not the same as beer, you know? Anyway, one case that stands out is a bastard who was into child porn. We get a call for an injured person and find this guy naked on the bathroom floor. He had fallen in the shower and broken his femur. He was able to get to a phone and call for help but not to his computer to shut it down."

"You mean you just walk into his bedroom and there's child pornography on a computer screen? That's sick," said Bryce, shaking his head.

"Well, the computer was in screen saver mode. I sorta bumped the desk as I was walking by, and it moved the mouse enough to bring the screen back up and there it was."

"Did he know you saw it?"

"No, I turned the monitor off before we brought him out of the bathroom. He ended up with a broken right femur.

Wanna guess what he was doing in the shower when he slipped and fell?"

Bryce chuckled and nearly spilled his Diet Coke. "No. No, I do not."

"Okay, but want to guess how much pain medication he received before we got to the hospital? I told you about choices of action and inaction. Some people actually deserve both. Child pornography harms kids both directly and indirectly. Anyone supporting it in any way should be killed."

He pondered what Clay had just revealed. Bryce was confident that Clay had been the one responsible for making Kent sick initially. He knew the CPAP machine was the vehicle used to get the bacteria into Kent's lungs that ultimately killed him. Now he knew the motive. Bryce recalled the landlord mentioning Kent's wife had thrown a laptop in the bathtub. Now it made sense. He decided to push Clay and see what else he could learn.

"Hey, is that a PCA machine they have you hooked to?" asked Bryce. A PCA pump is patient-controlled analgesia machine. A drug delivery pump with a button that a patient can press to deliver a small dose of pain medication. They became widely used in the early 2000s when the "no pain" campaign was in full swing. After steadily increasing addiction and death statistics were recognized, the PCA pumps became rarer, used only for those with excruciating pain conditions. Like a pressure washer injury to the ass.

"Yeah, 25mcg Fentanyl every fifteen minutes. Watch this," said Clay, holding up a small button on the end of a cable. He depressed it with his thumb causing the machine to beep and then an intermittent hum indicating the medication was being delivered by a rotary pump. "I can see how people get addicted to this stuff. It's amazing," said Clay, closing his eyes.

"You mentioned domestic violence calls. I absolutely hate seeing those patients in the ER. I get so mad at their abusers, but then I feel guilty because I find myself getting mad at the patients too. I know most of them are going to go back into the situation, and I can't understand it. I see their abuser sitting next to them in the room, answering all the questions for the patient who sits there meekly. I wish there was something we could do to punish the perpetrators, but I also know that trying to intervene often makes it harder on the victims. It just sucks all around."

"Tell me about it. I have a story about that too. It wasn't a run I was on since I was out sick, but my partner told me about a situation she was involved in. Some bastard who liked to beat on his girlfriend had pushed it too far. She needed to go to the ER and get her head fixed. Turns out that guy does animal rescue. Who would have thought? Maybe it was some psychological attempt to repay the universe for what he did to her. Some people are so sick and twisted, nothing makes sense."

Bryce swallowed hard. There it was. David Lewis. The case of the mistaken identity. The guy who truly was a good person struck down because he shared a name and an apartment complex with a low-life scum. Bryce looked over at the folder and felt his anxiety rise. He swallowed the last of his drink and crushed the can between his hands. He stood and tossed the can into the garbage, grabbed the folder, and walked to the side of Clay's bed.

Chapter Fifty-Five

Bryce stared down at Clay, his heart rate accelerating as he prepared his words carefully. His hands trembled. An enormous amount of built-up emotion was climbing its way through his body, like magma rising through a volcano. It started in his soul, and then his heart pumped it quickly upwards toward his mouth until his pursed lips could hold it back no more.

"David Lewis," said Bryce.

Clay's eyes snapped open, and he turned to see Bryce standing over him. The anger on his face was obvious. "What?" replied Clay.

"David Lewis was his name. The animal rescue guy. The guy who fell to his death in the woods just two weeks after your partner drove an abused woman to the ER for treatment. What a strange coincidence. Turns out her boyfriend's name was David Lewis."

Clay adjusted himself on the bed, bringing a fresh wave of pain. He reached for the button to deliver another dose of pain medication, but a loud series of beeps indicated an error.

"Sorry, buddy. Guess it hasn't been long enough since your last dose. You're going to have to listen to this without extra fentanyl. David Lewis received a call about an injured owl in the woods and responded to the remote location in a park. The next day he was found by a guy who was out geocaching. The coroner's report said he had fallen from a tree while attempting to rescue an owl. Coincidentally, the guy who saw the injured owl drove to the library across the street from your fire house to call in the report of the owl. And he has the same name and almost the same address as the guy your new partner told you about."

"How do you know about him?" asked Clay with a look of confusion.

Bryce couldn't stand still any longer and began to pace slowly back and forth. "I have spent the last few weeks trying to figure out what happened to my life. It all started falling apart about the time I headed down to the Bahamas. Turns out a patient I saw right before I left came back to the hospital and died. Kent Carpenter."

He paused and stared at Clay, hoping for a reaction. Clay sighed and sank back into the bed, his eyes closing in a prolonged blink. He pressed the button on his pain pump, but it denied him relief again.

Bryce continued. "When I saw him, he had a slight cough and had been sick for about an hour. Get out of here; don't waste my time, right? But then he came back nearly dead two days later. Guess what he died of?"

Clay didn't respond. He simply stared at the ceiling, refusing to make eye contact. "He died of multi-drug resistant Pseudomonas. And wouldn't you know it, the only other person in this hospital system who has had that same bacteria grow in culture is none other than Eleanor Livingstone. Someone you bring to the ER more often than you see your family. I found that same bacteria growing in Kent's CPAP machine. What a damn coincidence, wouldn't you say?"

Clay said nothing.

"I bet if I looked at your multi-tool I'd find a small screwdriver that would fit exactly inside the melted hole in the water reservoir of his machine, wouldn't I?" Bryce continued, "Want to know something else amazing? Kent was a healthy guy, except for a history of testicular cancer and a broken right femur. Seems he slipped in the shower and was brought to the hospital by you. That's a lot of people who die unexpectedly after crossing paths with you. Do you want to make a bet he was into child porn? Did he deserve to die, Clay?"

"You can't prove I had anything to do with any of this. People die all the time of weird things; you know that," said Clay, his confidence returning.

"You're right, I can't. But I don't have to. That's up to the prosecutor. How confident are you that cell phone tower logs won't prove you were in the area when both of these people were attacked?" Bryce held up the folder in his hand. "This folder has all the information I've put together on these two deaths. Even a rookie prosecutor could convince a jury that you did it."

Clay's heart monitor began to sound an alarm, indicating his heart rate had elevated above the warning threshold. Bryce looked at the monitor and smirked. "Those people deserved to die. They were bastards; both of them," said Clay.

"Yes, Kent was a bastard. But your actions against him nearly cost me my career, my marriage, and my life. And I have to disagree with you about David Lewis. He truly was a saint. He volunteered a lot of time with animal rescue and wouldn't hurt anyone, especially someone he was in a relationship with."

"That's not true. I looked him up. Arrest records for domestic battery and my partner saw what he did to his girlfriend," said Clay.

"That's where you screwed up. David Lewis is not all that uncommon of a name. Did you know there were actually two of them that lived in the same apartment complex? Until one," Bryce made air quotes with his right hand, "fell out of a tree and died."

"What are you saying?" said Clay, a look of confusion on his face.

"I'm saying you killed the wrong David Lewis, Clay. The bad David Lewis went on to kill his girlfriend the next month and is now awaiting trial. The good David Lewis left behind family and friends who probably still mourn his loss. At least the local Audubon Society named an award after him."

Clay laid still in stunned silence. He pressed thumb down and was rewarded with a single beep and the gentle whirring noise of Fentanyl being pumped into his arm. After the pump stopped, he turned to look at Bryce, fear showed in his eyes. "So what now?"

"That's up to you, big guy. You like to have all the power. To decide which way the train goes on the track. Do you want to go to safety? Or to the bridge out?"

"That depends. What does the safety side look like?"

"This is where it gets fun. Remember earlier I said only two patients in this hospital have ever had that same multi-drug resistant Pseudomonas? Well, that was a bit of a lie. It seems you are actually patient number three. They do not have you on the correct antibiotics. If you choose the safety side, I'll let your doctor know which antibiotic will work and your infection will get better. You'll need some rehab and physical therapy, but ultimately you should recover well.

The price of choosing the safety track, however, is that I deliver this folder to the prosecutor and you'll be arrested for two murders."

"You're a dick," said Clay, breaking eye contact. "What's the other track look like?"

"Oh, the bridge out track? That ends with you dying tragically from a severe infection you picked up because of your interaction with Eleanor. It seems you were likely colonized, and the bacteria just needed a way into your body to cause the infection. My careless trip with the pressure washer was all it took to give the bacteria an opening. You will be remembered fondly by everyone at the hospital and in the community. You'll get a hero's funeral by the city. And after you die, I'll burn this folder, and no one will ever know."

"What about David's family? Shouldn't they know he was murdered?"

"How would that help them? They are grieving and healing as the days go by. Remembering your loved one dying for something he loved is a much better memory than knowing he was murdered."

"So either way I'm screwed?"

"Well, you did murder two people; at least you get to make a choice in the direction your life goes. You didn't give them that chance."

Clay didn't move for nearly a minute. Then he slowly turned to look at Bryce. "If the police test your pressure washer, are they going to find Pseudomonas growing in it?"

Bryce shook his head slowly. "What a thing to suggest. I remember you pouring the bottle into the soap tank. In fact, I'm sure I have security camera footage of it. Who knows what might have been in there? But the pressure washer is long gone. Remember, I had to toss it in the pool to allow paramedics access to you? With all that sterilizing chlorine water soaked into every part of the engine and components, the only thing I could do is get rid of it. I can't even remember which dumpster I tossed it in."

Clay swore quietly. "Look, I have no real family. I lied earlier when I said I see Eleanor more than my family. I have none. The only friends I have are EMS crews and here at the hospital. If they find out about this, I'll have no one left," said Clay slowly. His voice was flat and devoid of emotion. "The only way to charge you with assaulting me would open me up to murder charges. I'm screwed."

Clay closed his eyes and cried. Slowly at first, and then the speed and depth of the sobs increased until his body was moving so much it strained his wounds and he let out a scream. "Hey, calm down. Let's get you a dose of pain medication." Bryce leaned over and pressed the button for Clay. Three quick beeps signaled a denial of the dosage. Too soon.

"Son of a bitch," said Clay, recovering enough to talk. "This is going to be a slow, painful death. Maybe I deserve it. I don't want to be alive if everyone is going to hate me."

"Perhaps I can help you with that." Bryce reached into his pocket and pulled out a 20ml syringe full of a clear fluid.

"What is that?" asked Clay, shifting slightly to the right in bed, further away from Bryce and the syringe. The body language didn't go unnoticed.

"Relax, it's like a boost of energy for your train headed down the bridge out track. It's Fentanyl and Rocuronium. The fentanyl will kick in quickly and knock you out. The rocuronium will ensure you never start breathing again. No pain. No agony. No murder trials. No prison time. No blemish on your legacy. But I'll only give it to you if you agree to wait fifteen minutes after I'm gone to inject it into your IV. Once it's in, just throw the syringe into the corner. It'll get picked up by the janitorial staff and no one will ever know."

"I can't believe this is where it ends," said Clay. "After everything I've done, taken out by a damn ER doctor."

"No, you were taken out by your own actions, both in the two murders and what you're about to inject into your arm. I simply called you to task for what you did. Let me ask you this, if you could go back and do it again, but this time kill the right David and not destroy my life, would you do it?"

"Damn right I would," said Clay, eyes staring directly into Bryce's.

"I figured you'd say that. And you know what? I probably would have cheered you on. I still think that deep down, you're a good guy. You just screwed up and hurt some people along the way. You'll be missed, my friend."

Bryce reached out a hand toward Clay, who grasped it firmly and held on. "You too, Doc. Don't tell anyone about this, okay? I'm sorry for what I did to David and to you and your family. If I could somehow fix it, I would." The sentences started strong but cracked near the end. Tears streamed down Clay's face, and he let go of Bryce's hand to wipe them away.

"I forgive you, and I promise to not say anything. Remember, give me fifteen minutes. I'll be back in the ER for my shift by then. I'll be sure to speak kind words about you to all present while I run your code." Bryce handed the syringe to Clay, collected his cooler and folder, and walked out of the room.

Chapter Fifty-Six

"Excuse me, Dr. Chapman? Do you have a moment?" Bryce spun around at the sound of a familiar voice behind him.

"Val!" he said with a huge smile. "What a pleasant surprise. What are you doing here?"

"Well, I was doing some shopping at that one store you always try to get me to go into at the mall..."

"Ooh, the one with the hot headless models?"

"Maybe... I realized it had been a while since we'd been on a date and figured why not tonight?" She held up an envelope as she finished the sentence.

"What's that?" asked Bryce.

"It's the test results from Tony. Negative for Hep C and HIV."

"I never expected those words to turn me on as much as they did. In fact, I'm a bit concerned," said Bryce.

"Relax, I also feel like it's been ages. There was something else in the envelope." She handed a letter to Bryce, who skimmed it quickly.

"What is it?"

"Niles Proffit sent us a voucher for an entire week on a private island in the Bahamas. All expenses paid, the entire staff on premises, full use of all water sports. And we can bring up to twenty people. He's flying us down there on his private jet."

Bryce wanted to scream. Or lift something heavy. Or ravage his wife. "I can't believe this! That's amazing!"

"Glad you approve," she smiled. "I got us a hotel room downtown and the kids are at my sister's." She leaned in and touched his face. "Now that the tests are back, I think we need to pick up where we left off in Exuma."

Bryce stood and gave her a tight hug, cradling his head in her hand. He whispered, "Looking for some more of that specially prepared bacon?"

Valerie giggled at the memory and twisted away as his touch sent a chill down her neck and arm. "Just try to get out of here on time. I don't want to have to start without you."

Bryce watched her walk down the hall toward the exit. Every fiber in his being wanted to run after her and skip the rest of his shift, but patient abandonment was frowned upon by the licensing board. Only twenty minutes to go, anyway. He wouldn't be picking up any new patients and was nearly finished with the few he had left. A week on a private island? *I know exactly who to invite.*

He scanned the tracking board and saw a familiar name. Had it only been ten days? It seemed like a month had passed since then. He smiled, jumped up from his chair, and jogged out to the triage rooms. One more patient wouldn't hurt anything. "Mattie!" he yelled when he saw the bundle of cuteness sitting on the bed, her right arm secured in a cast.

"Hi, Doctor," she said, her face stretched wide by a smile. "Look, they gave me a pink one." She held her arm up for Bryce to see. "Will you sign it for me?"

"I would be honored." He pulled a Sharpie from the triage desk drawer and wrote his name as neatly as one can hope for when writing on perforated fiberglass. "Now, let's get those stitches out." He quickly removed the sutures he had placed while she was sedated ten days ago. The wound was healing well.

"The other doctor said you did a really good job fixing my arm. I knew you would fix it; you can fix anything."

Bryce smiled at her and held back the tears. If only she knew they had fixed each other. "Well thank you, Mattie. I am glad I could help you out. But can you keep a secret?"

She nodded quickly, eyes scanning back and forth to see if anyone else could hear. "I had been having a really bad couple of days when I took care of you. I was very sad. But your confidence and trust made me feel so much better. Then I was able to fix a lot of things that were making me and my family sad. I still have a few to work on, but I'm getting there." He leaned in close and touched her head. "I think you also have the gift of healing." Her mother beamed at the compliment.

Bryce placed a band-aid over the wound, and she hopped down off the bed. "Bye, Doctor. Thank you for helping me," she said as her mother led her out of the room.

As the door was shutting, he heard, "Mommy, when I grow up, I want to be a doctor."

Epilogue

"Well, that was amazing. Can you hand me my phone? I want to give you a positive review on Yelp," said Bryce. He expected a smack and was ready for Val's arm coming towards him. He grabbed it and used her momentum to pull her on top of him.

"Nice move," she said, leaning in for a kiss. "Did you use something like that on those Duke boys?"

"Absolutely. I bet they've been in trouble with the law since the day they were born."

"Don't write that review yet. You haven't been served the final course." Valerie raised up into a sitting position, staring down at Bryce with a smile, her hands resting on his chest.

His reply was interrupted by the sound of an incoming call on his phone. "Let me get that for you; it might be about the kids," said Val, leaning over to the nightstand. Bryce held her tightly, with a dual purpose in mind. To stop her from falling, and to keep her in place. "Oh, it's the hospital," she said, handing him the phone.

"Hello, this is Bryce."

"Hey Bryce, it's Elisa. Sorry to bother you, but I wanted to give you some good news. I rounded on Clay after my last case of the day, and he is doing much better. His fever is down, his wound is draining less, and his pain is improving. I think the new antibiotics are starting to work. How did you know to change them?"

"I had a suspicion that he may have had the same bacteria as our chronic tracheostomy patient since he had transported her so many times. He was probably colonized already, and it just needed a way into his body. There's only one antibiotic that works on that bacteria. I gave him a bolus dose at the bedside directly into his IV and then scheduled the med with pharmacy after that."

"Absolutely brilliant. I think you saved his life, Bryce. It is strange though. He is fuming mad and keeps screaming your name. Says he needs to talk to you but won't tell anyone what it's about. I ordered a sedative for him."

Bryce laughed so hard Valerie had to steady herself to not fall off. She gave him a confused look and mouthed "What?" He shook his head and held up his index finger.

"Tell Clay I said I am terrible with a train switch, and that I'll stop by to see him soon."

"Okay, but what does that mean?" asked Elisa.

"I'll tell you some day. But stand back when you tell him. He will not like it." Bryce ended the call and threw his phone onto the couch. "Clay is doing better; sounds like he's going to make it."

"That's great news, honey. But what was that laughter and the train switch comment about?"

"It means he's going to be really pissed when I go to see him tomorrow. For some reason, I think he thought he was going to die today."

THE END

Mailing List Signup

I hope you enjoyed reading *Redemption*! Please take a moment to sign up for my mailing list to stay up-to-date on my new releases. As a free gift, you will receive a copy of *The Muddled Mind: An Eclectic Collection of Short Stories*. Seventeen individual short stories I have written across several genres. I hope you see you on the list!

If you enjoyed *Redemption*, find the next book in the Bryce Chapman series, *Deception*, available on Amazon in paperback and e-book format.

★ ★ ★ ★ ★ **Captivating**
Reviewed in the United States on July 18, 2022
Verified Purchase

Great book with an engaging storyline that keeps the reader captivated. Every twist and turn in the plot kept me eager for reading more. Can't wait to begin the 3rd book of this series. Well done.

Acknowledgments

You are reading this book through equal parts effort of myself and dozens of others who have encouraged me along the way. My wife, Cheryl, is my best cheerleader. Her encouragement and support through our eighteen years of marriage have been the rock I lean on in any situation.

To my father, mother, and the rest of my family who continued to encourage me and provide constructive feedback as beta readers. The emails, texts, and phone calls asking how the manuscript is progressing meant so much.

Eighteen months ago, I was a novice who had no idea how to write a short story, let alone a novel. The MeWe group "Aspiring Amateur Writers" has been an invaluable source for feedback and writing prompt projects. Thank you for reading my samples and being there through life's ups and downs.

Fellow emergency medicine physicians Drs. Tom Combs and John Robinson have acted as big brothers for me in the writing industry. Each have published multiple books in their premiere series and have offered me hours of guidance and support. Please look them up on Amazon and help me thank them by starting with book one in each of their series.

The second edition of *Redemption* features several grammatical corrections, as well as a new cover to match the other books in the series, *Deception and Vengeance.* I have self-published this edition through Doodle Media, LLC.

There have been many other groups and individuals who have supported and encouraged me through this process. To name a few would leave out many, so I'd like to offer a blanket "thank you" to all. I intend to pursue my author journey with the same intensity I brought to medical school.

Finally, I'd like to sincerely thank you, the reader. You have given up a few hours of your life to lose yourself exploring my imagination. I will do my best to make this an enjoyable experience for both of us.

About The Author

Dr. Brian Hartman is a practicing Emergency Medicine Physician in Indianapolis, Indiana. He is married to his wife Cheryl, a dentist with whom he has two boys, Evan and Andrew. They enjoy traveling to tropical locations, including several of the settings of Redemption. Brian began the formal pursuit of writing as a creative escape from the stress of the COVID-19 pandemic.

Redemption is the first novel in his medical thriller series starring Dr. Bryce Chapman. Brian has written dozens of short stories and has several independent novels in production. He transfers his experience as a practicing physician to the characters and events of the books, letting the reader see inside the mind and emotions of the team caring for patients. The lives of doctors and nurses do not stop when they leave the hospital and his books explore the events and back stories that make our lives interesting.

Brian enjoys interacting with his readers via email and social media. Find him online:

Website: https://www.brianhartman.me/
Email: brianhartmanme@gmail.com
Facebook: https://facebook.com/brianhartmanme.

Also By Brian Hartman

Bryce Chapman Medical Thriller Series:
Redemption (Book One)
Deception (Book Two)
Vengeance (Book Three)
Hanging By A String (Book Four, pre-order)

Psychological Thrillers:

Lake Sinclair
It Happened In The Loft

Short Story Anthology:

The Muddled Mind

Printed in Great Britain
by Amazon